CHANGE OF FORTUNE

A Miss Fortune Mystery

NEW YORK TIMES BESTSELLING AUTHOR

JANA DELEON

Design and derivative illustration by Janet Holmes using images from Shutterstock.

❀ Created with Vellum

INTRODUCTION

If you've never read a Miss Fortune mystery, you can start with LOUISIANA LONGSHOT, the first book in the series. If you prefer to start with this book, here are a few things you need to know.

Fortune Redding – a CIA assassin with a price on her head from one of the world's most deadly arms dealers. Because her boss suspects that a leak at the CIA blew her cover, he sends her to hide out in Sinful, Louisiana, posing as his niece, a librarian and ex-beauty queen named Sandy-Sue Morrow.

Ida Belle and Gertie – served in the military in Vietnam as spies, but no one in the town is aware of that fact except Fortune and Deputy LeBlanc.

Sinful Ladies Society – local group founded by Ida Belle, Gertie, and deceased member Marge. In order to gain membership, women must never have married or if widowed, their husband must have been deceased for at least ten years.

Sinful Ladies Cough Syrup – sold as an herbal medicine in Sinful, which is dry, but it's actually moonshine manufactured by the Sinful Ladies Society.

CHAPTER ONE

I WAS in that state somewhere between finishing up a dream and awakening when I heard the quiet shuffle of footsteps on the hardwood floor, but before I could bolt up and grab my gun, I heard Carter's voice.

"Don't shoot."

I opened one eye and looked up at him, just remembering that he'd spent the night at my place. Since I was now fully awake and there was no way my adrenaline was going to drop down enough to doze back off, I sat up and checked the clock. Eight a.m. Jeez, I'd actually slept late.

Carter shook his head. "I'm going to start hiding your gun when I stay over."

"I have a knife in my pillowcase and an assault rifle under the bed."

"Of course you do. Well, if the urge to shoot something has passed, I made coffee."

I stared. Carter had been downstairs to make coffee and I hadn't heard him? I was seriously slipping. I held up one finger and scrunched my brow for a couple seconds.

"Yep," I said finally. "I think I'm good."

"It would be funny if I wasn't sure you were telling the truth. Come on. I'll make some French toast."

I jumped out of bed in an instant. "You know how to make French toast? Why have you been holding out on me?"

"Because we don't usually spend breakfast together unless we're fully clothed and at the café."

I grinned. "Best thing about breakfast at home. I don't have to be fully clothed."

He grabbed me and pulled me in for a kiss. "Best part for me, too."

I gave him a shove and followed him downstairs to the kitchen, still smiling. When our relationship had moved past the kissing stage, we'd been secretive about it—never staying overnight, always parking in the garage—but really, there was no point. This was Sinful, and everything interesting in Sinful was a topic of conversation among Sinful residents. So we'd skipped convention the past couple times, deciding to throw caution to the wind and live in the twenty-first century.

Based on a couple of disapproving stares I'd gotten at church on Sunday, I was pretty sure our "secret" was officially out. I was just waiting on a call from Pastor Don, wanting to discuss the potential of impending nuptials. Sinful had some really old ideas on relationships and marriage. Of course, over half the population had an AARP card, so that probably factored in.

While Carter grabbed things needed to make French toast, I poured us some coffee, then took a seat at the kitchen table to watch him work. There was something about a man standing in your kitchen, cooking breakfast, and wearing nothing but boxers and a perfect physique that was certain to improve even the worst of mornings. Not that my morning was bad, but it was just getting started. Given my history in Sinful, I was going to wait a little before declaring it a success.

Carter had just put the incredibly aromatic slices of powder-coated greatness in front of me when his cell phone rang. I could hear Deputy Breaux's frantic voice booming out, but all I caught was "Main Street," "situation," "now," and then my favorite, "Celia Arceneaux." Carter closed his eyes and sighed.

"I'll be right there," he said finally. When he opened his eyes, he looked at me, and at the same time, my phone signaled a text from Ida Belle.

Emergency downtown. Get Gertie and hurry.

Carter raised one eyebrow at me. "Your buddies summoning you to the situation they created?"

"Maybe. What's the situation?"

"Apparently, Gertie's alligator friend is terrorizing Main Street."

Uh-oh.

Back when an alligator poacher was on the loose in Sinful, Gertie had "rescued" an alligator she'd named Godzilla and hidden him in her bathroom. After he'd destroyed the bathroom, chased me up a tree, and terrified the neighbors, the cat was out of the bag and Carter had insisted Gertie return Godzilla to the bayou where he belonged. Unfortunately, the gator had developed a taste for the fish casserole Gertie had been feeding him and kept popping back up, apparently in search of a home-cooked meal.

"Normally," Carter said, "I'd tell you to stay put and mind your own business, but since you're an accessory to this particular problem, I'm telling you to get the perp downtown as quickly as possible."

"You don't want to get her yourself?" I asked, feeling a bit confused over being officially ordered to insert myself into police business.

"I'd be happy to...assuming you'd like to go downtown and

figure out how to get Celia Arceneaux down from a lamppost. It's a blue underwear moon over downtown Sinful, according to Deputy Breaux."

I cringed, considering all the ways Carter might have to help her down. People tended to be like cats. They could get up something, but getting back down was where they got stuck.

"Yeah, butt-grabbing isn't on my list of things to do today," I said, "so I'll just get some clothes out of the laundry room and go fetch Gertie."

Carter shoved his pistol in his holster, his jaw set.

"I promise to be fast," I said. "Please don't shoot Godzilla unless you absolutely have to."

He raised one eyebrow. "And what constitutes 'absolutely' in your book?"

"If he's going to eat someone I like. Or a dog or cat. I like dogs and cats."

"But birds and Celia Arceneaux are fair game?"

I shrugged.

He struggled not to smile. "Hey, at least you know where you stand. I have no plans to gun down that gator in the middle of Main Street. It's not his fault Gertie ruined him, but once they become a nuisance, it's only a matter of time before bigger problems follow in their wake."

He turned and headed for the front door. I ran into the laundry room and pulled on yoga pants, a T-shirt, and good running shoes before hurrying out to my Jeep. I had a .45 in the glove box so I was covered where weapons that would stop an alligator were concerned, although I was hoping it didn't come to that. I didn't have an attachment to Godzilla the way Gertie did, but I had an attachment to Gertie, which basically put me in the same position.

Gertie was standing on the sidewalk outside her house,

with her ridiculously large handbag, and I figured Ida Belle had already tipped her off. "What took you so long?" she asked as she climbed into the Jeep.

"I had to get dressed and get a small lecture from Carter."

"Oh crap. Carter stayed over? I hope Godzilla didn't interrupt a good morning roll."

"Worse. He interrupted French toast."

She stared. "You cooked?"

"Carter cooked."

"That is worse. Carter's really upped his game from grilling hamburgers."

"Yes, well, Carter and his French toast are chilling for the immediate future, so tell me what your plan is. I assume you have bribes in that black hole of a purse?"

Gertie nodded. "A casserole. I didn't have fish so I hope he'll go for chicken. And if that doesn't work, I brought some cupcakes and a bag of Fritos."

"No dip?"

She shook her head, the sarcasm apparently escaping her. "He never went for the dip. I tried French and bean."

I had no idea what kind of response that comment merited, so I just nodded.

"How mad is Carter?" Gertie asked.

I knew what she was asking. She wanted to know if Carter planned on grilling gator tonight.

"He was pretty annoyed, and I don't think that's going to improve by having to help Celia and her blue underwear down from a lamppost."

Gertie grinned. "I know it's not funny for Carter, but when is that woman going to learn to wear pants? I keep thinking surely this has to be the last time she moons the town, but no. She always manages a new way to show her butt. Dr. Tyler has probably seen an uptick in profit, though."

I nodded. Dr. Tyler was the local shrink. Some things you couldn't unsee without professional help.

A crowd was gathered at the end of downtown, but not in usual form. This crowd was on each side of the road, standing on top of cars and in the beds of trucks. One look at the star attraction in the middle of Main Street and the elevated gathering made total sense. Godzilla was right in the center of the road, holding downtown hostage. Oh sure, you might be able to drive by without losing a tire, but then you'd miss the show.

Carter was parked at the end of the street at the curb, holding a ladder under the lamppost and trying to coax a reluctant Celia down. I glanced up and saw Celia, clinging to the post in a death grip, and knew there was no way she was coming down unless he went up the ladder and got her. I shook my head, still marveling that her completely non-muscular frame had not only hauled her plump body up the post but had managed to keep it there for so long. Adrenaline was truly a remarkable thing.

"Good God," Gertie said. "What was she thinking, wearing that shade of blue with a red-and-white dress? Even if her big butt weren't hanging out for all the world to see, that blue would have shown right through the white. She looks like a giant flag with those horizontal stripes."

"At least she's patriotic." It was the nicest thing I could think of.

Ida Belle ran up to the Jeep, her expression a combination of glee and forced restraint. I knew she was dying to laugh at Celia but couldn't until the gator situation was in hand. "About time you got here," she said. "Were you baking a cake or something?"

"Chicken casserole," Gertie said. "Lucky for us I had it out to warm for lunch or I'd have had to thaw it."

"I don't think she could have held for a thaw," Ida Belle

said, nodding toward Celia. "Fear only beats out gravity for so long."

Carter waved at us and I knew that was our signal to do something. "Okay," I said, "what's the plan?"

"Just park here and I'll get out the goods," Gertie said.

"And then what?"

"Then I'll get him to follow me to the bayou."

Ida Belle shot me a nervous look.

"That's a fifty-yard dash carrying a casserole," I said. "That gator can run circles around you, assuming he chooses to run."

Gertie waved a hand in dismissal. "Godzilla isn't going to hurt me. I'll just put down this casserole, snap on his leash, and get him back in the bayou where he belongs."

"Great. I'll stay here with a running engine and loaded gun," I said.

"Me too," Ida Belle seconded.

"Don't you shoot my gator."

"Tell him not to eat anyone and we won't," I said.

Gertie frowned and climbed out of the Jeep. She dug a small casserole and a pink leash out of her handbag and headed up the street. Everyone on the vehicles pulled out their phones and directed them at Gertie. In ten minutes, fifty videos would be up on YouTube. The question was whether they would be under the "Things You Can't Believe" category or the "Unique Ways to Die" category.

Ida Belle jumped in the passenger seat and stood, looking over the top of the windshield as I eased the Jeep up behind Gertie. I know she'd told me to park, and I didn't want to scare the gator, but I also didn't want to be so far away that Gertie couldn't sprint her way to safety if necessary. I got about twenty feet from the hissing gator, and he pushed himself up on his legs. That was my signal to stop. I pulled my gun out of the glove box, stood in the driver's seat next to Ida

Belle, and trained my gun on Godzilla. Ida Belle pulled a hand cannon out of her pants and did the same.

"Where the heck were you keeping that?" I asked. "You should be walking with a limp."

"We all have our secrets," Ida Belle said.

Great. Now I had to worry about what was in Gertie's purse and Ida Belle's pants. At least Ida Belle was a crack shot. Gertie fell more into the crackpot category, but somehow managed to come out of mishaps mostly unscathed. I was convinced she was part cat.

I drew in a breath and slowly let it out, stabilizing my breathing in case I had to fire. I didn't want to shoot Godzilla, but I wouldn't hesitate if it came down to it. Carter looked at Ida Belle and me and gave us a thumbs-up. We were officially clear to fire. It gave me a bit of gratification that Carter trusted me enough to light up a gator on Main Street if I had to. Even if he wasn't necessarily thrilled with my skill set, at least he trusted it.

I have to give Gertie credit. She walked right toward the gator with zero hesitation. She was either confident or crazy. I was leaning toward the latter. When she got close to him, he lowered back down and threw his head in her direction, probably getting scent of the casserole. Gertie leaned over and placed the dish on the ground a couple of feet away from the gator. Godzilla tossed his head in both directions, as if making sure he wasn't being flanked, then crawled to the aluminum pan and started eating.

You could have heard a pin drop as Gertie inched forward and gently placed the leash around the gator's neck. When she rose back up, a low rumble spread through the crowd and Gertie beamed, then snapped her fingers and tugged on the leash. Godzilla, having consumed the meal, foil plate and all, looked at her and began to follow Gertie down the street.

Ida Belle elbowed me. "By God, the old fool is going to do it."

She walked past the Jeep and grinned up at us and I whipped around, not wanting my face to show up in a million places on the internet. She continued to the end of the street and probably would have made it to the bayou, but some things simply aren't meant to be. In this case, two things happened at once. First, the audience got excited and someone started clapping, which led to more people clapping. Carter waved his hands, trying to get them to stop, but it was too late. The alligator had stopped in his tracks.

Then Celia lost her grip on the lamppost. The ladder was right there below her where Carter had positioned it, but despite Carter's coaxing, she'd never even attempted to use it. Now that time had come and gone. Her arms and hands gave out and she fell backward, plummeting toward the bed of Carter's truck.

If Carter hadn't been in the way.

I saw his eyes widen, but he had no time to move before she crashed down on top of him, screaming her lungs out. Or maybe it was Carter screaming. No one would have blamed him. All that blue coming straight for his face was probably more horrific than things he'd seen with the Marine Corps in Iraq. Celia fell on him like a ton of bricks and sent them both crumpling down in a heap of red, white, and blue. All the noise startled Godzilla, and he turned around and took off for Carter's truck.

Because Gertie always found a way to make an impossible situation even worse, she'd stuck her hand in the end of the leash and was being pulled by the gator as he hurried for the patriotic commotion. They flew by the Jeep, Gertie barely managing to stay upright as she got yanked along.

"I don't have a clear shot," Ida Belle said.

"Me either." Gertie was too close to the gator, and the risk of a ricochet into the crowd was too high.

I heard muffled yelling and looked over to see Carter shove Celia off of him. She flopped around a bit, then stumbled to her feet, promptly tripped over the ladder, and fell out of the bed of the truck and onto Main Street. When she saw the gator racing toward her, she let out a scream that was probably heard in deep space. Deputy Breaux jumped off the hood of a car and ran for Celia, but before he could get there, she'd sprung up faster than I thought she could move and made a beeline for the lamppost. Carter pulled out his pistol and trained it on the raging gator, but I knew he couldn't risk a shot either.

Remembering Gertie's backup food, I dropped down, pulled a box of cupcakes out of her purse, and tossed the bag of Fritos to Ida Belle. We jumped out of the Jeep and yelled at the gator as we ran, shaking our food offerings. I opened the box and tossed one of the cupcakes, scoring a perfect shot right in front of Godzilla. He stopped short and flung his tail around, tripping Gertie and sending her sprawling onto Main Street.

"Do not go up that post again!" Deputy Breaux yelled as Celia grabbed on to the post to start her ascent. Deputy Breaux sprang for her as she got a couple feet up and attempted to pull her back down. Unfortunately, he reached a little too high and all he came down with was the blue underwear. He made a noise that sounded partly like a scream and partly like a wail and flung the offending cotton behind him, smacking Carter directly in the face with it.

Godzilla finished the cupcake and turned his attention back to the fray in front of him. Someone in the crowd yelled for everyone to duck, and the next thing I knew, a flare flew over a line of people and landed right in front of the gator. I thought the stick of fire would send him running, but instead, he clamped down on it and flung his head back and forth as if working up a toss.

I ran up to him and waved the cupcake where he could see it. As soon as he caught sight of the food, he made a beeline directly toward me, still holding the burning flare, and I took off. Gertie had managed to get upright but still had her hand caught in the leash and was being pulled behind him. I just needed him clear of the crowd and the shops and then I could get a shot. It wasn't what I wanted, but sometimes a mission didn't go as well as one hoped. All the commotion had riled up the gator, and Gertie was a meal on a string. If he got to the water with her still attached, he'd pull her under and be gone before we could even scream her name.

I looked behind me and saw that the gator was a little too close for comfort and picked up the pace, praying that Gertie could keep up. Ida Belle dashed back to the Jeep, and I saw her digging in Gertie's handbag as I ran past. As we rounded the corner of the shops, Godzilla tossed his head to make the turn and pitched the flare into a snow-cone stand, sending a cardboard sign advertising the specials up in flames.

Once Godzilla straightened back out, he picked up speed and so did I. I just needed to get him far enough away to mitigate the potential damage of a ricochet. When I was about ten feet from the water, I threw the cupcake, spun around, and pulled my pistol from my waistband, leveling it at the charging gator. But before I could fire, Ida Belle jumped in front of me and sliced the leash clean with an enormous hunting knife. Godzilla dashed into the water, snagging the cupcake, and then disappeared below the surface, leaving only a trail of bubbles and chaos on Main Street in his wake.

Ida Belle and I dropped down next to Gertie, who pulled

the leash off her wrist, revealing a nasty burn. Her pants were a casualty of the fall, and her knees hadn't fared much better.

"Can you stand?" I asked.

Gertie nodded. "I'm fine. It's just some scrapes."

Ida Belle threw her hands in the air. "Are you kidding me? You won't be walking tomorrow without a round of aspirin and a couple shots of cough syrup. I swear, woman, one of these days, you're going to have a heart attack over your antics. Or give me one."

"Oh, stop your bitching," Gertie said. "You've been saying that for decades now, and yet here I am, still going strong."

I heard rumbling behind us and saw Carter round the corner, a small crowd a bit behind him. A billow of dark gray smoke towered in the air behind them. "We need to shelve this argument for now," I said. "We have a bigger threat at the moment."

Carter was seriously pissed.

He strode up to us and gave Gertie a once-over. He must have decided she looked good enough, because he didn't inquire about her injuries.

"Where's the gator?" he asked.

"Took off down the bayou," I said.

"Why didn't you shoot him?" he asked. "And don't bother trying to weasel out of it with excuses about no clear shot or worrying about your ability. We both know better."

"I *didn't* have a clear shot until right at the end," I said.

"So why didn't you take it then?"

"Because Ida Belle jumped in the way and cut Gertie loose," I said. It was sorta the truth. Ida Belle *had* jumped in the way. A little. I mean, I could have shot around them both, but there was no use admitting that. Not if I wanted to stay out of the doghouse.

"Cut her some slack," Ida Belle said, her voice low. "She's

used to shooting people, not gators. And probably never with an audience standing behind her."

Carter sighed. He was still mad but he couldn't argue with our logic. Unfortunately, the most illogical person in Sinful chose that moment to come stalking up to us and train a gaze of death on Gertie.

"I have a clear shot now," I whispered.

Carter hesitated a full second, then shook his head.

Celia stomped through the crowd, pausing to grab her handbag from a teen who'd held it out to her as she passed. I recognized him as one of the busboys from the café.

"You should be ashamed," Celia said to him, "trying to steal a lady's handbag."

The teen flushed with anger. "I'm returning your handbag, you ungrateful old crow. And don't even confuse yourself with a lady." He turned around and stalked off through the crowd.

"I want that woman arrested," Celia said as she stepped up and pointed at Gertie.

"For what?" I asked. "Trying to keep that gator from snacking on your big blue butt?"

Celia's face turned even redder, and she started to sputter. "That...that BEAST chased me down the street from the butcher shop. He ate thirty dollars' worth of deer steak that I'd just purchased."

"Shorty's got deer steak?" Ida Belle asked. "He's been holding out."

"Stop it!" Celia screamed, spittle flying out of her mouth and spraying all of us. "Stop all your blather. Do your job for once and arrest her."

The aggrieved look on Carter's face said it all. "She hasn't broken any law."

"She created a public nuisance," Celia ranted. "Or do you plan on letting that alligator take over downtown?"

"You're a public nuisance," Ida Belle said. "Carter should arrest you for attempted assault since he could have suffocated to death when you fell on him."

"There's also the whole blue-underwear-in-the-face thing," I said.

"Like I wanted any of that to happen," Celia said.

"Please," Gertie said. "That's the first and last time you've ever been astride a good-looking man. Don't knock the gift horse."

If Celia's head could have spun around on her shoulders, it would have. I actually saw a vein appear on her forehead. She raised her hand in the air and I swear she was about to lose it completely and attempt to hit someone when I heard a horse approaching.

I looked over and saw the ancient Sheriff Lee approaching on his even more ancient horse. Celia dropped her arm and smiled. "Finally," she said. "Someone who knows how to uphold the law."

I was fairly certain that Sheriff Lee was expending most of his energy upholding himself on the horse, but who was I to get in the way of Celia and her idea of justice? We all counted the seconds, then minutes, as the sheriff made his way over to us, and before he could even issue a greeting, Celia started in.

"First off," she said, "I want you to know that this town has become a tragedy ever since you turned the reins over to this sorry excuse for a deputy."

"What?" Sheriff Lee yelled and held one hand up to his ear, apparently trying to form a funnel to make things louder. "I've got the reins right here. What the hell are you talking about?"

"I want you to arrest Deputy Breaux for assault and personal property damage," she said.

Sheriff Lee stared. "Who'd he assault?"

"Me!" Celia yelled.

"What was the personal property damaged?" he asked.

"A blue parachute," Gertie said.

I tried not to laugh, I swear. I didn't want to make things worse for Carter, but when Ida Belle started chortling, I couldn't help myself. Then Gertie joined in and before long, we were a huddled mass, shaking with laughter. Exhausted from the stress, the run, and mostly from Celia's existence, I sank onto the ground and drew in a deep breath, trying to get control of myself. Gertie and Ida Belle dropped next to me and Carter gave us a disapproving look, but I could see his lips quivering.

"The deputy pulled off my undergarments," Celia continued. "Ripped them right from my body."

Sheriff Lee stared at Celia for a bit, then looked over at us, his expression one of complete disbelief and massive confusion. "So, er, you're not saying this was a sexual assault, are you?" he asked.

"That's exactly what I'm saying," Celia said.

"And where did this alleged assault happen?"

"Right here on Main Street."

Sheriff Lee shook his head. "I don't think so."

"What do you mean you don't think so?"

"I've known Deputy Breaux his entire life and unfortunately, that goes for you as well, and the only polite thing I can say is I don't buy it. You must be mistaken."

Celia put her hands on her hips and glared at Sheriff Lee. "What?"

"Dang woman, your hearing's worse than mine," he yelled. "I'm saying it must have been an accident because there's no way Deputy Breaux put his hands on your drawers on purpose."

Celia let out a strangled cry. "Well, I never!"

Sheriff Lee nodded. "That's what I'm saying."

Someone in the crowd that had formed around us took that moment to slingshot the blue underwear directly at Celia's head. She snatched the panties off her head and I swear if they'd been a bomb, she would have set them off right there, killing us all.

"There you go," Carter said. "Your personal property is recovered."

"No damage except the stretch marks from her wearing them," Gertie said, and collapsed in my lap.

Celia whirled around and stalked away. "You haven't heard the last of this."

I smiled up at Carter. "Still have a clean shot."

CHAPTER TWO

After Celia and her underwear stalked off, Carter waved at the crowd. "That's it," he said. "The show is over. Go about your business."

He looked down at me. "You know this is going to be all over the internet. Do I need to confiscate phones?"

I shook my head. "I don't think so. Ahmad's guys are good, but I don't think they could data-mine my face on a passing shot. And I made sure I turned around before Godzilla headed our way."

Ida Belle gave him a pointed look. "I think a bigger problem is going to be if your Special Forces buddies see it."

"He's in the clear," Gertie said. "First he was hidden by Celia's big butt, then he was hidden by Celia's big-butt panties."

He cringed. "Can we please cease all references to the panties from this moment forward?"

Ida Belle nodded. "I can appreciate the horror you must have experienced. May I suggest a bottle of whiskey and a round of therapy?"

"I'd just go shoot something," Gertie said.

"Don't tempt me," Carter said. "Because I have a target in mind."

Gertie frowned. "Godzilla doesn't mean to cause trouble. He just prefers home cooking to sushi. Given how much you like my casseroles, you can't really blame him."

Carter stared at her. "Oh, I'm not blaming the gator."

"Well, what was I supposed to do?" Gertie asked. "I couldn't let that poacher get him."

Carter sighed. "Look, I know you were trying to do a good thing, but this is one of those cases of no good deed goes unpunished. If that gator keeps coming around people, someone is eventually going to have to shoot him. Today, it could have been Fortune or Ida Belle. How do you think they would have felt about that?"

Gertie's shoulders slumped. "They would have felt bad and that's the last thing I want, but I don't know how to fix the situation."

"I think the only solution," Ida Belle said, "is to trap the gator and see about a wildlife sanctuary. He's gotten too used to people and isn't going to stop coming around them. Not when he knows we have tasty treats."

"I agree," Carter said and gave Gertie a sympathetic look. "I get it. I really do, and I think your intentions were good even though the execution didn't turn out so well. But that gator needs to be in a controlled environment or he's not going to be around much longer. One more incident and the townsfolk will be screaming for me to hunt him down, and there's not a good argument to make for the contrary. Chasing Celia down Main Street is one thing, but he also managed to take out the only snow-cone stand in the town. And it's going to hit a hundred degrees today."

"We'll figure something out," Ida Belle said. "If you can buy us some time on this one, I'll make some calls and see what I can come up with."

Carter nodded. "I know someone with a rescue organization. I'll call him and see if he has any ideas."

"I'm sure Tim has insurance on the stand," Gertie said, "but tell him I'll pony up the money for the deductible and his lost profits."

"I'm sure he'll appreciate that," Carter said.

"Well," I said, not liking so much gloom and doom this early in the day, "I think it's beyond time for breakfast, and since mine was interrupted, I'm starving. Maybe we could head over to the café and have some blueberry pancakes?"

Francine's blueberry pancakes were one of Gertie's favorites. She perked up a little.

"That does sound good," she said.

"I'm going to have to pass," Carter said. "I have a report to file, and I'd rather Wildlife and Fisheries hear about this from me before they hear it from Celia."

Ida Belle nodded. "And you know as soon as that woman gets home and puts on a new pair of drawers, that's the first thing she's going to do. She's not going to rest until Carter is out of a job and Fortune is run out of town."

"Then she's going to be very tired," I said. "I swear, I have never seen someone so determined to volunteer to lose."

"Celia is one of a kind," Gertie said. "So are those pancakes, and my stomach is rumbling. It's hard to come up with solutions with a rumbling stomach."

"Got that right," I said.

We left Carter and headed for the café. Despite being midmorning on a Monday, it was pretty busy. I figured that's because so many people had headed downtown to see Celia up the lamppost, then stuck around for breakfast, just as we'd decided to do. Our table in the back corner was open, so we headed that way and took seats. A minute later, my friend Ally came round to get our drink orders.

"I heard about Aunt Celia," Ally said, unable to stop grinning.

Gertie gave her a thumbs-up. "Sales of Sinful Ladies Cough Syrup are sure to skyrocket. The whole town saw her underwear."

"Again," I said. "There really should be some sort of law requiring you to keep your personals on when in public."

Ida Belle straightened up. "There is. The city council passed it during the Great Underwear Riot of 1948. Came in handy when streaking got popular in the seventies."

I had no idea what constituted an underwear riot or what prompted one, and I wasn't about to ask. I'd had more exposure to strangers' underwear in Sinful, Louisiana, than any one person needed in a lifetime, especially since the exposed underwear was usually attached to Celia. This pair just happened to be out parading around without her.

"Did Deputy Breaux really fling the panties in Carter's face?" Ally asked.

Gertie nodded. "Probably would have suffocated if he hadn't gotten them off so fast."

"He's probably on his way home now to shower in bleach," Ida Belle said.

"He could have packed them in a backpack and used them as a parachute," I said.

"Or a mainsail," Ida Belle said.

"He could have made tents for homeless people," Gertie said.

"He could have cut them up and stocked an entire sheet section of a Bed Bath & Beyond," Ida Belle said.

Ally reached up to wipe the tears from her eyes. "Stop. You're killing me, and we're too busy for me to take a break.

Can I drop by after work? I have something else I want to run by you guys."

"Of course," I said. "We'll be at my place, trying to come up with a plan to relocate Godzilla before Celia figures out a way to turn him into luggage."

Ally frowned. "There's a rumor going around that she went to New Orleans and bought a gun. I'm scared for all of us if she starts carrying it."

"That's definitely not good," Ida Belle said. "Celia does enough damage shooting off her mouth. The last thing she needs is real ammunition."

Ally nodded. "She's been weird lately. I mean, she's always been strange, but it's been worse. This morning she was in the first wave of customers, and I swear she smelled like raw chicken. Aunt Celia has a lot of quirks, but not bathing or laundering her clothes isn't one of them."

"Maybe she'd been cooking," Gertie said.

"Maybe," Ally said, and shrugged. "I'll go grab your drinks."

"Celia with a gun," I said. "That's a whole new level of worry we didn't have before."

"You should tell Carter," Gertie said.

"I will." I shook my head. Despite being a tiny bayou hamlet, Sinful produced enough crime to keep Carter hopping. The last thing he needed was more problems from Celia. She was already in the fat middle of most of the noncriminal sort of trouble in the town. If she'd just let her grudge match with Ida Belle and Gertie go, not to mention her desire to run me out of town, things would be so much more peaceful. But Celia seemed determined to chase those dreams into a coffin.

"Well," Ida Belle said, "looks like we need to find a place for that gator and figure out a way to trap him before Celia goes full-on Rambo with us. I've seen her try water pistols at the parish carnival, and it doesn't bode well for any of us."

"All we need to do is find him," Gertie said, "and I can tempt him near the boat with food. Then we heft him in with straps or something."

I shook my head. Gertie might have used a pair of her pants to cart the alligator into her boat before, but no way was I having any part of Reptile Fashion Week.

"I'm not riding around with that gator in a boat," I said. "He doesn't like me."

"You were going to shoot him," Gertie said.

"Because he was going to eat me," I said.

Gertie waved a hand in dismissal. "He was just playing around."

"When I feel like wrestling with an animal, I'll get a puppy," I said.

"Fortune's right," Ida Belle said. "It's not safe to ride around with him in a boat. We'll just coax him onto the bank and into a cage. I know a guy who builds them for Wildlife and Fisheries. I'm sure he'll lend us one."

"Great," I said, "but how do we get the cage out of the swamp?"

"Carter has a hoist on the sheriff's boat," Ida Belle said, "but I thought we might be able to entice him onto the bank in your backyard. Gertie's fed him there before, so maybe we can get him to return."

It was times like these that I wished I were hiding out in a high-rise condo. People practically never trapped alligators in the parking lot of condos. Except maybe in Florida. But from the things I'd read on the internet, Florida was just as unique as Louisiana when it came to certain things. Still, I supposed fetching an alligator in a crate in my backyard would be easier than hauling him out of the swamp.

"Fine," I said, "but no more adopting animals from the wild. Why can't you get a nice cat or something?"

"Remember the bobcat?" Ida Belle asked.

During one of our misadventures, I'd had the interesting experience of running into a pet bobcat. I'd gotten away, but my clothes hadn't been as fortunate.

"A domestic house cat," I clarified. "Preferably a small breed and with its nails trimmed."

My own adopted house cat, Merlin, liked to race across my head when startled out of sleep. Cat tracks across your face wasn't a great look. Didn't feel so hot, either.

"I don't like litter boxes," Gertie said, "and if they go outside they haul in dead things. It's too much mess either way."

I stared. "Says the woman who had an alligator in her bathtub. I was there—running for my life—when he tore the door off the wall. I have yet to see a house cat make that kind of mess."

"A house cat won't eat you, either," Ida Belle said.

"They will if you die," Gertie said.

"Yeah, but they won't be the one who kills you," I said.

"Maybe I'll get a bird," Gertie said. "One that talks."

"The last thing we need is a bird repeating stuff we say," Ida Belle said.

"I was just going to teach it to curse and call Celia names," Gertie said. "We can have meetings about secret stuff at Fortune's."

"A bird calling Celia names *would* be entertaining," I said.

"Fine," Ida Belle said, "she'll get a damn bird. But not until we get rid of that gator. I can only handle so many distractions at one time."

Gertie clapped. "The first thing I'm teaching the bird is the 'I see London, I see France' poem."

Ida Belle grinned. "Perfect."

I CLENCHED my cell phone as I walked back into the kitchen, then threw it across the room. Gertie picked that moment to turn around from the stove with a ladle of spaghetti sauce. The ladle and Ida Belle caught the worst of it. The cell phone smacked into the ladle, sending it flying right over Ida Belle's head, streaming the spaghetti sauce down on her as though it was crop-dusting. Ida Belle looked up from her *Guns & Ammo* magazine and frowned, sauce dripping from her hair.

Gertie stared at Ida Belle in dismay, then turned to me. "If you didn't want spaghetti, you could have said so an hour ago before I started cooking."

Ida Belle picked up a napkin and wiped her forehead. "I'm guessing the phone-flinging escapade has nothing to do with lunch and everything to do with the phone call. Given that you're one of my best friends, I'm happy to shoot someone for you. I just need to know who to aim at."

Gertie nodded. "And I'll dispose of the body. I'm out of casseroles and we still need to trap Godzilla. After all that running this morning, he's probably hungry."

I looked at both of them and couldn't help smiling, mostly because I knew they were only half-joking. With friends like these, you had life pretty much in the bag. I flopped down in the dining chair and grabbed the beer I'd abandoned earlier to take a big swig. Then I let out a long-suffering sigh.

"Carter?" Gertie asked as she rubbed Ida Belle's head with a damp washrag.

Ida Belle waved her off and frowned at me. "I thought you two were going to have The Talk."

The Talk being the one where I told him I would probably always do things he disapproved of and he had to learn to live with it because I didn't see myself changing. Or he could walk away. It was the Door Number 2 option that had kept me from broaching the subject, even though we'd said over a week ago that we needed to talk about our relationship.

"We were," I said. "We did. Sorta."

Ida Belle raised one eyebrow.

"Okay, fine," I said. "We were going to, but then I distracted him with other things so I could put it off."

"Interesting," Gertie said. "Most women put off other things because they want to talk. You're going against the grain here."

"Yes, well," Ida Belle said, "Fortune has never been your average woman."

"Neither have you," Gertie said. "And unless we want her following your example of keeping a perfectly good man at bay for a lifetime, you might want to try to push her a little more in the average direction. She could ruin this whole dating thing for the rest of us."

Ida Belle rolled her eyes. "What the heck are you talking about? Your last date was so long ago that he probably clubbed you and dragged you to his cave."

I waved my hand at them before they could get started. "It wasn't Carter on the phone, so all this discourse on my lack of womanly skills or the potential that I'm a complete coward when it comes to emotional things is not relevant."

Ida Belle and Gertie glanced at each other, their expressions serious. They knew as well as I did that only a handful of people had my phone number, and almost half of them were in the room with me. I'd already stated it wasn't Carter. Ally was still at work, and Walter was busy at the General Store. That left one other option.

"Harrison?" Ida Belle asked.

I nodded. The week before, my CIA partner, Harrison, had called to inform me they had eyes on Ahmad in Miami and were planning the takedown. He wanted to know if I was up for it, which was a stupid question, because there was nothing I wanted more. But then the time frame he had targeted came and went without a word from Harrison, and my phone calls went straight to voice mail and weren't returned. At first, I thought they'd decided to undertake the mission without me, which would have pissed me off, but I would have understood it in a bureaucratic sort of way. The government was rarely efficient or logical.

Then the phone call I'd been waiting on had come ten minutes ago, but it wasn't at all what I wanted to hear. I'd hoped Harrison was calling to apologize for leaving me out but would tell me that Ahmad was captured or dead and I was free to be me again. But that wasn't what he'd said at all. I took a deep breath and slowly blew it out, trying to calm myself so I didn't scream when I explained the problem.

"They lost sight of Ahmad," I said finally.

Gertie and Ida Belle let out a stream of impressive cursing that was definitely appreciated, even though I'd mentally gone through most of the same words while flinging my phone.

"What happened?" Ida Belle asked. "Harrison seemed so certain."

"He's not sure what happened," I said. "They had eyes on Ahmad at a hotel in Miami and knew the meeting place for an arms deal. They were planning on making their move as he was on his way to the meet, but the time came and went and he never left the hotel. They sent in an undercover posing as housekeeping, but the room was empty."

"How did he disappear like that?" Gertie said. "I mean, I know the CIA probably didn't have people in the room with him, but surely they were watching him closely."

I nodded. "They had six undercovers in the hotel including

Harrison—housekeeping, room service, front desk, maintenance—you name it, they had a body in place."

"He's good," Gertie said. "I guess he didn't get to where he is by being stupid. He got there by being slippery."

Ida Belle glanced at me, and I knew she was thinking exactly what I was—that Ahmad had inside help. "There's slippery and then there's slippery," Ida Belle said.

Gertie looked back and forth between Ida Belle and me, then her eyes widened. "One of the agents is compromised."

"That makes the most sense," I said. "And Harrison thinks so as well."

"On the plus side," Ida Belle said, "you've narrowed the mole to six people."

"Unless there's more than one," I said.

"Let's not make things harder than they have to be," Ida Belle said. "Not yet, anyway."

"Mole or no, someone needs to get a grip on Ahmad's slimy butt," Gertie said. "Fortune is running out of summer."

It had been on all our minds, and now that Gertie had said it, we all slumped in unison. Things were coming down to the wire. The real Sandy-Sue was going to have to head back to her job at the school library, which meant settling up Marge's estate. Which also meant I was officially outed and would have to go into hiding somewhere else. The question was, for how long? Weeks? Months? Possibly years? I had a hard time visualizing even one day of starting over with a new identity. I couldn't attempt to process months or years without sinking into depression.

Before coming to Sinful, my life had only been about my job, probably because it's all that I'd had. But now, all that had changed, and instead of being the only thing I lived for, my job was the last thing I cared about. Except for wanting out of it without having to look over my shoulder the rest of my life.

I jumped up from the table and retrieved my phone, happy to see it hadn't suffered any ill effects from my tantrum. I accessed Harrison's number and looked over at Gertie and Ida Belle, who were staring at me in complete silence.

"I'm not waiting for this to materialize any longer," I told them. "It's time to end this."

Gertie's eyes widened. "But how?"

Ida Belle shook her head. "She's going to become bait."

CHAPTER THREE

It wasn't long after my ultimatum to Harrison that my phone rang. Even though the number was Harrison's, I already knew he wasn't alone on the other end.

"Have you lost your mind?" CIA Director Morrow yelled as soon as I answered. "Never mind. The question is rhetorical and beside the point. There is no way in hell I am using you to lure Ahmad out."

I put the call on speaker and motioned to Ida Belle and Gertie to remain quiet. I'd been expecting this exact conversation, and although I already knew what I was going to say, it was still hard to show complete disrespect for the man who'd had my back since I was a teen.

"Sir," I said. "All due respect, but I'm doing this with or without the agency's resources. I will not spend another month living as a fraud. We both know how long the agency was after Ahmad before I even signed up for that task. I could spend years hiding with nothing changing except my life drifting away from me day by day."

There was a pause on the other end, and I knew Morrow

was processing what I'd said and trying to formulate a response that didn't begin with "I know you're right."

"Look, Redding," he said finally. "I know you hate being stuck in that tiny town, but that time is drawing to a close. I'll work on something that puts you in a bigger place with more options for a normal life."

"You're right. I did hate this place when I first got here, and I resented everything about being forced to be here." I looked over at Ida Belle and Gertie. "But all that changed. Sir, I need to tell you that when this is over, I plan on resigning from the agency, and I'm thinking of staying in Sinful."

I heard a gasp and then Morrow sputtered, "You...I...what?"

"As impossible as it is to believe," I said, "I think I might have found my place, and for the first time in my life, I'm certain about what I want."

Okay, maybe that last sentence was a bit of a stretch, as certainty and me weren't necessarily good friends, but I had a much better idea now than I had when I was living in DC and thinking only about my next mission.

"I...I don't know what to say," Morrow said. "I never expected this and quite frankly, I'm having a little trouble processing it."

"I imagine you are. It took me a long time to admit it to myself. But the reality is I have a life and friends here that I don't want to lose. I'd prefer that life to improve by living legitimately. I can't do that until Ahmad is out of commission. We did this your way and it didn't work. I don't blame you for that at all. I know better than anyone what you're up against. But I'm not willing to wait any longer. My expiration date in Sinful is fast approaching."

"Harrison?" Morrow asked, sounding as bewildered as I'd expected.

"I, uh, agree with Redding," Harrison said, completely surprising me.

"You agree with her?" Morrow asked, his voice ticking up several octaves.

"Yes, sir," Harrison said. "The reality is our best option for catching Ahmad is dangling Fortune in front of him. And we're not exactly keyboard punchers. We both know the risks."

"You think those risks are acceptable?" Morrow asked.

"If it's what Redding wants to do," Harrison said, "then the risk is acceptable to me."

"We need time to plan," Morrow said. "We have to determine the best location for staging and get another crew in place for backup."

"I want to do it here," I said. "In Louisiana. It's home turf now. I have the advantage."

"You want to expose yourself in the place you wish to remain?" Morrow asked.

"Yes," I said. "This thing with Ahmad is personal for him because of his brother. Once he's gone and someone else takes over, I won't matter any longer. You know as well as I do that the rest of his organization isn't happy about the heat he's bringing onto them over a personal vendetta. They won't make the same mistakes."

"So that's your plan," Morrow said. "We draw out Ahmad and capture him."

"Actually, I'm planning on eliminating him."

"And then you go on with the rest of your life, fishing and gazing at sunsets, or whatever else they do for excitement down there."

I looked over at Gertie and Ida Belle and smiled. "I don't think boredom is in the cards."

"What about the team?" Morrow asked. "I need time to vet people I can trust."

"You thought you'd done that last time, right?" I asked. "Put together a new A team and we'll take our chances. Unless there's more than one mole, you should be safe with new agents."

"And the mole?"

"I have some thoughts on that one that we can go over when we do a more intensive discussion of the takedown. But I want the rat out of the CIA. Anyone who can be bought is a danger to every agent. With Ahmad gone, they'll just look for the next payoff."

I heard a long-suffering sigh...the one Morrow reserved only for me.

"I hope you know what you're doing," Morrow said.

I nodded. "Absolutely certain."

And this time, I was telling the truth.

The call with Morrow and Harrison ended with them focused on putting together a plan for the ambush. When it was all over, I leaned back in my chair and blew out a breath. That had gone a little better than I expected, especially given that I was essentially twisting my boss's arm. He could have issued an ultimatum that would have left me with no choice but to attempt a takedown without agency approval or resources. I was relieved that it had gone in my favor.

"Holy crap!" Gertie yelled, and for a moment I thought the entire weight of the conversation had just hit her. But then she jumped out of her chair so fast, she sent it tumbling over as she ran for the stove.

I spun around and saw what looked like a stove massacre. Red sauce ran down the front of the stove and cabinets, and in the pot, giant red bubbles popped, sending sprays of sauce upward and outward. Gertie grabbed pot holders and moved the pot to the other side of the stove, then reached for the dial several times before finally managing to get it turned into the Off position. When she turned around to face us, her eyeglass lenses were completely fogged and the glasses and her face looked as if they'd both contracted a case of the measles.

"Did you burn the bottom?" Ida Belle asked.

Gertie glared. "I'm okay. Thanks for asking."

Ida Belle waved a hand in dismissal. "You're a little steamy and dirty. No worse than this mass of sauce in my hair. You'll live. More importantly, are we eating spaghetti with burned sauce?"

"A little burning just adds character," Gertie said.

"If it's so great, how come they don't bottle 'character' and shelve it next to paprika at the grocery store?" Ida Belle asked.

"I'm sure it's fine," I said. "And as much as I appreciate and am happy that I can avoid the work that goes into cooking, I've got bigger fish to fry."

"Now she wants a fish fry," Gertie grumbled.

Because I knew it's what she wanted, I smiled just a little. A little was all I could manage at the moment. I'd told Morrow I was absolutely certain about what I was doing, and that was true enough when it came to the part about being the bait that lured Ahmad into my sights. But there was one part I wasn't confident about at all.

Telling Carter.

The average man would have a heart attack over the woman he cared for offering herself up as bait, but with Carter's Special Forces past, he knew better than the average man exactly what I was letting myself in for. And then there was the part where I also had to explain why I wanted to lure one of the most dangerous men in the world into my home state. Logically, he'd know I was right, but emotionally, I wondered if he'd threaten to lock me in jail until I came to my senses. This was exactly the kind of thing Carter didn't want to deal with when it came to me, and I was pitching him the worst possible situation I could muster. All the shenanigans that Ida Belle, Gertie, and I got up to were about to look extraordinarily minor.

Gertie tossed the pot holders on the counter, righted her upended chair, and flopped into it. "What can we do to help take down Ahmad? I've got a pretty good stock of ammo and a reasonable amount of explosives."

"What constitutes a *reasonable* amount of explosives?" Ida Belle asked.

"Depends on your hobbies," Gertie said.

"And your friends," I said and grinned. Gertie's store of contraband explosives had come in handy a couple of times. Or caused problems. It depended on how you wanted to look at things.

"I'm pretty sure anything in your collection passes right by the line Carter considers reasonable," Ida Belle said.

"If Carter had his way, I wouldn't even own matches," Gertie said.

"True enough," Ida Belle agreed. "But one of these days you're going to blow up the block."

"I don't like most of them anyway."

I shook my head, thinking how much I loved these two women. Here I was, facing a showdown with one of the most dangerous men in the world, who just happened to be hell-bent on killing me, and they were doing arms inventory to figure out how to help. I knew with certainty that the thought of saying "nice knowing you" had never crossed either of their minds. It was both overwhelmingly comforting and a tiny bit scary.

"I appreciate the enthusiasm," I said, "and the offer of

explosives, which I might take you up on. But at the moment, that isn't my biggest concern."

"You have a bigger concern than death?" Gertie asked.

Ida Belle nodded. "Carter."

Gertie's eyes widened. "Oh. You're right. That is a bigger concern."

"Thanks for the vote of confidence," I said with a sigh.

"What are you going to tell him?" Gertie asked.

"If she knew that, it wouldn't be a problem," Ida Belle said. "Try to keep up."

"I don't have any options other than the truth," I said. "It's not like I can orchestrate a coup without him noticing. I know we've managed to fly under the radar a time or two, but this is totally different. I can't disappear for days or even weeks and then return after news of a shoot-out between federal officials and terrorists makes the rounds without him guessing something was up."

"Yeah, and I guess law enforcement might be the first to hear," Gertie said.

"Not to mention that she'll need Carter's help," Ida Belle said. "She'll need all of our help."

"Yes and no," I said. "I'll need you to talk things out with and all three of you to watch my back when this goes into motion, but the last thing I want is any of you in the middle of this. With the exception of Carter, no one is trained to do what this will take. I know you guys did your thing back in Vietnam, but that was a long time ago. Things are different now."

"You mean we're old," Ida Belle said.

"Who the hell are you calling old?" Gertie asked. "I'm only in my third act."

Ida Belle stared. "Going to live to be three hundred, are we?"

"If it pisses Celia off, I'm willing to try," Gertie said.

Ida Belle gave her a single nod. "Good point. But back to Fortune's problem." She looked at me. "You can't do this without allowing Carter to help, and that means getting him on board with your plan. In the past, we haven't wanted him involved, so everything was after the fact. You were asking for forgiveness, not permission."

"I'm still not asking for permission," I said, "but I get what you're saying. If I don't let Carter in on this right now, up front, it will probably be a deal breaker."

"Okay," Gertie said. "So here's what you should do. You tell him everything, but you do it wearing sexy lingerie and holding a pot roast."

Ida Belle threw her hands in the air. "You're not going to make it to act three, scene two, if you keep spouting nonsense. Are you even in the same conversation?"

"Are you?" Gertie asked. "At least I'm throwing out options instead of just insinuating dire things. Carter loves Fortune and pot roast. It's probably not enough to distract him from her offering herself up for potential death, but it might be enough to soften the blow."

"You give your pot roast entirely too much credit," Ida Belle said.

"And me in sexy lingerie," I said. "That's not exactly in my wheelhouse."

"Then how do you surprise him with a sexy date night?" Gertie asked.

"Naked and holding a beer?" I said.

"Seems reasonable."

"I've failed you."

They both answered at once.

"Look," I said, "I appreciate the suggestions and offering up of pot roast to the distraction gods, and I'm not saying it might not come to that, but I think I'm just going to start with the truth and go from there."

It sounded good and I was sure it was the right thing to do.

I was equally sure what the response would be.

I was saved from having to think more about the matter by a knock and then Ally's voice at the front door.

"Back here," I yelled, and a couple seconds later, she popped in the kitchen wearing her usual smile.

I really liked Ally. She was the first real girlfriend I'd ever had. I mean, Gertie and Ida Belle were my friends, but Ally was born within the same decade as me. It was different. I just hoped when the truth about me was out in the open, Ally wasn't too hurt by all the duplicity I'd laid on her since the moment we'd met.

"Spaghetti?" I asked, and motioned Ally into the vacant chair. "We're getting ready to have a late lunch. Gertie's outdone herself this time."

"And overdone the sauce a bit," Ida Belle said.

"The sauce is perfect," Gertie said. "Your palate simply isn't refined enough to appreciate it."

"My palate is as old as yours and knows burned sauce when I taste it."

"That's okay," Ally said. "After working a shift at the café, I usually can't eat for a couple hours."

"Really?" I said. "I don't think it would work like that for me. Looking at all that great food all day, I'd want to eat it all. You'd probably have to drive me around on a flatbed trailer."

"I thought the same thing," Ally said, "and then on my first day, Mrs. Fontenot took her false teeth out at the table and started cleaning them in her water glass. Seeing other people's table habits puts me off food for a while."

I cringed. "That false teeth thing might put me off food for a year or better."

"I did lose weight after I started working there," Ally said. "At first, I thought it was all the walking, but when I spent a week tracking calories, I realized it was because I'd cut my intake by about thirty percent."

"Then it all turned out all right," Ida Belle said.

"Not if they kept that glass the false teeth were in," I said. "You threw it away, right?"

Ally laughed. "We use strong cleaner and water so hot it would melt plastic. The glass is fine."

I made a mental note to start bringing my own cup to the café. Lord only knew how many seniors in Sinful were dipping their teeth in glasses. It was one of those problems you didn't realize existed until you were living in the middle of it. It was also one of those problems you wished you didn't know about.

"Anyway," Ally said, "I wanted to come by and tell you guys about the mystery we've got going down at the café."

"What mystery?" Gertie asked. "I haven't heard anything."

"Francine's keeping it all under wraps for now," Ally said. "But for two weeks straight, food has been disappearing from her freezer."

"Disappearing when?" Ida Belle asked. "During service?"

"Yes," Ally said, "but Francine thinks it could also be happening some nights after close. She first realized something was wrong when we ran short on bacon two days ago. She was certain she'd ordered enough, and when she checked the delivery that week against tickets, she estimated that two boxes were missing."

"That's an awful lot of cholesterol," Gertie said. "Anyone had a heart attack lately?"

"Actually, studies are claiming cholesterol is no longer linked to heart disease," Ida Belle said.

Gertie snorted. "Says who? Doctors? Please."

I waved a hand at the two of them, then looked at Ally. "I take it the bacon is not the only missing item?"

"Nope," Ally said. "When she was doing inventory for the food order yesterday, we were short two pot roasts, four whole chickens, and a case of potato chips."

"Someone's eating well," Ida Belle said.

I shook my head. "No dessert. Clearly an amateur."

"Clearly," Ally agreed. "Anyway, Francine was certain at least two of the chickens were there that morning because she'd moved them to reach some steaks. But that evening when she worked up the food order, they were gone."

"And I take it you hadn't cooked them that day," Gertie said.

"We already had enough for the day cut up that morning," Ally said. "Besides, these were frozen. We couldn't have cooked them right away."

"How did someone lift two frozen chickens from the freezer and waltz out with them in the middle of service?" Gertie asked.

"Maybe they didn't waltz out the way you're thinking," I said.

Ally nodded. "You're thinking it's an employee. Francine does too. That's why she's keeping it on the down low. Back a few years ago, she had an employee whose husband got laid off but who didn't tell anyone. Francine caught her taking food, but she was so distraught and had two little kids. Francine said she would have helped anyway if she'd known."

"So she's afraid for word to get out in case one of her employees is in a bind," Ida Belle said. "Francine's a good woman."

"The best," Ally agreed. "But I'm not convinced it is an employee. Like I told her this morning when she filled me in, people stroll through all the time when we're open. She leaves checks for vendors on her desk in the back office and they all know where to get them. The back door isn't locked when we're open, so they let themselves in and drop off stuff, then pick up their checks. It always seems like one of the appliance or computer guys is there, and friends and family of employees sometimes pop in the back for a private word."

"And since all of those people cycle through on a regular basis," I said, "and Francine can't pin down the exact time the food disappeared, it could be any of them."

"Exactly," Ally said. "It's making Francine a little crazy, not knowing if someone needs help. I knew something had been bothering her, but I never dreamed this was going on."

"Plenty of people have access during the daytime," I said, "but you said some stuff might be missing from overnight. How is someone getting in then?"

"I don't know," Ally said. "I mean, the employees who handle open or close have keys because we do the unlocking in the morning or final lockup at night, but if it's not an employee stealing, then I don't know how they're getting in. Nothing has been jimmied, and none of the windows are unlocked."

"If all the employees who open or close have a key," Gertie said, "that could be an awful lot of keys floating around Sinful. It wouldn't be that hard for someone close to an employee to pick one up and have a copy made. It's not like keys are stamped with the address on them. Walter wouldn't know a key to Francine's place from a key to my house."

"That's true," Ida Belle said. "Simple to swipe someone's key on their day off and have a copy made."

I nodded. "Why doesn't Francine have a security system?"

"She's never really needed one," Ally said. "And she doesn't want the monthly bill. Besides, if someone sets off the alarm, then the police come. If it is an employee and the police catch them, Francine doesn't get to decide how to handle it."

"Well, she should at least put up some cameras," I said. "They're inexpensive and can run off the internet. When something goes missing again, she can check the footage."

Ally nodded. "I told her the same thing. A friend of mine from high school did that in her sorority house because her snacks kept going missing."

"Was it one of her sorority sisters?" Gertie asked.

"Uh-huh," Ally said. "The one on a diet, of course. She didn't want anyone to see her buying junk food, but she had no compunction over stealing other people's."

Ida Belle shook her head. "I don't trust anyone on a diet."

"Is anyone working at the café on a diet?" Gertie asked.

"Every one of us off and on," Ally said. "We're not all blessed with Fortune's metabolism."

"I get a lot of exercise in unconventional ways," I said. It was the best way I knew to put it. I couldn't exactly tell Ally that I worked off my calories evading law enforcement and bad guys in Sinful and by even more nefarious means before my arrival here.

"I know about some of those unconventional ways," Ally said, and grinned. "And there's more rumors than you can shake a stick at, which is my whole point in telling you guys about this. I know you like a puzzle, and you don't call the police over every slight, so..."

"You want us to catch the thief?" Gertie bounced up and down on her chair, clapping her hands. It was a look I'd seen several times before and it had yet to end well.

"Wait," I said. "I thought you told Francine to get cameras."

"I did and she ordered them," Ally said, "but they won't be

here for a week. I thought that in the meantime, you guys might want to take a run at solving this."

"The Mystery of the Missing Morsels," Gertie said. "It has Nancy Drew written all over it."

"No way," I said. "This woman in some interview about books last week on the news said she missed Nancy Drew because she wore dresses and was well-mannered. That's not me."

"Ha!" Ida Belle said. "Got that right. But we are nosy, and we like to butt into things the police would rather we stayed out of."

"So you're saying we should try to catch a foodie thief?" I shrugged. "Why not? God knows we've done worse, and besides, I like Francine. If she thinks someone might need help, then there's no use making their plight public."

"Oh good!" Ally said. "What do you need from me?"

"A list of all the employees who have a key, for starters," I said. "And another list of the people you think might have done it."

Ally's eyes widened. "Me? Oh, no. I couldn't...I don't..."

"Sure you can, honey," Gertie said. "Just think about all those people and cough up the names of the ones you think might have money troubles or just be up to shady stuff. It's not hard. Ida Belle and I have been doing it all our lives."

"She's right," Ida Belle said. "If you're going to live in Sinful, and especially if you plan on ever opening a business here, you better hone your discernment skills. They'll save your hide."

"And your frozen goods, apparently," I said.

Ally laughed. "You guys crack me up. Okay, I'll put together the employee list and I'll think about the other one. But honestly, no one comes to mind."

"You're not thinking hard enough," Gertie said. "I saw

Myra drink half a bottled water last week and refill it with tap."

"Oh my God!" Ally said. "Myra's been there since Francine opened her doors. Please tell me you're joking."

Gertie shook her head. "But she was serving Celia, so I was okay with it."

Ally covered her mouth with her hand. "That's so wrong. I want to be outraged but I can't work it up."

"I want to buy Myra a drink," I said. "Maybe even flowers."

"I already baked her a blueberry cobber," Gertie said. "It's her favorite."

"Myra was an only child who inherited her mother's estate," Ida Belle said. "She could probably buy out the café ten times over, so she's definitely not the one in need. She still works there because she likes it. If you can believe that."

"If I could get one over on Celia on a regular basis, I'd like it," I said.

"Oh, Fortune," Ally said. "Your existence alone gives Aunt Celia heart palpitations every single day."

I grinned. "Then my work here is done."

CHAPTER FOUR

I WASN'T ABOUT to give Gertie's idea a try. At the first sign of lace, Carter would know something was up. But I figured it wouldn't hurt to put on something besides a sports bra, and since it was one degree cooler than yesterday, leaving my hair down wasn't completely odd. And it wasn't pot roast, but Carter always had a couple homemade hamburger patties in his refrigerator, for quick and easy dinner. So if I dropped by before he got off work and threw them on the grill, then that wouldn't be completely underhanded. After all, I usually spent at least one night a week at his house and we'd probably end up eating burgers anyway. Call it being efficient. Or proactive, because once Carter found out what I was doing, he wouldn't stop yelling until the burgers were burned to a crisp.

I wore jeans and a light turquoise tank over to his house. I wasn't about to admit that I was wearing that tank because the color looked good against my tan skin and blond hair or that it brought out the color of my eyes. And if my jeans had gone through a hot-water wash cycle and were fitting a little snug, well, accidents happened. Especially when Gertie was around. The tank had been her idea as well, but I'd drawn the line at lip gloss. That was just asking for suspicion as soon as he walked in the door.

I took a look at myself in the rearview mirror of my Jeep and sighed. Who was I kidding?

One look at my face and Carter would know something was wrong. I was a highly skilled undercover operative and a professional liar, but the deeper my feelings for Carter became, the harder it was to get things by him. It was both frustrating and somewhat comforting to know that I had the ability to care deeply enough to break down my brick wall facade. It was also scary. Caring about people put me in a position of vulnerability that I wasn't used to and hadn't been trained for. In so many ways, a CIA mission had been easier.

But all that was moot. This was my future, or at least, I wanted it to be. Which meant putting on my big-girl panties and learning to be a normal woman. Well, as normal as a former assassin turned potential private investigator with two former spies as sidekicks could manage.

I'd just pulled the burgers off the grill when Carter walked into the living room and saw me coming in from the patio with the steaming patties.

"That looks good," he said.

"Let me get you a cold beer and I bet it will look even better."

I put the patties on the counter and grabbed a beer. Carter had sunk into his recliner and looked completely beat. I immediately felt bad because I was about to make an already less-than-stellar day even worse, but it couldn't be helped. Now that Director Morrow was on board with my bait plan, things would move quickly, so I needed to inform Carter as soon as possible. And even though I could probably wait until tomorrow, what would be the point? What I had to say wouldn't change and neither would his reaction to it. Might as well get it over with.

I handed him the beer and sat on the coffee table in front of him. "There's something I need to tell you."

"I kinda figured that."

"Was it the cooking? Too much?"

He shook his head. "You like to eat. The cooking was bound to happen sooner or later. It was the fancy bra."

"It's not fancy. It's just not a sports bra."

"Your boobs are twice as large as normal. From where I sit, that's pretty fancy."

So much for subtlety.

"You might as well spit it out," he said. "Whatever Gertie has got you in the middle of this time can't be any worse than what I've dealt with before."

"Yeah, well, this time it's not Gertie."

He studied me for a couple seconds, then blew out a breath. "Ahmad?"

I nodded. "They lost him in Miami."

"Damn it!" He slammed his hand on the recliner, and I could see his jaw flexing. "There is no way he's slipping through the CIA's fingers without help."

"I know. I figure it has to be someone on the takedown team in Miami."

"Unless someone on the team blabbed to someone else."

"That's possible too, but either way, the leak had to start with someone in Miami because they were the only ones informed of who the target was."

"So what now?"

"Well, the CIA's plan was to locate him again and repeat but with a different team."

"Because they've been so successful with that plan thus far."

I couldn't blame him for the sarcasm. I was more than a little frustrated with the situation myself, and I knew firsthand how slippery Ahmad was.

"I feel the same way," I said. "So that's why I decided to push the issue."

"Push how?"

I was silent for several seconds, trying to decide exactly how to phrase what I had to say next, but apparently, it was broadcast across my face. He jumped up from his chair, knocking his beer off the end table, and threw his hands in the air.

"Have you lost your mind?" he yelled. "Don't answer that. It's clear you have."

I stood as well, refusing to let him have the dominant position of height, which still wasn't completely effective since he had a good four inches on me to begin with.

"I'm not crazy," I said. "What I am is done. I'm done waiting on them to locate Ahmad. I'm done sitting here, pretending to be someone else, while I hope other people do the job I'm best trained for. I'm done worrying about the fact that summer is almost over."

I could tell he was working up to a round of argument, but my last sentence stopped him. He stared at me for a while, his frustration and fear so apparent. Finally his shoulders relaxed a tiny bit and he sighed. Then he reached for me and pulled me in close.

"I get it," he said. "But I don't have to like it."

I wrapped my arms around him and placed my face on his chest where I could hear his heartbeat. I was twenty-eight years old and had completed eighteen successful CIA missions, but this one was different. This time I had something to lose. Something big and important. Something that I never imagined I'd have or was even capable of.

"I don't like it either," I said. "But I hate the alternative even more. You know better than most how this works. If I wait on the CIA to do this without my help, it could be years or never. As much as I hate to admit it, I am aware of a couple people who were in protective custody for decades. I can't do that. I can't bounce around from one place to another, pretending to be someone else and waiting for Ahmad to be captured or killed."

"I know. I'd do the same thing."

He pushed me back just a bit so he could lower his lips to mine.

"So do you think he's still in Miami?" Carter asked. "Do you plan on trying to draw him out there?"

I drew in a breath, bracing myself for the second round of yelling that was surely coming. "No. I want home-field advantage."

"You want to bring him here? To your home?"

"Not to Sinful, but to Louisiana."

"New Orleans?"

"It's the most likely. I know the city some, and there's something about doing it here that just feels right. Like it was always meant to go down this way."

"I want to be involved. I know the CIA will have a fit, but I'm insisting."

"Don't worry about the CIA. I've already strong-armed my boss into doing this because I told him I'd do it with or without resources. I can't promise you anything in particular, but I'll make sure you're involved."

He frowned. "Speaking of resources who want to be involved..."

"They know and are just as insistent as you, but don't worry. I'm not about to put them in harm's way. I don't mean to diminish their skills, which are numerous and varied, but

Ahmad is a criminal many generations younger than their prime."

"They're not going to sit home and knit while this happens."

I nodded. "I'll find them something to do that keeps them out of the line of fire."

"I'm sure you'll do your best."

"You don't sound convinced."

"Oh, I'm convinced that you'll make the attempt. I'm also just as convinced that those two are slippery as eels."

"There is that. If it becomes necessary, I'll put a protective detail on them."

"Good. But no pulling that crap with me. Unlike the two senior James Bonds, I am trained for exactly this sort of thing. I want to be there with you when this happens. To be honest, I want to be the one to put a bullet through Ahmad's head, but if the opportunity is there, I'm happy to defer to you on that one."

I smiled. "That whole new-age closure thing?"

"No. Just good old-fashioned revenge. He put a price on your head."

"I *did* kill his brother."

"You killed a human-trafficking pedophile. You're a hero, Fortune. One of the good guys. Don't ever forget that."

I leaned against him, not wanting him to see my eyes getting all misty. He never talked much about his service with the Marine Corps. I knew he was Special Forces and he'd given the barest of details about one mission that went bad, but no one became a great assassin without being a keen observer. I had zero doubt that Carter had been a complete badass, and that he'd done and seen so much that he'd spent three months roaming the country after leaving the military simply to get his head back round to civilian living.

So when someone like Carter LeBlanc called you a hero, you were allowed to cry a little.

Carter and I talked late into the night. Sometimes about Ahmad and the takedown. Sometimes about how my life would change after leaving the CIA and all the little things that you never thought about while you were neck-deep in the middle of a war. Things like taking a vacation. I'd been all over the world, but viewing it through a riflescope wasn't the perspective I wanted to take to the grave. Not to mention, the places I'd been weren't exactly a trip to Disney.

I'd always seen pictures of white sandy beaches, with clear turquoise water and drinks with little umbrella thingies. Back then, I would have rather had a root canal or maybe even a small bullet wound than sit around on a beach like a lump, doing absolutely nothing. Now it seemed like nirvana. I'd definitely changed, and sometimes those changes woke me up in the middle of the night, fearful that I was making a mistake. That I couldn't be normal people. Or at least as close to normal as Ida Belle and Gertie managed.

Carter seemed to manage normal very well, but then, he'd had a nice childhood right here in Sinful, with a loving father and mother, to give him that foundation that he could return to. I, on the other hand, was learning how to be a regular joe for the very first time. I had to admit that some of it had been a lot easier than I'd imagined. Like making friends. And having a relationship with a man, although that one still had a bunch of questions surrounding it. Still, when I remembered those things, I thought maybe, hopefully, it wasn't going to be as difficult as I imagined.

We talked about so many things, except the one thing that

we'd been avoiding for a while—us. A couple times, I started to bring it up and something stopped me. A couple times, I thought Carter was about to go there, but then he'd get quiet and never start down that line of conversation. The last time he went silent, he looked away for a moment, but when he looked back, he hadn't completely gotten his emotions under control and I saw what he'd been hiding.

Fear.

And that's when it hit me. He didn't want to bring us up because he knew there was a chance I wouldn't make it out of this alive. He was right, of course. Why put ourselves through a difficult conversation that might not ultimately matter? Why waste what might be our last days together at odds with each other? Everything Carter and I needed to say, needed to find equal ground on, could wait.

When we started yawning more than talking, we called it a night and went to bed. Carter had work the next morning, and had to be out early. No matter the time I retired, I rarely slept late, so I got up when he did, had a hot shower with a hot man, then headed to my house for breakfast and some morning contemplation.

Setting a trap for someone of Ahmad's caliber required three different elements—a location for the takedown, a team that could execute the takedown with extreme efficiency and prejudice, and a way to filter the location to the target without him suspecting a setup. I had no doubt that the team Morrow and Harrison put together would be first-rate. It was the location and the filtering that required more thought.

Fortunately, I had an idea for both, and that idea sprang from the same place.

I made myself a protein shake, grabbed the keys to my Jeep, and headed out the door, shake in hand. Breakfast on the go. It was only 8:00 a.m. but I needed to have this conversation without Ida Belle and Gertie there, and that meant cutting out before they were up and going. I just hoped the people I was going to see didn't have a problem with my early-hour arrival. Just to be sure, I sent a text.

Need to have emergency meeting. Can you meet me in twenty?

I sent the text, expecting a delay for the reply. After all, people had to hear the signal, get up, check their phone...heck, I might be there before they even got the message. But the reply was almost instant.

We will be there.

I pulled up to the warehouse that served as the office of Big and Little Hebert, the local mob connection, and as weird as it sounded to people who didn't know our history, people I considered friends. I saw their Hummer out front and one other vehicle that I recognized as belonging to their right-hand man, Mannie.

The front door was open so I entered the building and waited. I knew their security system had alerted them to my presence and they were watching me on one of the many screens housed in a room upstairs. It wouldn't be long before Mannie arrived to escort me to the office on the second floor, where I'd been before. Sure enough, about ten seconds after I walked in, Mannie got off the elevator and headed my way.

He gave me a huge smile and extended his hand for a shake. "Ms. Morrow. This is a surprise, but a nice one." We started for the elevator. "Mr. Hebert was excited to hear about your text but anxious about the content itself. Is everything all right? Ida Belle and Gertie?"

"They're fine. And so am I, at the moment. But I have a situation that I think Big and Little are specifically suited to helping me with, and I'm really hoping they're willing to."

"Big and Little are very fond of you, and they are rarely fond of anyone. I'm sure if what you need is within their ability to provide, they'll be happy to help. And please, let me know if there's anything I can personally assist with. You get involved in the most interesting situations. Really perks things up around here."

"Thanks, Mannie." I knew very little about the Heberts' top security guy. He was probably a stone-cold killer, but he was a very polite one. And for whatever reason, he'd taken a liking to me, Ida Belle, and Gertie, along with Big and Little. I wasn't quite sure what that said about any of us, but I figured that could be considered at more depth once this was all over.

"How's the leg?" I asked. The last time Mannie had helped us out, he'd gotten shot.

"It was just a scratch."

I wasn't sure whether to laugh or be scared. A bullet wound could hardly be called a scratch, but Mannie sure didn't show any signs that he'd taken a hit. Maybe he was a superhero. It would make as much sense as anything else in Sinful.

Big was in his usual place, on a park bench behind his desk. Even though the desk was massive, his sizable physique made it look more like a desk in a college student's dorm room than an executive's office. Little was standing behind the desk, conferring with his father, and approached with a smile and an extended hand as I walked inside. He gave Mannie a nod as he greeted me, and the bodyguard slipped silently from the room.

I was pretty sure Big rose from the bench only when leaving the room, but he gave me a huge smile that I returned. I knew that technically they were the "bad guys" but I couldn't help liking them. Plus, a while back, I'd formed a theory about their somewhat duplicitous behavior. I had no doubt they were indeed in charge of the region and that their distantly-related cousin Sonny Hebert, Louisiana's biggest mobster, was pulling the strings from Baton Rouge, but there was an undercurrent of something else. Something I thought I'd guessed and really hoped I was right, because it would make a difference in what I was about to do.

"Ms. Morrow," Big said as he gestured to the chairs in front of his desk where I took a seat. "It's always a pleasure to see you, although your message has me a bit concerned. Your stealthy sidekicks aren't here with you?"

"Not this time," I said. "I didn't want them to hear what I want to discuss, and if you agree to help me, I'm guessing you wouldn't want them to be aware of our discussion either."

Big leaned back. "Now I'm both intrigued and a bit worried. Are you in some kind of trouble?"

"Yes. But that's been the case since my arrival in Sinful."

Big laughed. "You can say that again. Your arrival has prompted the most entertainment that Little and I have ever witnessed in these parts."

"I'm sure it has, but that's not what I meant. I'm about to tell you something—something that could get me killed. And despite who you are, I am placing my trust in you to keep my secret. At least for now."

Big looked over at Little, who gave him a knowing nod, then he looked back at me.

"Little and I have had quite a few discussions about you," Big said. "Your hidden talents never seemed to align with your résumé. At first, we thought you were FBI, sent here to infiltrate the family, but as time passed, it was clear that wasn't your agenda."

Little nodded. "It was Mannie who suggested you had military training, and that made a lot of sense, both from an ability standpoint and from your desire to insert yourself into situations that a librarian would normally hide from."

If I was being honest, I wasn't really surprised. They were criminals. If anyone could spot my training, it would be the people whose future depended on flying under the radar when people like me were around. But hearing them lay their thoughts out was a relief.

"I suspected I might not have fooled you," I said. "For many reasons, I'd prefer not to go into details. But you're right —I'm not Sandy-Sue Morrow, and I don't think I've ever actually been in a library except for the time I was pursuing a target through one."

At the word "target" Big raised his eyebrows. "I'm going to assume that the real Sandy-Sue is safely tucked away somewhere while you fill her shoes and escape the view of whoever has forced you into hiding. I'm also assuming you have official protection?"

What he was asking me was if I was in witness protection, which meant a federal agency was involved in the placement and follow-up.

"Yes, and no. Two people are aware of where I am, but it's not on the books. Our security is compromised, and my boss felt this was a better alternative."

"That's not good," Big said. "When you have security problems within our sort of businesses or yours, people die."

"My plan has always been to avoid that, which is why I'm here."

"Has the traitor located you?" Big asked.

"No. But I'm done waiting for other people to handle things. I've decided to expose myself to draw out the man threatening me. But I need a location to do it in. And I need word to filter back to this man that I'm in that location."

"If there's a leak with your employer," Little asked, "why not filter the information through your coworkers?"

"Because there was a recent coup in place, and this man slipped away in a manner that suggests he was warned by the mole. If the tip comes through his spy, then he'll likely suspect a setup being pushed from higher up and won't show. This man has escaped our grasp for many years. He didn't get where he is by being foolish."

Little nodded. "I think I speak for both Big and myself when I say that we have several vacant properties in New Orleans, and you're welcome to use whatever best suits your needs. But what has me curious is why you think we would be able to filter information back to the man who seeks you? Or more importantly, why we'd be willing to?"

"Well, to answer the first question, I think your business interests give you exposure to the right people to get the information where I need it to go."

"Fair enough," Little said. "And the second?"

This was it. I was about to lay my cards on the table. I just hoped I had an ace in the hole and wasn't putting up deuces.

"In observing you," I said, "I've found some of your behavior, uh, inconsistent with my past experiences with gentlemen in your line of work. And there were a couple of cases of curious timing and beforehand knowledge that made me start to wonder." I looked at Little, then at Big. "I believe you're confidential informants at the federal level."

Big tilted his head to the side and studied me long enough to make me want to squirm, then he gave me a single nod. "I think we have a reasonable understanding of each other's status."

"And now you understand why I didn't want my friends to hear," I said. "They know about me, but it wasn't my place to let them in on my thoughts about you."

"Little and I appreciate your discretion. It speaks well for your character, not that it was in question. But we have a certain position to maintain with our organization, and the fewer who know about the things we do on the side, the safer we are."

It wasn't any of my business, but curiosity overwhelmed me and I couldn't help asking. "Does Mannie know?"

"Yes," Big said. "He is the only person in the organization who is aware of our other pursuits. But his loyalty lies with Little and me. Not with the family."

I wondered briefly what Big and Little had done to inspire such loyalty from a man like Mannie. I'd bet a case of ammo that it was more interesting than anything I could see at the movie theater. And I'd bet another case of ammo that the three of them were taking that story to the grave.

"And your deputy friend?" Little asked. "He's hardly a fool. I assume he's up to speed on your situation?"

"Yes. But not my visit here, and I've never told him about the other things we've worked on together. He has his suspicions, but he's never asked. I think he's afraid of the answer."

Big nodded. "Definitely a professional quandary for the lawman. Well, as Little already stated, we are happy to offer the use of any of our vacant New Orleans properties. I'll have Little prepare a list with descriptions and get it to you. The bigger issue, I believe, is going to be the filtering of information back to your target. In order for that to happen, we're going to have to know more about you than just your abilities."

"I need your word that if you can't get the information directly to the source, you won't even try. There's a certain group of, uh, contractors who would take advantage of the information and might cause a derailment."

Big narrowed his eyes. "There's a bounty on you?"

"I'm afraid so."

"How big?"

"One million."

Little whistled and Big frowned. Both looked slightly unnerved.

"Who is this man?" Big asked.

"His name is Ahmad. He's a Middle Eastern arms dealer."

Big exchanged glances with Little, and for the first time since I'd met him, he seemed slightly stunned. Finally, he cleared his throat and pushed himself up from the park bench. I was afraid he was about to shoot me himself and collect, when he walked around and stuck out his hand. I rose from my chair, uncertain about what was happening, and clasped his hand in mine. He grasped my hand and gave it a firm shake, at the same time reaching out to hold my forearm with his other hand. Then he leaned in and kissed me on each cheek.

I was completely overwhelmed. The handshake holding the forearm, the kiss on each cheek, was a sign of respect shown only among men of a certain level within organized crime. That this man had bestowed such an honor on me was both exhilarating and humbling.

Still holding my hand in his, he looked me straight in the eyes. "I know exactly who you are. You saved a child from being sold as a sex slave. You risked your own life and your mission for a single girl the same age as my goddaughter. That girl was taken from my grandfather's village in Italy. You have my undying respect, and Little and I will always have your back. All you have to do is ask."

"Thank you," I said, trying to keep my voice from breaking. "You have given me such an honor."

"Honor is earned, not given," Little said. "You deserve this."

Big nodded. "Now, let's get to work figuring out how to take this bastard down."

CHAPTER FIVE

By the time I finished up with Big and Little, it was already 10:30 a.m. As soon as I hopped in my Jeep, I checked my phone and saw two missed calls from Gertie and a text from Ida Belle asking me to check in because they were worried. I immediately felt bad. I hadn't meant to make them worry but given my current situation, I suppose it was only natural for them to assume something might be wrong if I disappeared first thing in the morning without telling them what I was doing.

On my way home now. Meet you in 30.

I sent the text, then directed my Jeep toward the highway, still amazed at the turn my meeting with Big and Little had taken. I would have never guessed that my actions had turned me into some sort of underground legend, but Little had made it clear just how big a deal I was among certain groups of people—mostly those who hated Ahmad and his business practices. Probably some didn't like the power he held in the arms dealing community, so to speak, but I learned that mostly people didn't like him because he was crazy unpredictable and his word meant nothing. When they'd found out he'd been trafficking children, many had refused to deal with him any longer.

Ida Belle and Gertie were already in my kitchen when I arrived, and I was thrilled to see Gertie unpacking a box of food. Ida Belle was sitting at the breakfast table, popping the top off of three beers.

"If that's for people," I said, "I will forever be in your debt."

Gertie pointed to the two pans covered with tin foil. "One for people. One for Godzilla."

"So we're set to go on that?" I asked.

Gertie nodded. "Carter talked to his friend this morning, and they're happy to take Godzilla at the preserve."

"And my friend is happy to lend the trap," Ida Belle said. "He's going to drop it off here sometime this afternoon."

"Cool. So what's the plan for getting Godzilla to pay us a visit?"

"We track him down by boat," Gertie said, "then entice him to your place. Once he's here, I can get him in the trap with a casserole. I have some chicken necks and Lay's potato chips to use to lead him here."

"Sour cream and onion?" I asked, teasing.

"No. He prefers barbecue."

I looked over at Ida Belle, who gave me the "don't ask" look.

"So what were you off doing so early?" Ida Belle asked.

"And without us," Gertie said.

"She doesn't have to take us everywhere, you know," Ida Belle said.

"Unless she was having a romantic time with Carter, I don't see why not," Gertie said.

"Maybe she was having her hair done," Ida Belle said, "or grocery shopping, or sitting next to the bayou contemplating life."

"Please," Gertie said. "We'd have to put a gun to her head to get her into a salon, although those extensions are starting to need work. And what few groceries she uses, Walter has Scooter deliver weekly, otherwise she wouldn't have anything in this house. As for contemplating life, she's got a bayou in her backyard, and the only thing I've ever seen her contemplate next to it was the back of her eyelids in that hammock."

Ida Belle inclined her head. "Touché."

"I had a meeting with Big and Little," I said, figuring I might as well lay it all out now.

"About what?" Gertie asked. "Did they contact you?"

I shook my head. "I contacted them. I thought they might be able to help with my situation."

"I think it needs a name," Gertie said. "All the cool missions have one. What about Operation Fortune Freedom?"

I smiled. "I like it. From henceforth, my situation will be referred to as OFF."

"Ooohhh, I didn't even think about the short version," Gertie said. "Very nice. I'm a genius."

"Obviously," Ida Belle said. "So back to the Heberts—what kind of help were you wanting from them?"

"A place to stage the coup, for one. I know they have properties in New Orleans, and I figure that's the best place to do this."

Ida Belle narrowed her eyes. "So you just strolled into their offices this morning and asked to borrow real estate? I know they are fond of you, but that seems a bit of a stretch."

"They know about me."

Ida Belle's and Gertie's eyes widened and they looked at each other, then back at me.

"Your cover was already blown?" Gertie asked.

"No," I said. "They already had their suspicions that I wasn't a librarian."

Ida Belle nodded. "Given their line of work, I suppose they'd have to be blind to miss your training. Did you tell them everything?"

"I didn't have to." I told them how the conversation went down, and when I got to my exchange with Big, Gertie gasped.

"You've been made," she said. "You're officially an underboss or something cool like that."

"I don't think that's how it works," I said, "but it was pretty overwhelming."

"I can imagine," Ida Belle said. "So you're famous in the underworld. Not really surprising given Ahmad's reputation. Do they have the ability to pass the tip along?"

"They're pretty sure they can get word directly to Ahmad's people in the Middle East."

"What if his people act on the tip and don't pass it on?" Gertie asked.

"Word is Ahmad's obsessed with killing me. None of his men would move on me in secret because Ahmad would kill them for taking away the joy he would get from torturing and killing me himself."

"Still, it's risky," Ida Belle said. "Someone in his organization could tell a mercenary, planning on splitting the reward."

"That's true enough," I said. "The whole thing is risky, but there's a serious lack of options and the others are riskier than this one."

"I'm sure you're right," Ida Belle said. "I know there's no level of certainty with this sort of thing, but I can't help wishing there was."

"Me too," I said. At one time, the uncertainty had been part of the excitement—one of the reasons I loved the job. Uncertainty meant I got to test my skill when things went off track. It meant every call and action was mine, and I'd experienced a lot of satisfaction from pulling off successful missions despite derailment.

But this one was different. If someone gave me a magic button to press that would dissolve Ahmad into dust, I would press it so fast, you wouldn't even see my hand move. As far as I was concerned, the only uncertainty I wanted to deal with anymore was everything in my life that would happen once Ahmad was no longer a factor. I figured living in Sinful, with all it provided, would be plenty to keep me off-balance.

"So did you get a list of properties?" Gertie asked.

"Not yet," I said. "Little wanted to do some asking around about the nearby businesses to make sure the location wouldn't put up any red flags due to things the neighbors might be into."

Ida Belle nodded. "Illegal activities tend to draw the interest of cops."

"Exactly," I said, "and Ahmad could spot a local cop from across the Atlantic. Anyway, Little is going to get a list to me as soon as he's done poking around."

"So what's the next move?" Ida Belle asked.

"Lunch," I said. "Or I'm going to faint. I only had a protein shake for breakfast."

Gertie, who'd been fixing up plates while we talked, shoved a huge serving of lasagna in front of me. "I didn't bring any bread with me. I don't know what I was thinking. It's not like you have regular groceries here."

"I don't need bread," I said. "There's enough carbs on this plate to power ten people."

Ida Belle looked at the plate Gertie slid in front of her. "Got that right. Good Lord, woman. Are you trying to give us clogged arteries in a single meal?"

"Stop your bitching," Gertie said as she sat with her plate, "or you can cook the next meal."

I'd eaten Ida Belle's cooking before and she wasn't half bad at it, but I was certain she'd rather spend her time loading shotgun shells, or sharpening knives, or waxing her SUV. She cut off a big piece of the lasagna and shoved it in her mouth, not about to say another word. I didn't have to worry. No one wanted me to cook. It was strange how being inept sometimes gave you an advantage.

"This is awesome," I said, both to pacify Gertie and because it was the truth. Gertie had many talents, but cooking was right up there at the top. She hadn't made a single thing I hadn't liked, even the time I accidentally ate designer dog food kibble she'd baked for a neighbor. How was I supposed to know it wasn't granola? Anyway, it tasted good on yogurt. The neighbor's dog thought so as well.

"Did you tell Carter about your upcoming acting job as bait?" Ida Belle asked.

I nodded. "Last night."

"What did you wear?" Gertie asked. "Did you go with my suggestions?"

"Who cares what she wore?" Ida Belle asked.

"I do. Because what she wore is probably indicative of how it went," Gertie said.

Ida Belle rolled her eyes. "She could have been standing in the middle of his living room completely naked and holding Kobe steak and a five-hundred-dollar bottle of whiskey and it still wouldn't make what she had to say go down any better."

"If a hot naked man wanted to stand in my house with steak and expensive whiskey, he could tell me anything he wanted," Gertie said.

"If a hot naked man was standing in your house, it would be because he got the address wrong."

"Not necessarily," Gertie said. "I could order up one of

those strip-o-gram men. I hear that even though it's not an option online, you can tip them into taking off their G-string."

I didn't even want to know why Gertie was aware of the online menu or the secret tipping policy, and from the look on her face, Ida Belle was terrified she was going to tell us anyway.

"All door-to-door stripping aside," I said, "the conversation went better than I thought it would. Carter isn't happy about the situation, but he understands my reasoning and admitted he would do the same thing if he were in my shoes."

"He's showing remarkable restraint," Ida Belle said. "Especially given that you wanted to involve the Heberts."

I shifted in my chair. "I didn't exactly tell him that part. I didn't want to say anything to anyone until I knew they were willing and able to help. And honestly, I don't think I'm going to tell him now."

"I don't blame you," Gertie said. "No use fanning the flame unless you have to."

"Finally, we agree on something," Ida Belle said. "Took long enough."

"Anyway," I said, "if I say nothing, Carter will assume the CIA set up the place for the takedown. It's not that I like lying by omission, but Big and Little are doing me a huge favor, and I'd rather not have them officially dragged into this unless it's absolutely impossible to prevent. I owe them that."

Ida Belle nodded. "Look, I get why you're conflicted, and it says a lot about your character that you are. But the reality of your line of work—and Carter's—is that you will always have informants and other connections that you keep secret. Otherwise, the law enforcement business doesn't run so well, and technically, you are still a CIA agent. It's for your protection as well as theirs. If it meant mission success, Carter would do the same thing."

"I know," I said. "And you're right. I need to get used to

keeping professional secrets now. It's not like Carter shares the details of his work with me."

"It would make things easier for us if he did," Gertie said.

"I think that's the point," Ida Belle said.

"Whatever," Gertie said. "He can bitch all he wants, but the reality is every time we've been involved, the bad guys have gone down. We have a one hundred percent success rate. How many law enforcement officers can claim that?"

"Probably not many," I said.

"So what happens when we get the list?" Gertie asked.

"Recon," I said. "We'll take a day trip to New Orleans so I can assess each one and determine the most viable for what we need to do."

"And what exactly will we be doing?" Ida Belle asked.

"Oh, I hope it involves explosives." Gertie bounced up and down in her seat.

"God forbid," Ida Belle said. "I don't think the Heberts are lending a building so that the Feds can blow it up. Besides, that's a little risky."

"But permanent," Gertie said. "Very few people survive a good explosion."

"A valid point," I said. "However, official policy is to capture the bad guys in case you can convince them to give up information."

"You plan on capturing Ahmad?" Gertie asked.

"Hell, no!" I said. "I plan on putting an emptying an entire magazine into him. Maybe even reloading and going again."

Ida Belle held up her beer bottle. "I approve of that plan."

We clinked our bottles together, and I polished off the last bite of lasagna, somewhat surprised that I'd eaten the entire thing so quickly. I was just about to head to my refrigerator and dig out the last of a chocolate pie Ally had made for me when Gertie's cell phone rang. She looked at the display and frowned, then answered.

"Hi, Walter," she said.

I looked over at Ida Belle, who shrugged. Walter, the owner of the General Store and lifetime, ill-fated pursuer of Ida Belle, wasn't much for talking on cell phones. Normally, I would have chalked it up to an order Gertie had placed at the store, but her frown had tipped me off that she wasn't expecting to hear from Walter either.

"What?" Gertie's voice rose several octaves. "When? Thanks for letting me know."

She disconnected the call and slammed her phone on the table. "That bitch!" she yelled.

I didn't have to ask. There was only one person who could make Gertie yell and slam cell phones. "Celia?"

"What's she done now?" Ida Belle asked.

Gertie was so mad her face was flushed red. "Walter said his buddy who owns the feed store in Mudbug called him and said Celia was in there shopping."

"What the heck is she doing all the way in Mudbug?" Ida Belle asked. "There's no love lost between her and Walter, but that hasn't stopped her from shopping at his store."

"Exactly," Gertie said, "which is why Walter's buddy thought it was strange, especially when Celia claimed Walter's stock was lacking and she had to shop elsewhere."

I didn't like where this was going. "Did Walter's buddy say what Celia purchased?"

"Poison!" Gertie said. "And since Walter darn sure has the same one on the shelf in his store, I can only think of one reason she'd be trying to hide that acquisition."

"She's going to try to poison Godzilla," Ida Belle said. "I knew she wouldn't wait for the professionals to handle this."

I wasn't convinced the three of us were professionals—at

least not when it came to alligator wrangling—but I understood Ida Belle's point.

"She's not looking for a solution," I said. "She wants revenge."

"Killing Godzilla isn't going to make the town unsee her big panties in Carter's face," Gertie said. "And it's not going to erase those videos on YouTube."

"There are videos on YouTube?" I asked.

"Maybe a few," Gertie said. "You're not in them. I checked."

"No. It won't change any of that," Ida Belle said. "But killing Godzilla would make you miserable, and that's exactly what she's shooting for."

"I never understood that whole misery-loves-company thing," I said. "Wouldn't it be easier to just get a life?"

Ida Belle shook her head. "I think people like Celia have been miserable for so long, they don't know how to do anything else."

"I don't suppose we could convince her to move," I said.

"Gertie and I have been trying for years," Ida Belle said. "If you can figure out how to make it happen, I'm willing to do it."

"The bigger plan is going to have to wait," Gertie said. "Celia also bought melt."

"What is melt?" I asked.

"Cow innards," Ida Belle said. "You leave them sitting out a bit and they stink to high heaven."

"Which means Godzilla will be able to smell it from far away," Gertie said. "She's going to poison him. I'm certain of it."

Gertie was so worked up she was almost to the point of tears.

"Now, let's calm down a minute," I said. "What Celia plans to do and what she's capable of are two different things."

"She's right," Ida Belle said. "All the stinky bait in the world isn't going to help her find that gator. She can't even drive a boat."

"She can't?" I asked, a little surprised. "I figured that would be a law here."

"It is," Gertie said. "Everyone is supposed to prove the ability to swim by three years old and the ability to drive a boat by five."

"Okay," I said. "That's a little aggressive, even for Sinful. So why can't Celia drive a boat?"

"She can, sorta," Ida Belle said, "but it's never ended well, for her or the boat."

"Or Mr. Pitre's truck," Gertie said, "or that coop of chickens."

"We could go on," Ida Belle said. "Ultimately, the city decided to give Celia a pass, but she's not supposed to drive a boat."

"Perfect," I said. "Problem solved. Surely the fine and upright Celia Arceneaux wouldn't break the law?"

"No," Ida Belle said. "But she could ask someone else to drive for her."

"There's always a work-around," I grumbled. "Which one of her brainwashed followers has a boat and would be willing to help her chase an alligator?"

"Dorothy."

They both answered at once.

"Her cousin?" I asked.

"That's the one," Gertie said. "Just the sight of the woman gives me indigestion."

I'd "met" Dorothy when she dumped a tray of iced tea on me at the café. On purpose. She apologized later, when I'd saved Celia's life, but since that little bit of reality had long since passed from Celia's mind, I was going to hazard a guess that I was back on Dorothy's shit list as well. On the plus side, Dorothy didn't seem like the type that would be all that competent with boating, but Sinful held a few surprises in certain arenas, so I wasn't willing to bet on it.

"Dorothy can handle a boat?" I asked.

"She's no Jacques Cousteau," Ida Belle said, "but she can manage to get a bass boat around without too much trouble."

"Does she own a boat?" I asked.

"She inherited one from her father," Gertie said. "He was never much of one for fishing, but back then, everyone was required to own a boat, so he kept one in his backyard."

"Maybe we'll get lucky and it won't run," I said.

"It runs," Ida Belle said. "Dorothy's nephew has been borrowing it. I've seen him out in that floating junk pile a couple times now."

"Well, then we'll just have to beat them to it," Gertie said.

"How are we supposed to do that?" I asked. "We don't have the trap yet."

"I could tether him to the tree out back," Gertie said.

"You want to tether a gator like he's a dog?" Ida Belle asked. "That's a ridiculous suggestion, even for you."

"Yeah, I'm going to have to go with Ida Belle on that one," I said. "Tying up a gator like he's an angry rottweiler is only going to make him frantic. Then we'll never get him in the cage or even back in my yard. Which now that I think about it, isn't the worst idea. Maybe we could scare him off and this whole thing will blow over."

Ida Belle shook her head. "I'm afraid we're at the point of no return with this one. Celia won't let it go until Godzilla is dead or out of her grasp. The gator isn't really the issue at this point. Getting even with Gertie is."

"Then we're back to the containment problem," I said. "Assuming our plan works and we get Godzilla into my yard, I don't think we can keep him here for hours with potato chips. Eventually, he's going to head back into the water."

"We could lock him in your shed," Gertie said.

"He tore right through your bathroom door," I said. "I don't think my shed is up for a match with a prehistoric predator."

"Actually," Ida Belle said, "it's not a horrible idea. Marge built that shed like a bunker. It's all steel frame. The door is wood, but it's solid hardwood, not that flimsy crap they put in houses these days, and Gertie had that bathroom door replaced when she remodeled a couple years ago."

The thought of trapping Godzilla in the shed presented so many ancillary issues. For starters, technically, it wasn't even my shed. So if the gator tore it up, we'd have to replace it. Then there was the stuff inside the shed. It didn't belong to me either, and even though the estate paid for lawn maintenance so I had no use for the equipment, that didn't mean I should let it get eaten by an alligator. Which meant relocating everything he could reach. Which meant more work. The bigger problem, of course, was if we managed to get him locked in the shed, I knew he wouldn't be happy about it. Which meant a raging alligator would be trapped on the property I occupied. What if he got out and decided he wanted to take revenge on me? My backyard would never be safe again.

There was also the issue of real estate value. The real Sandy-Sue would have to settle her aunt's estate soon. I had serious doubts that an angry alligator lurking about would be beneficial to property value. And I was pretty sure that if the shed was destroyed by an alligator, the real estate agent would have to disclose that little tidbit.

"Okay," I said. "Let's just assume for a moment that we waltz Godzilla into the shed like the Pied Piper and he doesn't level the place. How do we get him out of the shed and into the cage?"

"I have an idea," Ida Belle said. "We put the cage in front of the shed door, back far enough to swing the door open. We leave the door on the cage up and put some of Gertie's alligator goodies inside. I can get some sheet metal from Walter and we can brace it on both sides of the door from the shed to the cage."

"So make a tunnel?" Gertie said. "That's smart."

"What do we brace the sheet metal with?" I asked. "If that gator charges, he'll barrel right through most things."

"Vehicles," Ida Belle said. "We'll park your Jeep and my SUV on each side and prop the sheet metal against them. No way he can move a vehicle."

"And if everything goes wrong," Gertie said, "we have a way to get away."

"It sounded better until you talked," I said to Gertie.

Unfortunately, our best-made plans often went awry. This one didn't even count as best made. I was pretty sure it fell in the "certain suicide" category, but I also couldn't come up with anything better.

"What the hell," I said. "Let's do it. What's the worst that can happen?"

"We have to build Sandy-Sue a new shed or someone gets eaten," Ida Belle said.

"Well, I'm the fastest runner, so it won't be me that gets eaten," I said. "Still, I wish I would have known about this before I ate my weight in pasta."

"Maybe we can burn off the calories," Gertie said.

Ida Belle shook her head. "I'm rather hoping we don't have to."

So was I, but I wouldn't bet on it.

"What about you?" I asked Gertie. "You took some scrapes yesterday. Are you up to the fifty-yard dash if needed?"

Gertie nodded. "I have a heating pad and painkiller. I'm good to go."

That didn't sound quite right, but I was going to roll with it anyway.

"Okay," I said. "We have a plan. Everyone head out and gather supplies and meet back here in thirty minutes."

After all, it had been a whole twenty-four hours since I'd done something death-defying.

CHAPTER SIX

I'D DIRECTED everyone to get supplies and meet back at my place, but then when they'd gone, I realized I had no idea what "supplies" might entail on my end. Ida Belle was acquiring the sheet metal, and Gertie was bringing the gator snacks and God only knew what else. I was furnishing the airboat and the shed, not to mention myself, which I supposed was plenty, but I still felt like that person showing up at a gun range with no rounds.

While I mulled over things that might happen and items we might need because of things that might happen, I cleaned out the shed, then changed clothes. Leggings, muscle shirt, and running shoes. It wasn't a lot, but that meant there wasn't a lot to weigh me down if things headed into the bayou. Thinking of taking a dip in the bayou made me remember that silly movie Gertie had made me watch with the Australian crocodile dude, so I went into Marge's secret closet and grabbed a large hunting knife and belt from her stash.

I put the belt on, shoved the knife in, then hurried to the bathroom to check myself out. I took one look and shook my head. Ridiculous. I looked like some soccer mom having a nervous breakdown while on her way to the gym. I ditched the knife and shoved my pistol in my waistband. I'd grab some bottled waters from the kitchen and call my supplies complete.

I was out back getting my airboat ready when Ida Belle arrived with the sheet metal. She drove her SUV around into the backyard and parked in front of the shed. I headed over to help her slide the long, heavy metal pieces from the back of her SUV.

"Did you empty the shed?" Ida Belle asked as we laid one of the pieces on the ground.

"Uh-huh. Lucky for me Marge wasn't much into tools and such. I just put the mower by the porch. The other stuff is on built-ins a good four feet off the ground. If he reaches that stuff, we've got bigger problems than replacing some lawn tools."

"Keep your voice down when you say things like that. This entire thing could easily become a bigger problem. As far as I'm concerned, we're already starting out in the negative."

"I can't believe we're going to intentionally invite that gator onto my property. I made Gertie stop feeding him here so he'd go away. Quite frankly, I was a little concerned for Merlin. And myself."

Ida Belle nodded as we pulled out the second sheet. "Gertie thinks that gator is stuck on her cooking, but he'd make a quick snack out of that cat if he could get a hold of him. Fortunately, Merlin's too smart to get that close. Smart animals have an instinct about such things."

"Well, apparently I'm in the dumb animal category. I went to put the ice chest back in my boat last week after washing it, and Godzilla crept right up the bank. I never heard a thing. He was just sitting there staring at me when I turned around to get out."

"He probably thought you had goodies in the cooler."

"Probably. Also Gertie's fault."

"So what did you do?"

"What any sane person would do. I struggled for ten minutes to push the boat off the bank with an oar, then left. What I should have done was shoot him and hide the body."

"Did you have your pistol on you?"

I stared at her for a second.

"Never mind," she said. "You'll probably be buried with it."

"Now that you mention it, I ought to put something in writing."

"I figured given what you did for a living, all that would have been taken care of years ago."

"Why bother? I didn't have anyone to leave stuff to. And since I'd be dead, it wouldn't matter anyway."

"Rational and efficient. That's one of the many things I like about you."

"What are the others?"

Ida Belle paused, seriously considering my question. "Well, for starters, I love that you go along with Gertie's crazy ideas about things. She's a royal pain in the butt at times—like this gator thing, for example—but she's got a good heart. And I couldn't ask for a more loyal friend."

"Let's hope this one doesn't devolve as quickly as some of the others."

My back door opened and Gertie walked out, pulling a duffel bag behind her.

"Someone come give me a hand," she yelled. "This thing is heavy."

I looked over at Ida Belle. "Should snacks weigh that much?"

"Not even close, but I'm afraid to ask what else she has in there."

"We're about to get in a boat with her."

"Not if we ask what's in that bag."

"Good point."

We headed over, and Ida Belle and I each picked up an end of the duffel bag and started carrying it to the airboat. I could have handled it alone but it definitely weighed more than some casserole and chips should weigh.

"I brought a couple extra things," Gertie said. "Just in case."

She didn't elaborate on the "in case" part, and Ida Belle and I didn't ask. I just nodded and made a noise as we hefted the bag into the bottom of the boat. The fleeting thought of mentioned explosives crossed my mind, but I didn't think Gertie would take that kind of chance with Godzilla. I could, however, picture her lobbing a stick of dynamite at Dorothy's boat, which pleased me a bit more than it probably should have. Ultimately, I decided not knowing was better. I'd just watch closely if Gertie moved toward that zipper and came up with anything but food.

Ida Belle climbed in first and took her position as chief airboat driver, aka Lightning on Water, and Gertie took up residence in the bottom of the boat on a new cushion I'd ordered specially for her.

"Hey," she said as she sat. "This is nice."

"It's memory foam," I said. "I told you I'd fix you up."

There was only one other official seat in the airboat, and that was the one next to Ida Belle. I wasn't about to relinquish my spot—partly because it was my boat and I shouldn't have to, but mostly because it offered the best location for a sniper shot, and that was sorta my wheelhouse. Then there was the part where Gertie couldn't necessarily be relied upon to remain in the seat. Not with Ida Belle driving. She was the Dale Earnhardt of the swamp.

Since the bench in the middle was almost level with the sides, it had also presented problems on the ejection-of-Gertie side of things. So for her own safety, and my sanity, I'd started insisting she ride in the bottom of the boat with her back against the bench. We'd had fewer out-of-boat incidents since then, but even perching on a life jacket, Gertie had left every boat adventure unable to sit without a cushion for a couple days.

So I'd talked to Walter and we'd found a cushion specially made for office chairs for big and tall men. Not that Gertie was big or tall, but given that people tended to bang around in the boat far more than they did an office chair, I figured the extra support would be needed and appreciated.

Gertie squirmed around a bit on the cushion, then leaned back. "Firm but also comfortable. I can't even feel the bottom of the boat or the back of the bench."

"Wait until I start driving," Ida Belle said.

I untied the boat, shoved it off the bank, and jumped inside. Then I took my spot next to Ida Belle and braced myself for launch. As soon as the boat had enough clearance, Ida Belle started up the engine and we took off, the boat practically leaping out of the water. I clung to the arms of my seat as Ida Belle sent the boat sideways around a bend in the bayou, and I noticed that Gertie seemed fairly fixed in place tucked into the foam. If only I could put a racing harness on my seat without Ida Belle calling me names.

When we got to the point where the bayou dumped into a huge lake, Ida Belle cut the engine. "Okay, Gertie," she said. "You're up. I didn't see any sign of Godzilla on the bayou, so where do you think we should start?"

"I didn't see anything but the world coming at me at warp speed," Gertie grumbled.

"But I bet your butt feels great," I said.

"It is rather comfortable," Gertie agreed. "I might need

one of these for my recliner. It's getting old and my butt goes to sleep when I sit in it for more than an hour."

"You bought that recliner when you bought the house," Ida Belle said. "It's not old. It's prehistoric."

"Further discussion of recliners and butts will have to wait until another time," I said. "Preferably a time when I'm not with you. Gertie?"

Gertie rose from the bottom of the boat and glanced around. "There's a bit of wind today. I've never found him in open water when it's choppy."

"So one of the bayous?" I asked. There were only about six billion of them in the area. How hard could it be?

"Where did you find him last?" Ida Belle asked. "Alligators are territorial. He's probably found one place away from town that he hangs out in."

"That's true," Gertie said. "I found him a couple days ago in the bayou off Rabbit Island."

"Sit down," Ida Belle ordered as she fired up the boat. Gertie had barely gotten her butt back on the cushion before Ida Belle launched the boat across the lake toward Rabbit Island. It wasn't a long trip, but we made it in probably half the time normal people would have. When we reached the opening of the bayou, Ida Belle threw the boat sideways and we slid across the top of the water, bouncing as we went across the waves, then she shot forward into the bayou and immediately cut the throttle.

It was a good thing I was holding on to my seat, because I was about one inch from pitching out of it. "Do you have to do that?" I asked.

Ida Belle grinned. "I don't have to. I *like* to."

"I'm getting a seat belt," I said. "I don't even care anymore if you call me a pansy."

"You can call me a pansy all you want," Gertie said. "As long as you don't take the foam from me."

"Grab the binoculars out of that bench and get to looking," I said. "As much fun as this is, I don't want to spend all day looking for Godzilla."

Ida Belle nodded. "Especially when the real work comes into play once we find him."

"Don't remind me." I still wasn't completely sold on the alligator-in-the-toolshed plan.

Gertie handed Ida Belle and me binoculars from my bench stash and then opened her giant bag. Ida Belle and I gave each other worried glances, but she came out with a riflescope.

"I find this works better," Gertie said.

"I don't care if you use smoke signals and a magnifying glass," I said. "Just find that gator."

Ida Belle guided the boat slowly down the bayou, occasionally lifting her binoculars to scan the water. I moved my head back and forth, figuring the three of us probably looked as if we were at a tennis match, but nothing stirred on the surface. We continued a good mile down the channel before Gertie finally shook her head.

"I've never found him this far back," she said.

"Maybe he's still somewhere close to town," I said.

"It wouldn't surprise me," Ida Belle said. "I'm sure he prefers the easy meal to the one he has to acquire himself. I checked the bayou off Main Street when I picked up the sheet metal, but didn't spot him. Walter said he's been checking and he asks everyone who's been out on the water, but no one has seen Godzilla since the panties-in-the-face incident."

"Maybe one of the offshoots that wraps toward homes?" I suggested. "To Godzilla, people equal dinner. Even though they're not all tossing them out like Gertie, sometimes they're carrying tasty treats, like Celia with her butcher shop package."

Gertie frowned, clearly worried. "I overheard one of the teens downtown talking about seeing a gator when they were playing in the swamp behind the park."

"And you didn't think to tell us?" Ida Belle said. "This is so not good. If that gator turns up anywhere around kids, someone will shoot him for sure. Everyone take your seats. We'll head back to Sinful and cover the channels around the town."

Ida Belle turned the boat around, and we jetted back to town. I usually tried to do a round of sit-ups before bed, but I was skipping tonight. Riding in the boat with Ida Belle driving was all the core workout I needed. On the plus side, despite her obvious worry about Godzilla, Gertie had managed to escape the day bruise-free so far. But I didn't want to pat myself on the back for my cushion acquisition just yet. There was still daylight left.

When we hit the channel behind my house, Ida Belle slowed and we scanned the water and the bank, looking for any sign of the wayward gator. We continued all the way up to where the channel ran behind the shops on Main Street, and Ida Belle pointed to an offshoot of the main channel that headed to the right.

"I'm going to start here," she said. "This one runs behind part of the neighborhood and the park."

She took the turn and we continued our scan for several miles of channel, but there was no sign of the hungry gator. After thirty minutes of checking side bayous and marsh, Ida Belle finally stopped the boat and looked down at Gertie, shaking her head.

"I don't know where else to look," she said.

"Me either," Gertie said. "He's never been this hard to

find." Her eyes widened. "You don't think someone's got him already, do you?"

"Let's not jump to conclusions," Ida Belle said, although I could tell by her worried look that's exactly what she'd been thinking. "Maybe all the recent excitement was too much for him and he's lying low for a while.

"Or maybe he's full," I suggested. "How often do alligators eat?"

"They don't have to eat often," Ida Belle said.

"I've heard they can go years without eating at all," Gertie said. "By living on their fat stores."

"If that worked for people, there's some I know that could live into the next life," I said.

"Sadly for us mere mortals," Ida Belle said, "I don't think it works that way. But the food point is a good one. Given the number of easy meals he's acquired lately and with all the noise surrounding those meals, he might have made himself scarce."

"I'm guessing that if an alligator doesn't want to be found, he won't be," I said.

"In these swamps?" Ida Belle said. "We've had people disappear in these bayous for years, then pop back up just when everyone figured they'd moved or died. If people can stay off radar that long, then I'm certain a gator can, especially if that's his goal."

I blew out a breath. I knew Ida Belle was as worried about Gertie as I was. Despite the fact that it was completely ludicrous, the reality was Gertie had formed an attachment to Godzilla and she would take it hard if something happened to the gator. Mostly because she'd blame herself for creating the situation in the first place by feeding him. It had probably seemed harmless to toss him some bait while fishing, but then the poacher had shown up, and things had escalated to where we were now.

Unintended consequences. The story of my life.

"Let's head home," I said. "We'll all feel better after a shower."

"Not to mention sitting in a non-moving chair for a bit," Ida Belle said. "My butt is going numb."

Gertie just nodded. I could tell she was disappointed, but at this point, there wasn't anything else we could do. We could spend the rest of our lives roaming the bayous and Godzilla could spend the rest of our lives dodging us. There were too many places for him to hide, especially when one of them included under the murky water.

We had just cruised past Main Street when Ida Belle tapped my arm and pointed up the bayou. I picked up my binoculars and focused on a boat in the distance, but it only took a glance to zero in on Celia's bad haircut and tacky pink outfit.

"I'd know that polyester anywhere," Ida Belle said.

"And that old lady hair," Gertie said. "Celia and Dorothy."

"Don't worry about it," I said. "We've been out here for hours and haven't so much as caught a glimpse of Godzilla. No way they found him."

"Not on purpose," Gertie said. "But Celia could have called in a favor."

"A favor from whom?" I asked.

"Satan," Gertie said. "You know they're in cahoots."

"Isn't that a rather harsh statement for a Southern Baptist?" I asked.

"The alternative would be lying," Gertie said. "I figure that's worse."

"Stop your truth-telling and look," Ida Belle said. "They're up to something, because no way Celia would be standing in a boat otherwise. What's she got in her hand?"

I lifted my binoculars and zeroed in on Celia's clenched

fist, then watched as she flung whatever she held across the bayou. I shifted in the direction of the toss and my heart dropped when I saw the alligator moving toward whatever she'd just tossed in the water.

"It's Godzilla!" Gertie said. "Go! Go! She's killing him!"

CHAPTER SEVEN

Ida Belle grabbed a handful of throttle and we launched toward Dorothy's boat at breakneck speed. As the boat grew larger and larger in my blurred vision, I kept thinking surely Ida Belle was going to cut the throttle, but she kept barreling at them as if she intended to run the other boat right over. For a split second I thought about bailing, but in the time it took to consider it, we'd covered so much distance it was too late.

Then Ida Belle swung the boat sideways and it dug into the bayou as it tilted, throwing a blanket of water over Celia and Dorothy. I heard them scream and looked over at the two drenched women. Both were furious.

"I'll have you arrested," Celia ranted at Ida Belle. "You could have killed us."

"Don't be stupid," Ida Belle said. "If I wanted to kill you, I'd shoot you. I wouldn't tear up a perfectly good boat to do it."

Gertie, who'd finally discovered the grip breaking point for the cushion, picked herself up from the bottom of the boat and glared at Celia.

"You're trying to kill Godzilla!" she yelled.

"Darn right I am," Celia said. "That alligator is a menace and so are you. Unfortunately, I can only get away with killing one of you."

"Bring it on," Gertie said. "It would give me a reason to put you down."

I held my hands up. "Now, let's everybody calm down."

I didn't think for a moment that Celia could actually kill Gertie. Not with her bare hands, but there was that rumor about her buying a gun, and I had a lot of concern about what Gertie had in that huge duffel bag of hers. If Celia pulled a gun out, I had no doubt we'd find out.

"Don't you open your mouth, you harlot," Celia said. "Cavorting with the police like a cheap floozy. We all know that's why you're not in jail, but I've filed my complaints with the state, and when they investigate, you and Carter will both go down."

"Last time I checked," I said, "dating wasn't illegal." I looked over at Ida Belle. "Is it?"

"Not really," Ida Belle said. "There's some rules about the lunar eclipse and triple-X tides that come with a full moon, but since Carter's not a shrimper, you're good."

"No one cares!" Celia yelled, her face beet red. She reached down and grabbed something nasty-looking from a bucket and flung it out in the bayou. Godzilla had wisely disappeared, but that didn't mean he wasn't lurking beneath the surface.

"You hateful bitch!" Gertie yelled and pulled what looked like a bazooka out of the bag.

Holy crap! While Ida Belle and I were busy arguing with Celia, Gertie had opened the bag of doom and the end days were upon us.

Dorothy took one look at the giant cannon-looking device and twisted the throttle on her ancient boat. I leaped off my seat to tackle Gertie, but she managed to get off a shot. I grabbed her shoulder, and we both went down in the bottom of the boat. I heard screaming and jumped up to look, figuring at least they weren't dead.

Yet.

A wave of relief washed over me when I saw that the bazooka was a net gun. And Gertie's shot had been a direct hit. The net had landed right on top of Celia and Dorothy, and now they flailed around in the boat, trying to get it off them as the boat turned and faced our direction.

"Something's wrong," Ida Belle said. "The boat is still moving even though Dorothy's not touching the motor. The throttle's stuck. Hold on!"

Ida Belle gunned the engine and we shot away, Dorothy's boat scraping the side of mine as it flew past. The net draped over them had hooked on the side of the boat and was probably the only thing preventing them from pitching out into the bayou.

"Look out!" Ida Belle shouted and pointed at the bank.

Dorothy looked up and then grabbed for the motor, but it was too late. The boat hit the bank and flew up the grassy incline as if it were simply another bayou channel. A thick row of azalea bushes completely hid the backyard of the house, but the boat didn't even appear to slow as it plowed through the bushes and continued into the yard. Gertie glanced at the torn bushes, then looked skyward, and I figured she was either praying no one was in the backyard, as I was, or that Celia had died of a heart attack. I was betting on the second option.

The two women had screamed the entire ride up the grassy slope but now, more voices joined the fray. So much for hoping no one was in the yard. An occasional "floozy" and "sleaze" drifted our way but the rest of the conversation was too garbled to make out. I could only assume that Celia was up there blaming the entire incident on me.

"We should call 911 and then get out of here before someone calls the sheriff," I said.

Ida Belle pointed down the bayou. "Too late."

I looked over to see Carter approaching in the sheriff's department boat. Crap. No way we were getting out of this one.

Ida Belle motioned to Gertie. "For Christ's sake, put that hand cannon down. And where the heck did you get that thing?"

"eBay," Gertie said. "You can get all kinds of things on eBay. The same guy that made this one also makes one that shoots six-foot subs."

I tried to come up with a good reason for launching a sandwich into the air but short of a stadium full of hungry people who couldn't move, I couldn't come up with anything.

"You better start working up a story," I said. "You've got about two seconds."

"I don't need a story," Gertie said. "Celia deserves whatever she got and so does Dorothy for helping her."

"But whoever was in that backyard didn't," Ida Belle said. "And you're on the hook for it unless you come up with some reasonable story about why you fired a net on them."

I slouched back in my chair as Carter approached. I didn't need binoculars to know he was frowning. I knew this entire situation with the alligator wasn't going to be trouble-free, but I'd hoped to stay off law enforcement radar for a couple of hours. I figured the next call was going to be from my neighbor Ronald, reporting a monster in my shed. Instead, it was round four million eighty-two of the Gertie and Ida Belle Versus Celia Chronicles.

If their feud kept affecting other people, the Sinful City Council was going to write some new laws. Probably starting with forcing them all to either leave town or make a schedule for leaving their homes so their paths never crossed. Although now that I thought about it, Sinful residents did seem to enjoy the entertainment value. Maybe not seeing Celia's butt, but in a perverse way, I could see where people might find some things hilarious. If I weren't smack in the middle of them, I would still be laughing.

Carter slowed his boat as he approached and pointed a finger at us. "Don't move. I'm going to want to talk to you."

He drove his boat onto the bank where Celia and Dorothy had taken flight, then jumped out and headed through the bushes. Ambulance sirens echoed across the bayou and I hoped it was a cursory call and not a necessary one. The shouting had lessened to occasional name-calling. I could make out three women's voices and one man.

"Whose house is that?" I asked.

"Leonard Walsh," Ida Belle said.

I stretched my memory to church, the General Store, and the café—the places I usually came in contact with Sinful residents. "Sixties? Mole on his forehead?"

Ida Belle nodded.

"Is he married?" I asked. I usually saw him at the café with a couple of other older men, but that didn't mean anything. Most of the groups of older men in Sinful had wives that they were trying to escape for a bit. Same for the women. The café was a regular meeting place for both. The men early in the morning and the women later.

"Widowed," Gertie said. "About a year ago."

"Family in town?" I asked.

"No," Ida Belle said. "He had an older sister, but she died of cancer fairly young. His parents are long gone, and his kids moved out of state right after high school."

"Interesting," I said. "So do either of you recognize the voice of the woman in his backyard?"

They both shook their heads.

"I wonder if Leonard was having a soiree in his backyard," Gertie said. "The old coot. Couldn't even wait until his wife's body was cold."

"Her body was cold forty years ago when they married," Ida Belle said.

"I thought you weren't supposed to speak ill of the dead," I said.

"Then I wouldn't be talking a lot about dead people," Ida Belle said. "His wife was a harsh woman who spent their entire marriage bossing him around like a drill sergeant. Did the same to her kids, which is why they left the day after high school graduation and rarely come back to visit."

"Now you've got me interested," Gertie said. "Maybe we should go see what's going on back there."

"We'll do no such thing," Ida Belle said. "And instead of wondering what's going on in that yard, you better figure out a good reason why you're not to blame for it."

"Here comes Carter," I said. "I hope you've got your alibi ready."

He pushed his boat off the bank, then drove over next to us and grabbed hold of my seat to keep from drifting.

"Is anyone hurt?" I asked.

"Is it Celia?" Gertie asked, a little too excited at the prospect.

Carter frowned at her. "No one is hurt. At least, not in the 'needing medical transport' sense, although I imagine Celia and Dorothy will be rather sore tomorrow. Any of you want to tell me what happened?"

"What did they say happened?" Ida Belle asked.

Good, I thought. It was always more efficient to figure out what you needed an alibi for before you started making stuff up. It saved a lot of creative energy.

"They said Gertie shot a net over them, causing Dorothy to lose control of her boat. They said that you were trying to knock them out of the boat and into the bayou so Godzilla could eat them. They said I should arrest Gertie for attempted murder and Fortune for being a floozy."

"Hey, I guess I got off this time," Ida Belle said.

Carter shook his head. "According to Celia, you're the ring-leader and ultimately, all of this is your fault."

"As long as she recognizes me as the one in charge," Ida Belle said.

Carter sighed and looked at Gertie. "Did you shoot them with a net?"

"No," Gertie said. "Well, yes, but that wasn't my intention."

Really? I leaned forward in my seat. This was about to get good.

"Celia was throwing poisoned melt at Godzilla," Gertie said.

"Poisoned?" Carter glanced over at me and Ida Belle, and we nodded. "And you know this how?"

Gertie told him about the phone call from Walter and Celia's purchases at his friend's store. I could see Carter's jaw clench and knew Walter would be getting an earful from his nephew for going straight to Gertie with that bit of information.

"So I shot the net at Godzilla," Gertie said. "I figured if I could get him trapped in the net, we could haul him to a preserve and then he'd be safe."

"But you didn't hit the alligator with the net," Carter said.

"Unfortunately, I didn't have time to train with the gun beforehand," Gertie said. "This was the first time I used it. I guess my aim was off."

I shot an approving glance at Ida Belle. Gertie had managed to say all of that with a completely straight face.

"See?" Ida Belle said. "It was an accident, and one that isn't even remotely against the law. Unlike flinging poisoned melt into the bayou where anything could pick it up, not just that gator. As for the boat part of things—Dorothy's throttle stuck."

"You're sure about that?" Carter asked.

"Positive," Ida Belle said. "She didn't even have her hand on the tiller when they flew past us and hit the bank. She was too busy yanking on the net."

I nodded. "Dorothy only touched that thing Ida Belle said —the handle on the motor—once, then let go, but the boat kept coming. If Ida Belle hadn't moved us out of the way, they'd have run right into us."

"You know good and well Dorothy doesn't maintain that boat," Ida Belle said. "The darn thing shouldn't even be registered. Clearly, it's a danger to everyone on the water and on the bank."

"What happened up there anyway?" I asked, unable to control my curiosity any longer. "There was a lot of yelling. Was Mr. Walsh in his backyard? I heard Celia yelling about floozies and figured she was blaming it all on me."

Carter rubbed his jaw, and I could tell he was trying to decide what, if anything, to tell us. He must have figured we'd hear about it anyway because finally, he dropped his hand and I could see his lips quivering.

"Yes," he said. "Mr. Walsh was home, and he was not alone. He was in his pool with Ms. Morehead...naked...when Dorothy's boat flew through the azaleas and crash-landed in the pool next to them."

"Ms. Morehead? As in Dorothy's sister?" Gertie asked.

Carter nodded. "I have recently been made aware that Dorothy had been secretly dating Mr. Walsh and was less than thrilled to find her sister in the buff with him."

Gertie hooted. "Oh boy!"

"How did we not know about any of this?" Ida Belle asked.

Carter couldn't hold it any longer and the grin finally broke through. "So, for once, the floozy calling wasn't about Fortune."

"I wonder how many women ol' Leonard is 'secretly' dating?" I asked.

"I have a feeling we're about to find out," Carter said. He studied Gertie for several seconds, then sighed. "I suppose the entire thing is your word against hers."

"Except for the poisoning," Ida Belle said. "If you test that melt, you'll know for sure."

"And I plan to," Carter said. "That's public endangerment, and I'm not about to let it slide. That melt could have washed up on the bank and been picked up by someone's pet."

"We're not far from my house," I said. "Merlin could have gotten a hold of that. If that witch hurts my cat, I'll shoot her with something worse than a net."

"Don't worry about Celia," Carter said. "She won't be throwing any more poison meat in the bayou. As soon as I have proof of the poisoning, I'll let her sit in jail for a day or so."

"Then you'll have to listen to her mouth," Ida Belle said.

"I'll have the sheriff cover the office those days," Carter said. "He won't hear anything."

"I want my net back," Gertie said.

"It's in shreds," Carter said. "They got pitched out of the boat when it crash-landed. Walsh had to cut them loose before they drowned."

"It's a shame he was home," Gertie grumbled.

"Is that gator still around?" Carter asked, scanning the bayou.

"I don't think so," I said.

"He probably took off because of all the commotion," Ida Belle said.

Carter nodded. "Which is exactly what you three should do. And do me a favor—find something indoors to do the rest of the day. Something that doesn't involve weapons or explosions or animals that can kill people. Just one evening of peace and quiet. Is that too much to ask?"

We all shook our heads. That had been my plan anyway. I desperately needed a shower and I wasn't alone. And despite the huge plate of lasagna I'd eaten earlier, I was starving. All the excitement must have burned off my lunch. I checked my watch. Three p.m. Seriously? It felt as if we'd been out here at least a week.

"Okay," Carter said. "Well, I've got to go grab that bucket of meat before it disappears." He looked at me. "I'll see you later tonight, but I don't know what time. I have to deal with this, and I have a feeling I'm going to be hearing about it for quite a while. Especially as I'm not hauling any of you to jail."

"I'm going home and staying put," I said and held up two fingers. "Scout's honor."

"You wouldn't have lasted five minutes in the Scouts," Carter said before pulling away.

"I wonder how they're going to get the boat out of the pool," I said.

"It's small enough," Ida Belle said. "They can probably get some guys to lift it out."

"Well, at least the boat is out of commission," Gertie said. "I can't imagine that trip through the hedges and into the pool did it any good, and apparently, it was already on its last leg."

Ida Belle nodded. "We may have a reprieve on Celia's water access. And since Carter is going to pursue the poisoned meat thing, maybe she'll back off."

"Celia will never back off," Gertie said. "She hates us too much for that."

"Maybe she'll back off long enough for us to relocate Godzilla," Ida Belle said.

It sounded good, but I had my doubts. We were talking about Celia here.

She'd finally figured out a way to hurt Gertie. She wasn't going to let it go that easily.

CHAPTER EIGHT

I HAD a thirty-minute cold shower and a big roast beef sandwich, then cleared the dishes and debated what to do with the rest of my day. It had been a long one already, and it was only late afternoon. At the rate I was going, I'd age ten years before I went to bed. I was just deliberating between a *Justified* marathon or a nap on the couch when my phone rang. It was Ally.

"Are you home?" she asked.

"Home and not about to leave unless it's on fire."

"Did Carter put you on house arrest?"

"You heard?"

"The whole town heard," Ally said. "Mr. Walsh in the buff with Dorothy's sister...that's gossip that will travel for a good month."

"I have a sneaky suspicion Dorothy's sister wasn't the only other widow in town ol' Leonard was sneaking around with. This one might carry through to the holidays."

"We can only hope. Maybe that will drown out Aunt Celia's nonsense. Anyway, the reason I called is that I have that café list you wanted. I was going to drop it by. Is now a good time?"

"Absolutely. I'll see if I can round up Ida Belle and Gertie. Since they know all the people involved, they'll have more thoughts on the matter than I will."

"Cool. I'm going to stop at the General Store and pick up an order, then I'll see you in about fifteen minutes."

I disconnected and got Gertie and Ida Belle on the horn. Both had showered and had a snack and were up for discussing the Case of the Missing Morsels with Ally. Gertie also offered to bring cobbler. I have no idea why she still insisted on getting permission. There was no way I was ever turning down homemade cobbler.

I headed into the kitchen and did a quick assessment of beverages. I had some beer and a bottle of wine, but I was running low on diet sodas. I made a mental note to assess my pantry later on and put a list together for Walter. If I was low on soda, I was probably low on or completely out of other things. Oh well. Worst-case scenario, I wouldn't have enough diet soda to go around and someone would have to drink beer. After the day I'd had, I was happy to volunteer. I had a feeling Gertie and Ida Belle would be requesting an alcoholic refreshment as well.

Everyone arrived at the same time and I waved them into the kitchen.

"I'm taking drink orders," I said.

"Beer me," Ida Belle said.

"That sounds good," Gertie said. "Make it two."

I pulled three beers out of the fridge. "Ally?"

"Diet soda for me," Ally said. "I have to drive to New Orleans this evening. I'm having dinner with a pastry chef there to pick his brain."

Ally had left Sinful after high school and gone to nursing school in New Orleans, even though it wasn't what she really wanted to do. When her mother got sick, she returned to

Sinful to care for her and took a job waitressing at the café. Finally, her mother had gotten too ill for Ally to handle and she'd moved to a nursing home in New Orleans. Ally decided to stay in Sinful and save her money, hoping to fulfill her dream to one day open a high-end bakery.

"That sounds like fun," Gertie said as they all sat at the kitchen table. "Are you going to talk recipes or business?"

"Business," Ally said. "Chefs never talk recipes. They'd lend you their lover before they would their baking secrets."

I put the drinks on the table and slid into my seat. "You don't need any baking secrets. You have all the ammunition you need."

Ally blushed. "Thanks. I'm happy with several of my items, but I need to learn more about the actual store part. You know, leasing a space and handling employees...advertising. If the only thing I needed to know was baking, it would be easy."

Ida Belle nodded. "You're smart to study the business. Most people fail when they go out on their own because they didn't do that legwork."

"That's what Walter and Francine both say," Ally said. "They've been really helpful with things. Walter is a whiz at the numbers end of things and showed me his payroll and accounting software. And his CPA is happy to take me on when I'm ready. Francine knows all about the health code and food supply services and contracts. But I needed to talk to someone who owns a bakery because the product offering is so specialized."

"Are you planning on staying in Sinful?" Gertie asked.

"I don't know," Ally said. "At one time, I would have told you heck no and been gone like the wind as soon as possible. But now, I kinda like it here. The problem is I don't know if I can have a profitable business in Sinful."

"What about special events catering?" Ida Belle asked. "Or

shipping certain products? The internet has a never-ending supply of hungry people. You just need to figure out how to target them."

"Those are both items I've been thinking about," Ally said. "I'm hoping the chef will be able to give me the up and down sides of both. But enough about me and my dreams of high-end cupcakes." She pulled a folded sheet of paper from her purse and pushed it across the table to me. "In talking with Francine, she narrowed down the window on one of the thefts to between closing one night and opening the next morning."

"Which means they had to have a key," I said.

Ally nodded. "So I just listed the employees that have a key. Francine updated all the locks about a month ago and gave those of us that handle open or close new keys, so there isn't any issue with any old ones floating around."

"So if someone made a copy of an employee's key," Ida Belle said, "it had to happen in the last month."

"Exactly," Ally said.

I pulled the list over, then looked back up. "The first two names are you and Francine."

"I was being thorough," Ally said.

"Well, I think we can eliminate both of you," I said. "That leaves us with Myra, Jordan, Clarissa, Marco, and Cora." I looked at Ally. "So who's your guess?"

Ally looked pained. "I know you told me to give it a try, but honestly, I just don't see it with any of them. I'm afraid I'm not good at the Nancy Drew thing at all."

"You're young and nice," Ida Belle said. "When you're old and jaded, you'll be able to find a reason for anyone to do anything."

"I'm not old and I'm jaded," Gertie said.

Ida Belle rolled her eyes. "You're so old, 'jaded' wasn't even a word when you were born."

"Okay, jaded old woman," I said to Ida Belle. "What's your assessment? You've already given me Myra's background and she seems unlikely. What's the skinny on the others?"

"Cora is the wife of the music director at the Catholic church," Ida Belle said.

"So I guess that leaves her out?" I said.

"I never said that," Ida Belle said. "If we gave everyone a pass because they sat in church on Sunday, few people in the South would ever be arrested."

"The guilty have more to confess," Gertie said.

"So husband has a stable job and she works, too," I said. "Probably not in a situation where they need to lift food."

"I doubt the husband makes good money at the church," Ida Belle said, "but with her tips, I think they're probably doing okay. He inherited his aunt's house, so no house note, which is usually the biggest expense."

I grabbed a pen from the kitchen counter and made some notes next to Cora's name. "What about Marco? He runs the kitchen, right?"

"Francine runs the kitchen," Ally said, "but Marco is her lead guy. He's been with her since she opened, though. I can't imagine him stealing from her."

I looked at Ida Belle. "What do you say, Jaded? Does Marco have any vices?"

"He dated a woman in New Orleans for a while," she said, "but I think that cooled some time back. He still heads to the city a couple times a month, but single-lady pickings are slim in Sinful and Marco is midforties and not getting any younger."

"I don't think he's looking for women in New Orleans," Gertie said.

"Really?" Ida Belle asked. "Then what's he doing?"

"One of the women in my knitting group said he liked to gamble. Said that's why the woman broke up with him."

"And is this information reliable?" I asked.

Gertie shrugged. "The woman in my group heard it from her niece, who knows the woman that dumped him. As reliable as these things get, I suppose."

I made a note. "Marco wouldn't be the first or last person to get in a bind over gambling. What about Clarissa?"

Ida Belle, Ally, and Gertie looked at one another, but no one spoke.

"All righty then," I said. "Based on those looks, I can only assume that Clarissa might be trouble. Someone want to clue me in?"

"Clarissa is the younger waitress with the brown bob," Gertie said.

"The cute one who wears her T-shirt a size too small and has boobs up under her chin?" I asked.

"That's her," Ida Belle said. "Clarissa has always been a bit loud and rumor has it she's a bit wild. Smoking dope, hanging out with undesirable types at the Swamp Bar...the sort of thing Sinful frowns on."

"Why would Francine employ someone with a questionable reputation?" I asked.

"Clarissa is her second cousin," Ally said. "Her mother died when Clarissa was thirteen and her dad tried to raise her right, but I don't think he knew how to handle her. She ran a little wild in high school, and I don't think she's stopped."

"Then why don't you suspect her?" I asked Ally. "She sounds like a perfect suspect to me."

Ally shrugged. "Her dad works in the oil field and does fine. Geologist, I think. She still lives at home and doesn't have any bills to speak of. Her dad bought her car and pays her insurance, so the only things she's on the hook for are gas and her cell phone. From what I can see, she spends the rest on clothes, makeup, and booze. Maybe worse. But I can't see her stealing food from Francine, and especially not potato chips. She's hypersensitive about her weight. Eats like a bird."

I nodded. "All of that is well reasoned, but the men she's hanging out with probably don't have nearly as good a setup. All they'd need to do is get a hold of the key and make a copy."

"Oh no," Ally said, clearly dismayed. "I hadn't even thought of that. I told you I wasn't any good at this."

Gertie patted her hand. "You'll get more cynical with age. You'll also get crow's feet, so don't rush it."

"So Clarissa and her questionable men definitely warrant looking into," I said, then directed my gaze at Gertie. "But no trips to the Swamp Bar."

"Party pooper," Gertie said.

"Moving on," I said. "Last up is Jordan."

"Nice kid," Gertie said. "Horrible circumstances, though."

"Who is Jordan?" I asked. "And what happened to him?"

"Jordan is a busboy and does some prep. Young guy with dark brown hair and pretty green eyes," Ally said.

"He's shy but one day, he's going to be a heartbreaker," Gertie said.

"Oh, I know who you're talking about," I said. "He looks like he should be fronting for a boy band or staring in a remake of *Twilight*. Celia accused him of trying to steal her purse yesterday."

"That's him," Gertie said. "He's eighteen or nineteen and originally from New Orleans. Father was a loser who took off when he was a baby. His mother worked two jobs and did a good job raising him despite doing it alone, but she was killed by a drunk driver a couple years ago. Jordan came to live with his uncle here in Sinful."

"Who's his uncle?"

"Carl Whiting," Gertie said. "Older guy, silver hair. Always wears a blue suit to church and sits in the second pew."

I nodded, recalling the quiet, nondescript man who sang in a nice baritone. "What's Carl's story?"

"Chronic bachelor," Ida Belle said. "He had a childhood girl that he intended to marry and set up house with here in Sinful. She had other ideas but never told Carl that until the day of high school graduation. Right after the ceremony, she took off for the city. Her family moved away a couple years later, and I don't know what happened to her after that. But she's never been back."

"Carl never married anyone else?" I asked.

"Carl never even dated someone else," Gertie said. "Like some General Store owner we know, he's hopelessly devoted to a woman who will only continue to break his heart."

"This isn't about me," Ida Belle said, changing the subject. "This is about Jordan and offhand, I can't think of any reason for him to steal."

"How's the uncle set for cash?" I asked.

"He's a truck driver for a dairy," Gertie said. "Weekday route so he's home nights and weekends to see what Jordan is up to. I think he's reasonably comfortable. He doesn't live large. Had the same pickup for twelve years. The one blue suit for at least ten."

"Jordan's out of high school, right?" I said. "What are his plans for the future?"

"He wants to go to college," Ally said. "Engineering. He got a scholarship to pay for part of his tuition, but it wouldn't cover it all and then there's living expenses. He decided to stay in Sinful and save some money. Meantime, he's taking some of the basics online."

Gertie sighed. "There was a time when a person could work part time and cover living expenses for college. But nowadays, you need full-time income to cover things, especially when you're making the minimum."

Ally nodded. "Why do you think I stayed? No rent is a big perk. I'm saving way more here than I was in New Orleans, even though I was making more there."

"Okay, so Jordan needs money," I said, "but for school, not for food. Assuming his uncle is funding the grocery bill, I can't see where stealing food would give Jordan what he needs. It's not like the items stolen would bring in enough cash to make it worthwhile."

I made a few notes, then leaned back in my chair. "I have to admit. None of these look overly promising. Certainly no one stands out as secretly starving or needing to bring home food to feed their family."

"Employees eat free on shift anyway," Ally said. "Limited menu items, but it's still a hot meal. So there's that as well."

"So no loading up on steak?" I asked.

"Steak, shrimp, or desserts," Ally said. "Francine said she's providing fuel, not taking us out on a date."

I smiled. Francine was my kind of woman—direct and a sense of humor. "Okay, and the missing food was two boxes of bacon, two pot roasts, four whole chickens, and a case of potato chips. Anything else to add to that list?"

"I'm amazed you remembered all that," Ally said. "I guess it's all that time spent around books."

"Something like that," I said. "Well, I suppose this is a place to start. None of them look good for it exactly, but we might as well start eliminating those with the most opportunity. If we don't turn up anything, then we'll broaden the search."

Ally leaned forward in her chair. "Yes, but how are you going to eliminate people?"

"If I told you that, I'd have to kill you," I said.

Ally laughed. "No, really."

"Really," Ida Belle said. "Well, maybe not death but sometimes the less you know the better when it comes to our extracurriculars."

"I don't understand," Ally said.

"She means if you don't know anything," I said, "then you can't be required to testify against us."

Ally's eyes widened. "Oh! Ha. Then I'll just wait to hear something." She rose from her chair. "I need to run or I'm going to be late, but if I can help with anything, let me know."

We said goodbye and as soon as the front door closed, I looked over at Ida Belle and Gertie. "Well? What's the plan? Kidnap and torture? Break into the houses and look for the stolen goods?"

"The kidnap and torture is efficient," Gertie said, "but more problematic. Breaking into houses will take longer but there's probably less chance of going to prison."

I stared at her. "I swear, sometimes I have no idea whether or not you're joking."

"You don't want an answer on that one," Ida Belle said.

I looked back at Gertie. "Since clearly, I was joking, does anyone else have an idea?"

Gertie shrugged. "We could try surveillance, but even with three of us we can't watch all of them all the time. And the only way to catch them stealing on shift is to sit in the cooler. I still say it would be easier to hop into those homes and check out the fridge. Unless there's something weird going on, no way someone ate two cases of bacon in that short of a time frame."

"She's right," Ida Belle said.

"You too?" I asked.

"Not about breaking in," Ida Belle said. "The reality is this is just an exercise for us. Even if we did nothing, Francine will get her answer as soon as those cameras go in, and it's not like anyone's life is on the line or anything."

"Then why bother at all?" I asked. "It's not like we don't have other things to do."

"But we have downtime in between," Ida Belle said. "And I see this as an opportunity for us to address the problem like a PI would if Francine had hired one."

"Ah," I said, finally getting her point. "You think because this isn't critical, we should use it as a test run for honing our investigative skills."

Ida Belle shrugged. "Why not? If you move forward with the PI idea, you're going to need our help with background information and we're all going to need training."

"What we're going to need is some get-out-of-jail-free cards," Gertie said.

"Well, don't count on my dating Carter to get us any of those."

"With your lack of girlie talents," Gertie said, "I wouldn't count on you to get me out of a parking ticket."

I would have argued, but she was right. "Okay, so you guys have given me your thoughts. Obviously, if we had a legal way to search the houses, that would probably be the quickest way to figure out who has a lot of bacon and chips, but we still couldn't prove it was from the café."

"Yes, we could," Ida Belle said. "I've been talking to Francine while she checked a delivery. They stamp her name on the boxes. The bacon boxes I saw were white with red lettering."

"Great," I said, "but we're still back to not having a way to legally search the houses, so it doesn't help us. And surveillance on the employees at home seems unlikely to yield results as the food is probably going to be consumed in place, not moved again. So?"

"So we figure out a way to get inside the houses legally," Ida Belle said.

"Oh!" Gertie perked up. "I have a shirt from the cable company with my name on it. Just like the employees wear."

"Why?" I asked.

"Because I might need to pretend to be a cable guy," Gertie said. "I saw it on one of those police shows."

"I'm pretty sure everyone in Sinful knows you don't work for the cable company," I said.

"That's definitely a negative," Gertie said.

"That's definitely a no," I said.

Ida Belle whistled and we both looked at her. "Dressing like the cable guy wasn't what I had in mind," she said, "although I'm going to keep it in reserve if we go undercover somewhere else."

"So what did you have in mind?" I asked.

She pulled out her phone and dialed. "Hello, Braxton? This is Ida Belle. Yes, thank you, I'm doing fine. Listen, this is out of left field, but do you still have that decorative tile work that Destiny did in your kitchen? Yeah? I'm working on updating my own kitchen and wondered if I could drop by and get a picture. It's just the sort of thing I'm looking to do. How does fifteen minutes sound? Great. See you then."

She closed the phone and smiled. "There you go. We've got access to the kitchen where Clarissa lives and it's perfectly legal. We just have to do some creative snooping once inside."

"I take it Braxton is Clarissa's father, but who is Destiny?"

"Her late mother," Ida Belle said.

I frowned. "That doesn't sound like a Sinful sort of name."

"It's not," Gertie said. "Braxton broke rank and married a New Orleans stripper. And he wonders why Clarissa is wild."

Ida Belle nodded. "She did this perfectly horrible tile work in the kitchen. So horrible it actually makes you want to diet. But Braxton is notoriously cheap so I figured there was no way he would pay to have it redone."

"Destiny had horrible taste," Gertie said. "Made Celia look fashion-forward."

"I can't wait to see this tile then." I looked over at Ida Belle. "Nice work."

"That's only one," Ida Belle said. "If we don't find what we're looking for there, we'll have to come up with some way to get inside the other houses."

"My money's on Clarissa," Gertie said. "Walter said Destiny used to lift things from the General Store. He could never catch her, but he was sure it was her. She had the money to buy the stuff, mind you. Some people are just wired wrong."

"And sometimes they pass that wiring on to their children," I said.

"She's a logical choice," Ida Belle said, "but if this summer has taught me anything, it's that reality is rarely logical."

"Since this is the only house we have access to," I said, "let's hope this one is the exception."

CHAPTER NINE

WE HEADED out to my Jeep and Ida Belle directed me to Braxton's house. It was only a couple blocks away and looked like most of the other homes surrounding it. Part brick, part siding. Could use a face-lift but given Ida Belle's comment about cheapness, neat was probably as much as the neighbors could ask for.

Ida Belle knocked on the door and a couple seconds later, it swung open and a man waved us inside.

Late forties. Spare tire on the middle. Barely enough muscle tone to walk. Looked more like an accountant than someone who married a stripper.

"You remember Gertie," Ida Belle said as we walked inside. "And this is our friend Fortune. She's Marge's niece."

He nodded. "Sorry about your aunt. She was an, uh...interesting woman."

"Yes, she was," I agreed. "Thank you."

"Anyway," he said, "the tile is still in the kitchen, although why you'd want to put it in your house, I have no idea. It doesn't seem like the kind of thing you'd go for."

"I'm exploring all kinds of options," Ida Belle said. "I remember it was custom, right? An artist painted the tiles?"

Braxton nodded. "Paid a fortune to be tacky, but I've been looking at it for twenty-five years, so I can't see tearing it out now. Probably have to if I ever decide to sell. It tends to offend people."

My curiosity launched into overdrive. I understood if decor wasn't to one's taste, but I'd yet to see any I found offensive. And then we walked into the kitchen.

"Wow," I said, unable to keep silent.

"It's hard to find a nicer word, right?" Braxton asked.

The tile was a backsplash that stretched the entire length of the kitchen counter and went all the way up to the shelves mounted on the wall. The background of the tile was white and the "custom" part was black ink drawings. Nudes, to be exact. I couldn't fathom the tile looking right anyplace other than a strip club or a brothel, but here it was, on a kitchen wall in Sinful, Louisiana.

"How is this not against the law?" I asked. "I mean, with all Sinful's strange laws and all."

Braxton nodded. "There was a bit of a kerfuffle when Clarissa got old enough to have friends over. The parents refused to let their kids in our house until I covered all the tile with cardboard and promised them it wouldn't come down until Clarissa graduated from high school. There were still some holdouts, even with the cardboard."

I figured the holdouts were more about the mother than the tile, but they sorta went hand in hand. What I couldn't figure at all was why Braxton let her install the tile to begin with. There was cheap and then there was this. And this was beyond words. Clarissa's mother must have had all kinds of talents that didn't extend to her taste in decor.

"I don't suppose you remember the name of the artist?" Ida

Belle asked. "I know it's been a while."

"Not offhand," Braxton said, "but if you give me a minute, I might be able to come up with it. I'm fairly anal with my receipts. I probably still have the original."

"Take all the time you need," Ida Belle said. "I'm just going to take some pictures, if that's all right."

Braxton nodded and headed out of the room. Gertie crept to the doorway, then turned back and pointed up, indicating he'd gone upstairs. I heard the floorboards above us creak a few seconds later and we all flew into action. Ida Belle dashed into the laundry room to dig through the deep freezer. Gertie opened the top of the refrigerator and I flung open the pantry. Several seconds later, we all collected in the kitchen again, each of us shaking our heads.

Bummer. We'd struck out.

The floorboards upstairs creaked again, so Ida Belle pulled out her cell phone and started taking pictures of the horrible tile. Seconds later, Braxton came back into the kitchen with a name and phone number written on a sticky note.

"I found it," he said, looking pleased with himself. I assumed that was because of his record-keeping prowess and not because he wanted to recommend the tile artist.

Ida Belle took the sticky. "Thanks. I think I have enough pictures. We'll get out of your hair. Sorry to drop in on you this way."

"It's no problem," he said. "I wasn't doing anything anyway."

"Is Clarissa on shift at the café?" Gertie asked.

He frowned. "I don't know where Clarissa is. She stopped checking in with me about the time she turned fifteen and discovered boys. I guess the problem would be men now, although given their behavior, I'm rather loath to give them the title."

“She’s not making good choices?” Gertie asked, sounding sympathetic as only Gertie could manage.

“No,” Braxton said, “but then she never has, so my expectations were low to begin with. The truth is I haven’t seen Clarissa in over a week, except for one morning when I had breakfast at the café. And even then, she switched tables with Ally so she didn’t have to wait on me.” He sighed. “I swear I did everything I could, but that girl took after her mother. Marrying Destiny was a mistake, and I compounded it by having a child with her. She wasn’t exactly wife and mother material.”

Gertie patted his arm. “You did the best you could, but at some point, you just have to cut them loose and pray for the best.”

“All the prayers in Sinful won’t give that girl a lick of sense,” Braxton said. “Last week, I got a phone call in the middle of the night and I just knew it was the police calling to tell me something bad had happened. Turned out it was a wrong number, but short of a miracle, I know that call is coming.”

“Well, if there’s anything we can do,” Gertie said, “please let us know.”

“I appreciate it, but I think that train left the station years ago. You ladies have a nice evening.” He looked at Ida Belle. “If you come up with a good tile person, let me know. It’s time I changed all of this. Past time, actually.”

“I’ll let you know,” Ida Belle promised, and we headed out.

As soon as we drove away, Ida Belle pulled out her cell phone.

“What are you doing?” I asked. “Making notes?”

“No. I’m deleting those horrible tile pictures before my phone locks up in protest.”

“I may bleach my eyes,” I said. “Why didn’t he leave the cardboard up? Or wallpaper over it? Heck, coloring it with permanent marker would have worked even and couldn't have looked worse. Seriously, no one is that cheap."

Ida Belle nodded. "My guess would be he didn't take it down because of Clarissa. Destiny was certainly no prize parent, but she was still Clarissa's mother."

"Well, it sounds like Clarissa is following in her mother's questionable footsteps," I said. "And we still can't eliminate her from our suspect list. If she hasn't been home for a week, then the stolen goods wouldn't be at her dad's house."

"As far as I'm concerned," Gertie said, "this moves her straight to the top of the suspect list. I guarantee you she hasn't been hanging out with any reputable young men."

"Maybe Francine will know who Clarissa is seeing," Ida Belle said. "I don't think she'd be stupid enough to bring them around the café, but people talk."

Gertie nodded. "And given that Francine is Clarissa's cousin and her employer, any responsible person would have filtered that information to her. Especially if she's running with men from the Swamp Bar."

"Well," I said, "sounds like we need to get some more intel and come up with a way to check out the other freezers. And honestly, I don't think I'm going to be any help today. I think I'm out of energy for anything else."

Ida Belle glanced at me and I could tell she was concerned. It wasn't normal for me to run low on energy, and she was smart enough to know that it had nothing to do with the physical activities of the day and everything to do with the mental ones. Mostly, all the thinking I was doing about the Ahmad takedown.

"Sounds good to me," Ida Belle said. "I need to wash the SUV and do some grocery shopping or I'm going to be eating ramen noodles for the next week."

Gertie nodded. "And I had just put some dough out to rise before you called."

"Dough?" I asked. "If you tell me you're making coffee cake, I will be your slave for a day. Maybe two."

Gertie laughed. "The enthusiasm is very flattering but the offers of servitude are not necessary. I'm making two—one for me and Ida Belle and one for you."

"How come I have to split one with you?" Ida Belle asked.

"Because as much as I hate to admit it," Gertie said, "you and I don't burn off calories sitting still like Fortune does."

"She'll age and suffer along with the rest of us one day," Ida Belle said.

"If suffering comes with coffee cake, sign me up," I said.

I pulled into my driveway. and the two of them headed to Ida Belle's SUV, waving as they pulled away. I headed inside, my head overflowing with so much information that I knew if I didn't give it a rest, I was going to end up with a migraine. It was time to take a much-needed break. Between Godzilla and Ahmad, I was done with worrying and thinking. I'd thought keeping busy would keep me distracted, but all it had done was give me more to think about. It was time to escape. And there was no better place for that than my hammock with a good book.

I had finished the last novel up a couple days before and went upstairs to cruise through Marge's collection for another. The last had been a spy novel, and while entertaining, I didn't need a reminder of the upcoming Ahmad takedown, so I swept past that section. The next was fantasy, which I considered for a moment, but then decided that dragons were too much like Godzilla, which wasn't the escape I was looking for. I finally settled on a good old-fashioned PI book, figuring I might be able to pick up some tips about my potential future employment.

I headed out back with a bottled water and the book and climbed into the hammock. Merlin took up residence in the lawn chair beside the hammock that was reserved for Carter, but Merlin had decided it had been placed there for him. He spent a lot of time napping in that chair. I opened the book to the first chapter and began to read. I hadn't even made it three pages in before I nodded off.

I awakened to a hiss and then a frantic cat running across my forehead. I tried to bolt up, confused about where I was and what was happening, and remembered, a little too late, that I was in the hammock. I pitched out the side and fell facedown on the ground. I was just about to yell at Merlin when I realized something was moving nearby. Something large and definitely not my cat.

I lifted my head and found myself face-to-face with Godzilla.

I let out a scream that could probably be heard all the way back in DC and leaped up from the ground, then scrambled for one of the trees the hammock hung from. I shinnied up it like one of those pineapple pickers in the tropics, hitting Merlin on my way up and knocking him onto a lower branch. He grabbed the branch, his bottom end dangling, and I saw the gator race for the tree and hiss.

I reached down to grab Merlin by the scruff and pulled him back onto the branch below me. He repaid my efforts by racing straight up my body and taking roost on the top of my head, claws digging into my skull. I reached for my cell phone and realized it was sitting in the chair Merlin had vacated.

But I didn't even take a nap without my pistol.

I pulled it from the holster at my waist and took aim at the gator. This entire thing had gone from ridiculous to downright dangerous. I'd take the body out into the bayou and dump it. Gertie would blame Celia when she couldn't find him, and the natural order of enemy fire in Sinful would go on as usual. I sighted in the spot on his head I knew would kill him and started to squeeze. But something stopped me.

He was looking at me, and I swear he was smiling.

All those teeth in that enormous mouth looked like a smiling jack-o'-lantern and Lord help me, I couldn't pull the trigger. What the heck was wrong with me?

I took a deep breath and blew it out, then aimed again. Then I moved the pistol to the side. Maybe if I fired a warning shot, he'd leave. Then I could pretend this never happened. And maybe the warning shot would be enough to scare Godzilla away from the area. I didn't believe that for a minute, but it sounded good.

Just as I squeezed the trigger, Merlin shifted and one claw dug directly into my forehead. I yelped and the shot went wide, hitting the chair and flipping it over. The gator hissed but didn't seem fazed. I shoved the pistol back in my waistband and tugged the cat off my head, wincing as he clawed across my scalp. That was definitely going to scar. I plopped him onto a nearby branch and pulled out my pistol again.

I sighted in a spot right next to the gator's head and was about to fire when I heard yelling. I looked over and saw my neighbor, Ronald Franklin Jr., come through the hedges between our lawns. He was wearing a Confederate soldier uniform and I swear what looked like women's pumps. His face was as red as the shoes, and he stomped across the lawn with far more grace than I could have managed in five-inch heels.

"I've had about enough of your shenanigans, missy," he said as he approached.

"Stop!" I yelled. "Don't come any closer."

"Don't you dare try to pull that trespassing thing on me. Your screaming is a public nuisance, and firing a gun is highly illegal. I've called the police, so hiding in that tree won't help you."

He continued to push forward, not even noticing the alligator sitting in the ivy at the base of the tree. Okay, so maybe he blended, a little, but if Ronald hadn't been on his high horse, he would have spotted him.

"It's dangerous," I said, and pointed down. "Alligator."

"Don't be foolish," he said, continuing his walk toward me. "I've lived here my entire life and never had an alligator come up into my lawn. You're not getting away with nonsense this time. I don't care who you're dating. Don't think I haven't seen Deputy LeBlanc's truck parked in your driveway at indecent hours."

"There's an alligator down there," I insisted. "Just look, you fool!"

Maybe it was the yelling, or maybe it finally occurred to him that I sounded serious and there wasn't a good reason for me and the cat to be clinging to the tree like a lifeline. He took one look down and gasped, but it was too late. Godzilla homed in on him and rose up on all fours. Ronald screamed so loudly he made mine sound weak, then dashed for the tree that held the other end of the hammock. Godzilla whirled around and headed straight toward him.

Like any good horror movie heroine, Ronald refused to kick off his heels when he bolted for the tree and then scrambled up the side. The heel of the right shoe snapped off as he climbed up the tree, and I heard him yelp in pain. I wasn't sure if that was over the broken shoe or the bark that was probably eating off his bare ankles. He got to the first branch, a good ten feet above the ground, and stood there, hugging the tree as though it had been gone off to war and he hadn't seen it in years.

"You could have gotten me killed," he said.

"I tried to tell you. And besides, who hears a bloodcurdling scream and dashes toward it? In heels, I might add. And what the hell are you wearing? Are you doing one of those reenactment things?"

"This is what I wear for afternoon tea."

I didn't even know what to say. I mean, aside from it was probably a good thing he normally wore that getup inside his house. The Confederate soldier uniform was bad enough and the heels weren't doing anything to improve the image.

"Well, don't just stand there," he said. "Do something."

"What do you suggest I do? I've already fired a shot at it. He's not scared."

"Then fire another and kill it."

"I thought you called the police."

"And what do you think they're going to do?"

He had a point. Carter was somewhat sympathetic to Gertie's unorthodox attachment to the gator, but he couldn't let that get in the way of keeping the rest of Sinful safe. Regardless of what Gertie believed, Godzilla was still a stone-cold reptile who could easily kill a human and then drag them off to the watery depths to be tenderized for later consumption.

Still, there was always the cowardly train of thought. Gertie would take it better if Carter shot the alligator than if I did. But then, she'd probably blame me for not scaring him away before Carter arrived. Jeez, this situation had far too many things to consider, especially now that I had a witness. And the answers weren't exactly obvious while clinging to a tree.

"Don't just stand there, you idiot," Ronald said. "Shoot it!"

I pulled my pistol out, and for a split second, I considered doing us all a favor and shooting Ronald, but I figured that wouldn't be the best foot forward into my future. I took aim at the gator and squeezed off a round right next to his head. He didn't even flinch.

"You missed," Ronald said. "Don't you know how to shoot?"

I pretended to fumble with the gun and fired off a round toward Ronald, taking the heel off his remaining intact shoe. "Sorry," I said. "I haven't practiced in a while."

"You're going to buy me a new pair of shoes."

"I'm not buying you anything. You trespass on my property, you get what you get. Next time you hear me scream, maybe call the police, then stay in your own yard."

"If you can't shoot him, then throw that cat down and give him something to eat while we get away."

Okay. Now I wanted to shoot him for real.

Merlin glared at him and hissed, as if he'd understood the entire exchange.

I heard the splintering sound, but it took me a second to realize what it was. The branch Ronald was standing on was starting to break. "Get off that branch!" I yelled.

But it was too late.

A loud *snap* echoed across my lawn as the branch broke pitching Ronald out of the tree and directly into the hammock. All the commotion startled Merlin and he jumped back on top of my head, covering one of my eyes with his paws. I shoved my pistol sideways in my mouth and flailed around a bit, trying to pull his paw off my eye without blinding myself, but I only had one hand to work with since I was using the other to hold on to the tree.

"Good God Almighty." Carter's voice sounded below me.

I looked down with one eye, wondering why Godzilla wasn't attacking, but all I saw was a very unhappy Ronald climbing out of the hammock, clutching what was left of the red pumps, and a clearly confused Carter. Godzilla was nowhere in sight, which figured since he was the one who'd caused all the problems to begin with. Merlin decided the world was safe again and sprang off my head, leaving tracks across my forehead as he went.

Ronald glared at Carter. "I want this woman arrested."

I pulled my pistol out of my mouth and shoved it in my sports bra. "Get in line."

Carter gave Ronald a once-over. "What did she do?"

Ronald held up what was left of one of the pumps. "She shot off my heel."

"That was an accident."

"You *accidentally* shot his heel?" Carter asked, and I could see his lips quivering.

Ronald pointed a finger up at me. "The woman is a menace. Marge was bad enough with her *Guns & Ammo* life-style, but at least she only cleaned them outside. She didn't go shooting them off in her backyard and never at other residents."

"Perhaps she never got to know you well enough," I said. "Anyway, since he was trespassing not only in my yard, but up my tree, and I wasn't trying to shoot him, I don't think he has a case."

"Uh-huh," Carter said. "And you're up a tree shooting because..."

"That beast was in her yard," Ronald said. "The one that terrorized downtown yesterday. That old coot Gertie keeps feeding it. It's a menace that needs to be stopped."

"Godzilla was in your yard?" Carter asked.

Ronald glared at Carter. "You've named it? What kind of lawman are you?"

"Gertie named it," I said. "Godzilla startled me out of my nap and Nosy here called you when I screamed. And if he'd stayed on his own lawn, where he belonged, the situation wouldn't have gotten out of hand and he wouldn't have had a shoe casualty, although that's probably a blessing. And I only shot one of them. He broke the other one climbing the tree. Therefore, I'm not buying him new shoes."

"I don't think anyone's suggesting that you would," Carter said.

"I absolutely think she should buy me new shoes," Ronald said. "This entire mess is her fault."

"He's trespassing," I said. "I want him arrested for that and for the damage to my tree. That branch can't be repaired."

Carter had apparently heard enough. He held up his hands. "No one is getting arrested. Mr. Franklin, I suggest you go home and find a different pair of shoes to wear. In fact, you might want to reconsider the entire outfit if you plan on leaving your house. Fortune, get down from that tree before you *accidentally* shoot your gun again."

"You haven't heard the last of this," Ronald said as he stalked off. "I'm taking this up with the sheriff."

Carter shook his head as I climbed down from the tree. "Why did you shoot his shoe?"

"He was irritating me."

"Is that really all it takes?"

"Some days."

"Maybe I'll start wearing my steel-toed boots when you're around."

"Maybe I'll start aiming higher."

He laughed.

"That butthole Ronald suggested I toss Merlin out of the tree to distract Godzilla so he could get away," I said. Technically, I'd shot off the heel before he'd suggested feeding my cat to Godzilla, but I saw no reason to mention that.

"Ah," Carter said. "I'm surprised you only shot off his heel. So the gator was in your yard?"

"I'm afraid so."

"I would have thought after all that commotion earlier, he would have headed for less crowded waters."

"I thought so too, but clearly, we both underestimated the power of Gertie's cooking. I was having a nap and woke up with an unwanted sleeping partner, except he wasn't sleeping."

"I assume the shooting scared him off…as was intended."

"Actually, the shooting didn't faze him. I have no idea why he left. If a peek at Celia's bare butt and Ronald's outfit didn't do it, I'm not sure what will. Tell me the truth, Ronald's a former mental patient, right?"

"He's, uh, what my mother would call eccentric."

Carter's mother was exceedingly nice. "Uh-huh, and what would you call him?"

"Batshit crazy."

"I'm still not buying him new shoes."

"I never thought you would. Anyway, I've got some real work to do, so if the drama is over, then I'm going to get back to it. In the meantime, maybe you could go inside and sit quietly in the living room until I get off."

"You think that will work?"

"If Ida Belle and Gertie aren't here, you stand a fighting chance. Try another nap, maybe on the couch. You can give me the blow-by-blow tonight over dinner."

"Do you plan on eating or laughing?"

"Okay, after dinner."

"Fine, but I'm not cooking. I shouldn't have to provide the meal and the entertainment."

"I'll pick up something from the café. You can provide the entertainment…and the dessert." He winked and headed across the yard.

I blew out a breath. Just another steamy August afternoon in Sinful, Louisiana.

CHAPTER TEN

It took Carter several hours to wrap up his paperwork, mostly because he had Celia down at the sheriff's department ranting. She claimed that the meat wasn't intended for the alligator at all. She and Dorothy were going crabbing, and therefore, Carter had confiscated her bait illegally and she demanded that he return it. The entire mess had ended with Carter threatening to call Wildlife and Fisheries and have her arrested for poaching, which probably wouldn't have been enough to get rid of her. But when he said he'd go one step further and ask the governor for a commendation for Gertie for catching her, that did it. She stomped out of the sheriff's department, threatening to sue Carter, the sheriff, Deputy Breaux, the dispatcher, and even the janitor who had the misfortune of picking that time to wash the windows.

I took pity on his awful day and fixed up some more roast beef sandwiches instead of having Carter stop for dinner. I figured he was probably worn out on people and even giving a food order was just one more conversation he wasn't interested in having. Not to mention that word of the naked pool invasion had already started filtering through town, so everyone would be asking him to elaborate if he stopped at the café for a to-go order.

I gave Carter the blow-by-blow of the hammock-alligator incident over dinner. He'd had a good laugh at both my and Ronald's expenses, but I could tell he was concerned with the gator's lack of fear of humans and guns. Ida Belle and Gertie had shown similar reactions when I'd relayed the story to them by phone that evening. Ida Belle's friend had been delayed but had delivered the cage at dusk. We'd made tentative plans to have another go at Godzilla the next morning.

Carter had early shift at the sheriff's department, so he decided to go home, probably thinking we'd both get more rest that way. I didn't figure it would work out for me, but I appreciated the thought. Plus, as much as I liked being with Carter, I wasn't ready to be around him full time. I was still too much of a loner to adjust my entire lifestyle to accommodate another person in it 24-7.

After a somewhat fitful start to sleep, I finally crashed in the wee hours of the morning. Despite the lack of quality rest, I awakened at six a.m. I looked over at the alarm clock and groaned. Of all the mornings to sleep late, this would have been a good one, but I knew it was pointless. Once my mind got going, it was impossible to go back under. And my mind was definitely going. Between Ahmad and trying to capture Godzilla, and now the case of the missing bacon, I had a million things to think about. And when I'd exhausted all ideas on those three subjects, my mind jumped to the future. The one where Ahmad was dead and I was free to do whatever I wanted.

At one time, thoughts of that future would have concerned me more than the takedown or the gator, but now I found myself anxious to get started. I was ready. I wasn't at all sure Sinful was ready for me, but it was happening.

I flung the covers back and swung my legs over the side of the bed. There was no use lying there when there were chocolate chip cookies and coffee downstairs. If I felt really ambitious, I might cook up some eggs after the cookies. I gave my face a quick rinse, threw on yoga pants and a tee, and headed downstairs.

When I stepped into the kitchen, I choked back a yelp.

Mannie was sitting at my kitchen table, holding a cup of coffee and a newspaper. "I made a whole pot," he said and gestured to the counter.

"Thank you?" I wasn't sure what the etiquette was when someone had broken into your house and then offered up your own coffee. I didn't even bother asking him how he'd gotten in.

Mannie grinned. "I was surprised you weren't awake. You were more of a morning person at the beginning of summer."

I poured myself a cup of coffee, grabbed the container of cookies, and headed to the table. "I didn't sleep all that well."

"I'm sure you've got a lot on your mind." He pulled an envelope out from under the newspaper and slid it across the table to me. "That's the list of properties and the keys to access them. I did reconnaissance on everything the Heberts own. The ones on this list will do what you need. It's just a matter of you choosing which one is best for your arrangements."

"You know?"

He nodded. "The Heberts don't keep secrets from me, but you don't have to worry. I don't talk. And besides, I would have done the same thing in your situation."

I cocked my head to one side and studied him a couple seconds. "Who are you, exactly? Former military? Fed? Mercenary?"

"My past is long and varied, but one day, I might tell you some of it."

"Superhero? One of those dark and tortured ones like Batman, but without the money and the cool gadgets."

"I don't wear tights."

"I doubt anyone would give you grief if you did."

He grinned again and rose. "I have some other business to attend to, so I'll vacate your kitchen. If you need anything else, please let us know. And if I can be of personal assistance, for recon or as an extra shooter, I would be happy to help."

"I appreciate it. I'm going to assume that if someone took a cursory look at the chain of ownership, Big's and Little's names are hidden in layers of corporations?"

"Not planning on letting the boyfriend in on it, are you?"

It bothered me, just a little, that he'd clued in to that so quickly. "No. I don't talk either. Not when I give my word, and especially not when people are sticking their necks out for me."

"I can respect that. Hopefully, the good deputy can as well. The Heberts are well protected from general exposure. If someone at a state or federal level wanted to go digging, they could probably turn up something eventually, but it would take some work."

"Cool. Tell Big and Little I said thank you, again, and I'll try not to destroy their property. I don't make any promises, though."

"They'd probably be happy if you leveled one of them. They buy them depressed and insure them for more than they're worth."

"Of course they do," I said as Mannie slipped through the back door. The Heberts didn't miss a trick.

I opened the envelope and dumped the contents out on the

table. Six keys and several folded sheets of paper lay in front of me. I picked up the papers and unfolded them, surprised to find not only the location of each building, but a satellite image of the property and surrounding area and notes on the nearby properties and their tenants, if occupied. Additional marks on the satellite images noted where security cameras were in place.

I had no idea how many properties Mannie had scouted, but he'd done a very thorough job in very little time. And now that we had a list, the priorities for the day needed to change. Finding Godzilla was important but it would have to wait. I needed to pick a location before we could begin extensive planning on the coup. Everything was on hold until the location was set.

I grabbed my phone off the kitchen table and sent a text to Ida Belle and Gertie.

Change of plans for today. Got the list. Meet here at 9.

They were probably already awake, or would be soon, but 9:00 a.m. gave them time to take care of anything minor they had outstanding or reschedule anything larger. Until then, I'd go over Mannie's notes with a fine-tooth comb and put together a list of concerns to check on when we did our review of the properties. I popped open my laptop, shoved an entire cookie in my mouth, and started reading.

At 9:00 a.m. I was dressed and ready to go—which meant I had put on tennis shoes and was armed. I packed a duffel bag with supplies and headed downstairs. I'd reviewed the property list and ruled out one based on the nearby occupants, leaving five for us to research. I had a list of items to cover for each of the remaining five, and I figured the best way to get it all down was to haul my laptop with us. My intention was to take a ton of pics with my phone and make very detailed notes about each property. Typing on a phone beyond a text message was limiting and annoying, and I planned on recording every observation I made.

Then I'd take everything home and go over it again and again, running through every possible scenario in my head. Reviewing every potential problem. And ultimately narrowing down my choice to the one location that I thought would provide the best opportunity for success. Then I'd send the info to Harrison and he'd do the same thing I did but on the one property. Then he and Director Morrow would call and we'd all hash it out, hopefully ending the call with a set location and a plan.

Ida Belle and Gertie arrived in Ida Belle's SUV, and she insisted on driving to New Orleans. "My vehicle is a lot more comfortable than yours," she said.

"Got that right," Gertie said. "Have you spent much time on the back seat of that Jeep? It could use one of those foam mattresses like you got for the boat."

Ida Belle nodded. "The passenger seat isn't winning any awards. Besides, I could outrun that Jeep on foot. If we need to make a quick getaway, my SUV can handle it."

Ida Belle's pride and joy, a Chevy Blazer that I'd nicknamed Warp Speed, had been hopped up by local engine genius, Hot Rod. I had no idea how fast it would go and didn't want to know. At least, not firsthand. I'd already lost a couple of lives from riding in it before, and despite providing him with the good canned food, I hadn't yet convinced Merlin to lend me any of his.

"This is just recon," I said. "No getaways required."

"You always say that," Ida Belle said. "And then..."

Yeah. "I'm fine with you driving. It allows me to pay more attention to the surrounding areas and make notes as we go. Besides, the SUV has better cupholders than my Jeep."

"Clear liquids only in my vehicle," Ida Belle said.

Gertie rolled her eyes. "You have one little mishap with a strawberry soda and you spend the rest of your life paying for it."

"I have bottled water and diet Sprite," I said.

"Got any Red Bull?" Gertie asked.

"Red Bull is not clear," Ida Belle said.

"It's almost clear," Gertie argued.

"The last thing Fortune and I need is to be locked in a car with you for hours, with you high on Red Bull. The last time you drank one, you were up for two days."

"I know," Gertie said. "I repaired all my loose hems, baked twenty-six loafs of banana nut bread, and painted my back porch."

"Maybe save the Red Bull for when we get back," I suggested. "Or even better, when I'm on vacation."

Gertie frowned. "That's rather hypocritical coming from someone who ate two loaves of the bread."

"Can't have perfectly good food going to waste."

"That's exactly what I said when Walter was going to throw out all those overripe bananas," Gertie said.

"No Red Bull in the SUV," Ida Belle said. "I'll give a pass on the Sprite but only because it's diet. Sugar attracts bugs."

Gertie grabbed three Sprites from the refrigerator, which I found amusing since I was pretty sure she didn't even like Sprite. But she wasn't about to give Ida Belle the pleasure of drinking water. I loaded up my duffel bag, my laptop, and Mannie's notes, and we were off. I went over the properties with them on the way to New Orleans and covered my list of questions about each location. They surprised me by pointing out a couple of things I hadn't considered, but then, they knew the city a lot better than I did. I'd originally asked them to do the property review with me so that they felt involved, but now I could see they were going to help give me every advantage. When we reached the city limits, Ida Belle asked which property we were looking at first.

"The one she likes best, right?" Gertie asked.

"No," I said. "Actually, it makes more sense to start with the last on my list first. I have to see them all anyway, and starting at the bottom allows me to add other items to my list of undesirable attributes."

"Okay, then last it is," Ida Belle said, and directed her vehicle off the interstate.

We spent the next three hours reviewing the bottom four of the properties, then finally headed for the one I'd flagged as the best option. On paper, anyway. It was also Mannie's favorite, and he'd made a couple comments as to why. Comments that read so much like military recon that it made me wonder again what his background was.

"This is it," Ida Belle said, pointing at a large industrial building at the end of the road. "Looks like one way in. That's what you want?"

"That means one way out, right?" Gertie said.

"Not exactly one way," I said. "There's a canal behind the building."

"I would think that's more problematic," Ida Belle said.

"Pursuit in a boat is more difficult, as we all know," I said, "but insertion into the facility is improved. In this case anyway." I pointed to a picture Mannie had taken. "See this? It's an overflow grate that starts in the basement of the building and connects to the channel. Ahmad's men will be watching the facility closely and using thermo-imaging equipment to do it. I don't want to take the time to build out rooms to house operatives inside, so that means deploying them after Ahmad makes his move."

Ida Belle nodded. "And you're thinking they can access the building through the tunnel and then they won't be seen."

"I've checked everything available online and through the city," I said. "There's no way for Ahmad to find out about the water access unless he's in the building. He'll keep men on the outside, ready to alert him if operatives approach."

"But no one will be looking underwater," Ida Belle said. "That's genius."

"It's only genius if it's viable," I said. "So let's go check out that tunnel."

Gertie's eyes widened. "You're going in it?"

"Someone has to," I said. "I brought diving gear. Marge kept some in her secret closet."

"Marge had quite the haul in that closet," Gertie said. "Anything else we should know about?"

"You don't need to know about any of it," Ida Belle said as she parked in front of the warehouse. "You're dangerous enough with eBay."

I grabbed my duffel bag out of the back of Ida Belle's SUV and we headed inside. The first thing I wanted to locate was the water tunnel, so we found the basement access and we pulled out our flashlights and started down.

The opening for the tunnel was covered with a metal door. It was rusted a bit, but I'd brought lube so we had it moving in no time. It took me and Ida Belle to twist it open, but finally we got it pulled back and I stared into the three-foot-square hole.

"It's kinda narrow," Gertie said.

"Not when you're built like Fortune," Ida Belle said.

"I could be built like a stick figure and that would still be narrow," Gertie said. "That coffin you stuffed me in was bigger."

"I didn't stuff you in a coffin," Ida Belle said. "We had to get out of Sinful secretly. That was the best way to do it."

"That coffin rolled away and I almost died," Gertie said.

"Then you were in the right place for it," Ida Belle said. "Besides, you got a hot dog out of the deal."

"It was a good hot dog," Gertie conceded. "But that's still narrow. Is it safe?" She looked at me.

"I guess that depends on your definition of safe," I said as I pulled a dry suit and small tank and mask out of the duffel bag. "It's big enough for an operative to get through, and it should widen by a foot or so. Given that it's got water in it and it's not any more stagnant than what's in the canal, I'm going to go with no blockage. Nothing major, anyway. If it's clear all the way to the canal, then it's enough room to maneuver in, at least for professionals."

"You certainly meet that requirement," Ida Belle said as I pulled on the suit and equipment. "But wouldn't it be better to enter from the canal and swim inside, like the operative will do?"

"Yes, but there's an occupied building on the other side of the canal. If someone sees a person in a dive suit jump into the canal, they'll probably call the police. And since there's no logical reason for me to be diving back there, the police will definitely suspect something nefarious and might flag the location for regular drive-bys."

"Which would eliminate it as a possibility," Ida Belle said. "Makes sense. So what do you want us to do?"

"Are you getting a cell phone signal in here?" I asked.

"Not much of one," Gertie said. "But it's there off and on."

"That will have to do," I said. "I want one of you to head out to the channel where the tunnel empties. You won't be able to see the exit, as it's several feet below the surface, but there should be a ladder or at least evidence that one was once there. I want the person who stays inside to start timing me when I leave. When I surface, I want the person outside to signal the inside person that I'm there and note the exact time I surfaced. I'll need an estimate for Harrison."

"I'll go outside," Ida Belle said.

"Why do you get to go outside?" Gertie asked.

"Because there's less chance of you falling into that three-foot hole than the entire canal," Ida Belle said.

"You act like that happens all the time," Gertie said.

We both stared at her.

"Fine," Gertie said. "Go outside. I'll stay in here and play *Candy Crush* or count sewer rats or something equally riveting."

"Okay, Ida Belle," I said. "Head out and send a text when you locate the exit. If we haven't heard in ten minutes, I'll assume you found it and head out."

I finished suiting up while we waited on Ida Belle to signal Gertie that she was in place.

Found the exit. About thirty yards from building to canal.

Gertie read the text and I nodded. That was what I'd estimated when I'd looked at the satellite images.

"Okay," I said. "It's going to be easier if I go in headfirst, so I'm going to lean over the side, then I need you to lift my legs up and help me get in. Text Ida Belle once I'm gone."

I leaned over the side of the hole, putting as much of my body over as I could to remain balanced, pulled the mask on, and signaled to Gertie. I felt her grab my legs and slowly begin to lift. My weight shifted and I pushed off the side with my arms, diving headfirst into darkness. I clicked on my underwater flashlight and took a couple seconds to get my bearings, which was a bit harder when upside down.

I saw the bottom of the hole about ten feet down and swam in that direction; the tunnel then made a ninety-degree turn and headed straight for the canal. I was happy to see the width was the same in the tunnel as it was in the opening. I twisted at the bottom and headed into the tunnel, swimming as quickly as the murky water allowed. I couldn't afford to move too fast and risk injury on an exposed piece of metal or other trash that might have gotten caught inside. If something happened down here, there was no one to rescue me, and my tank was only worth an hour of breathing time.

The amount of trash collected on the bottom of the tunnel was minimal, making me think a grate was still in place at the end, but I'd brought a small metal saw with me. Given the amount of time the grate would have been submerged, it shouldn't be difficult to remove. Worst case, I'd have to turn around and go back, then locate and remove the grate from outside the tunnel, in the canal, and hope that no one saw me. Fortunately, if it came down to that, the tunnel was wide enough to allow me to change directions.

I had been estimating my time as I swam and figured I was drawing close to the end of the tunnel, so I slowed a bit more. The flashlight only allowed me a foot of visibility in the murky water. I didn't want to collide with the grate or anything that might be lodged in it. About ten seconds later, I saw the end.

The grate was metal and some of it had completely rusted off, explaining how some of the smaller trash items had gained entry. I stuck my hand through one of the holes and felt the perimeter of the grate. As expected, large bolts held it in place. I pulled the handsaw from my backpack and went to work on the strips of metal. It didn't take but a couple strokes to cut through each slat, then I pushed the center of the grate loose and it sank below me.

I eased through the opening, careful not to scratch my body on the edges of the grate, then headed straight for the surface. About fifteen feet up, my head broke the surface of the water and I saw Ida Belle standing next to a stone gate and looking down at me as I drew in a huge breath.

"A minute twenty," she said. "It seemed like a long time."

I pulled off my mask. "I had to cut off the grate, and I went slower to make sure it was clear. Cut fifteen seconds off of that, at least, and we're probably good."

She nodded and pointed to metal rungs that crept up the side of the cement wall. "The steps are still in place, but I don't know how sturdy they are."

"Not an issue. No one will be using them. The team will enter the water far enough away that they won't be seen. Head back inside before someone sees you and gets suspicious. Go ahead and start timing me again now."

I put my mask back on and let myself sink until I saw the tunnel opening, then I flipped over and headed into the tunnel, my pace faster now that I knew the tunnel was clear. It wasn't long at all before I twisted onto my back and bent upward to exit. A couple seconds later, my head emerged and I grabbed the sides of the exit hole.

Ida Belle and Gertie each grabbed an arm and helped hoist me out, and I sat on the side of the hole, removing my gear.

"One minute three seconds," Ida Belle said. "You were right on the money."

"How was it?" Gertie asked. "Did you see any snakes?"

"Fortunately, no," I said.

"You're scared of snakes?" Gertie asked.

"I'm not scared of them," I said, "but I have no desire to hang out with them. Usually, they hear something large coming and leave, which is just the way I like it."

"So you think it will work?" Ida Belle said.

I nodded. "It's plenty wide and there are no obstructions. A team could easily drop in a bit down the bank and make the swim no problem."

"And a thermal imaging camera won't pick them up in water?" Gertie asked.

"Not in the tunnel, and even if they put off a little heat signature in the canal, the person running the camera won't be looking there. They'll be scanning inside the building and the landlocked perimeter."

"What else do you need to see?" Ida Belle asked.

"Let's do a round in the building and get a feel for the layout. I'd also like to take some pictures. Somewhere in here has to be my home base, so I'll need a room set up for that."

"Mattress on floor, camping stove, ice chest, that sort of thing?" Gertie asked.

"Exactly. Ahmad may have someone check out the tip before he shows up."

"You think they'll come inside to scout?" Ida Belle asked. "That seems risky on their part."

"They'll check for heat signature in the building and then enter when they think I'm not there," I said. "It's not a sure thing, but it's something that has to be considered."

Gertie frowned. "If they don't check, how will they know for sure you're here? I mean, it could be a homeless person, right?"

I nodded. "Once I have word that Ahmad's men are on the ground in New Orleans, I have to make sure they see me enter the building."

"You're going to drive up and go inside?" Gertie asked. "What's keeping one of them from shooting you then?"

"For one, because Ahmad would kill any of his employees who took his glory. And if Ahmad's men are on sight, mercenaries won't risk the job because they don't want him as an enemy."

"You *think* they won't," Ida Belle said.

I blew out a breath. "Guys, I know the risks, and yes, there's a lot of them. There are a lot of unknowns. There's a lot of dependence on people acting rationally, and I'm aware more than most that terrorists and the type of people that terrorists employ aren't always thinking long term. But no matter when or how this goes down, it's going to have a lot of risk. There's no way around that. Not given the man who wants me dead."

"If I thought it was possible," Gertie said, "I'd tell you to change everything—your facial structure, your name, your location—and just disappear. Even if it meant we never saw you again, I could live with that as long as I knew you were safe."

Ida Belle nodded, and I felt my chest constrict because I knew they both meant every word Gertie had said. If the situation were reversed, I would feel the same way. Although it would hurt like heck to never see them again, knowing they were safe would be enough. Still, all it did was reinforce that what I was doing was the right call. This limbo that I'd been living in had to stop. It was affecting more lives than just my own.

"If there were another option," I said, "I promise you I would take it. But there's just not. At least, none that is acceptable to me."

"Then let's finish up here," Ida Belle said. "So you can get home and review everything, then speak to your people. I know they're used to putting these things together quickly, but they still need some time to do it correctly."

"And we definitely want their best effort," Gertie said. "I mean, I'm ready to shoot whoever needs shooting but I've only got two hands."

I stuffed my wet gear back in the duffel bag and hefted it up. "I'll drop this in the entry upstairs and we can finish exploring. This warehouse is fairly large, so lots of options for placement."

"When you canvass these buildings, what are you looking for, exactly?" Ida Belle asked.

"Everything, really," I said. "I'm looking for the most logical point of entry—and by that I mean logical by Ahmad's standards, not normal people."

"So probably not the front door?" Gertie asked.

"Probably not," I agreed. "Once I make a good guess as to his entry point, then I try to predict the search path he'd take and ways I might be able to direct him where I'd like him to go."

"Like a heavier trail of footprints in the dust in one direction but not another?" Ida Belle asked.

"That's it exactly. Nothing obvious. Just the things that would exist if I were really hiding out here. Ahmad is an experienced tracker. I don't have to leave him a trail of bread crumbs to get him where I want him."

"Then aren't we messing things up by walking through all these buildings?" Gertie asked.

"No. He would expect to see some footprints other than just mine. Even empty buildings are periodically checked on by owners, city inspectors, and the like."

"Or they could be for sale or lease," Ida Belle said. "Not everything is listed online."

I nodded. "Once I've picked a building and decided on the location of the ambush, I'll use ground-up rock to create a light layer of dust over the older footprints, then make newer prints for him to follow."

Gertie and Ida Belle looked at each other, and I could tell just how worried they were. They'd been upset from the beginning, although they'd done their best to hide it. But canvassing these buildings and being faced with the harsh realities of the takedown and all the variables that came with it had made it all too real. Ida Belle and Gertie were having trouble coming to terms with believing I was invincible and all the things I was up against. More than anything, I wished I could take away their worry. Their fear. But I knew it wasn't possible. When you cared about someone, that was just the way things were.

I understood that all too well now. And it made my next step even more important.

Figuring out how to keep them out of harm's way.

CHAPTER ELEVEN

When we arrived back at my house, I considered a boat ride to look for Godzilla, but Gertie immediately refused, insisting that I had bigger fish to fry. She figured exposing Celia's poisoned meat plan had bought us a reprieve so the gator didn't have to be a top priority. Still, because Godzilla had turned up again on my lawn, I insisted on getting the cage in place and baiting it with some frozen chicken wings. I figured the wings would thaw and while they weren't as tasty as Gertie's casserole, they would probably still do. Gertie had started prepping a casserole that morning and promised to bring it over later that afternoon.

We said our goodbyes and I headed inside with my laptop and duffel. I put the wet stuff in the garage to finish drying and cleaned the mask in the laundry room sink. I had a quick shower to rid myself of the stinky canal water, then headed back downstairs to the kitchen for lunch and to start my review of the properties.

I'd pretty much decided on the last property for the take-down. The advantage of the water tunnel was too big to pass up and too easy for a qualified crew to pull off. I gave the other properties one last cursory review while polishing off leftover lasagna but still couldn't find an argument for any of them over the last one. So I grabbed a pad of paper and went to work on a layout of the building.

I'd done a rough sketch as we'd walked and taken measurements in some places so that I'd be able to do a better drawing later to scale. Now I took that preliminary sketch and slowly redid it, appropriately sizing rooms and hallways, and making notes of dimensions as I went. I started on the ground level, and there were so many rooms that it took me an hour to get it done. I rose from the table and stretched, then took a walk around the house a couple times before settling back down to start on the basement.

When the basement was well documented, I did a cursory layout of the second floor, mostly noting points of egress to the lower floor. Given that the team would enter from the water tunnel, I had decided that the best place for the ambush would be in the basement, but I still needed to secure the first level. There were too many windows that weren't boarded and that would have to be addressed first, preferably with aged plywood and nails. New products would stick out like a sore thumb, but I needed to eliminate the possibility of Ahmad taking an easy leap through a window to escape or his men coming inside from every angle and flanking Harrison's team.

The basement provided only three ways out—the stairs, an elevator shaft, and the water tunnel. Ahmad was ballsy enough to try the water tunnel, even without gear, but one of the entry agents would close the opening once they were inside. Even if Ahmad managed to get past the team, opening the tunnel would take time, and that gave us time to take him down.

Once in the basement of the building, the hallway led to four different rooms. The first was the one where the water tunnel was located. Then the hallway extended past the water tunnel location, made a ninety-degree turn right, and led to the remaining rooms. All of them were formed from concrete, with no exit point. The last one was where I would hide. That forced Ahmad farther down the hallway and left him blind as far as men exiting the tunnel room went. Once he made that bend in the hallway, the operatives could close in and he'd be trapped. No getting out unless he shot his way through all of us.

I sat back in my chair and blew out a breath. It was all solid, except for one thing. The thing I hadn't mentioned to Ida Belle and Gertie and never planned to.

A bomb.

If Ahmad had explosives on him, he wouldn't hesitate to kill himself in order to get me. I'd known that from the beginning, and placing myself in a no-exit situation meant I'd go up in a blast with him if he was prepared to do it. Harrison wouldn't love the idea. Morrow would hate it. But neither of them would be able to come up with something that produced better odds. My way offered the best possibility of Ahmad's death.

I just hoped I didn't have to go along with him to make it happen.

I FIRED up my laptop and sent Harrison an email with all the building info. We'd taken precautions to hide our email communication, even from Director Morrow, but he was going to have to know about it now. Not that it mattered any longer. Either this mission was successful and the whole mess was over or it was unsuccessful and I had to leave Sinful.

Once the email was delivered, I sent Harrison a text, asking him to review the docs and call me when he and

Morrow could get a secure place to talk. I got a text back thirty minutes later saying they would call in another ten minutes. In that ten minutes, I'm pretty sure I wore the finish off part of the hardwood floors. I must have paced back and forth from the kitchen to the living room a hundred times before the phone rang.

I grabbed the phone and plopped into a chair at the kitchen table before answering, my laptop and all the handwritten notes sitting in front of me.

"You've been busy," Harrison said.

"I just want this over with," I said.

"We can see that," Morrow said. "What I want to know is why I'm bothering to put together a team. How about we just save the taxpayers the money and I shoot you myself?"

"Sir?"

"These plans make you a sitting duck!" Morrow yelled. "Sitting in a concrete basement, with no entry or exit other than the one you want Ahmad to step through. I knew last time we'd talked that you'd made a departure from your usual self, and you've always been on the wrong side of cautious. But this plan of yours is downright suicidal."

"If I can't get out, neither can Ahmad."

"He can take you both out," Morrow said, "and you know it. He'd just as soon send himself, you, and that entire city block sky-high as let you get away if he's got you in his sights. He missed an opportunity once before. He's not going to play it safe this time."

"I have to agree with the director on that," Harrison said. "Word's been filtering back. Key members in Ahmad's organization have some concerns about his mental state."

"They're just now concerned?" I asked.

"You know the drill," Harrison said. "There's a different level of sane for a terrorist, but reports are Ahmad's moved well beyond what his people are comfortable with. He's obsessed with vindicating his brother's death."

"So we give him the opportunity," I said. "And those concerned members can either die along with him like fools or hang back and fight over his business interests when he's gone. Tell me again what other options I have. Go ahead. I'll wait."

There was dead silence for several long seconds and finally, I heard Morrow sigh. I'd recognize that sigh anywhere because I'd heard it so many times. "It's not just you I have to think about," Morrow said. "I'm putting agents at risk."

Technically, it was true, but it was also a weak argument. If that's the best Morrow had, then I had won this round. "Agents are always at risk," I said. "We know that when we take the job. The risks of this operation are no greater than anything I've taken on in the past."

"Are you forgetting the mole?" Morrow asked. "We're assuming he was working the Miami team, but what if he's not the only one?"

"I haven't forgotten," I said. "I've just figured out a way around it."

"I can't wait to hear this one," Harrison said.

"Simple," I said. "You don't tell the other members of the team who the target is."

"Then what the hell am I supposed to tell them?" Morrow asked.

"You tell them it's a kidnap recovery mission. That the wife of a foreign dignitary has been abducted and your intel places her in the building."

"And when they see you? Or Ahmad?" Morrow asked.

"Since I look nothing like I used to, they'll think I'm the wife," I said. "If they see Ahmad, they are under orders to take the kill shot. Unless that's changed."

"No," Morrow said. "That order stands. But I still think it's risky sending them in blind."

"How many operatives?" I asked.

"Three aside from yourself and Harrison on the inside team, three more on the perimeter," Morrow said. "None of them were on the job in Miami."

"So don't keep them blind forever," I said. "Let them enter the building, then tell them who the target really is. Even if there's more than one mole and he's in the new group, it will be too late to get word to Ahmad about the ambush."

"The mole could still take out the other agents, in order for Ahmad to escape," Morrow said.

"He won't do that," I said. "He's a coward who's interested in money. Faced with the choice of allowing Ahmad to be killed or exposing himself, he'll fire the bullet personally."

"She's right," Harrison said. "In fact, it's perfect. And that's on the long chance that there's more than one mole, which I don't believe. I think it's one person, and I think it was an operative in the last group."

"But even if this is successful," Morrow said, "he'll still remain unknown."

"Not necessarily," I said. "I have an idea about that too."

"What's the idea?" Morrow asked.

"We know Ahmad will send out a crew to recon if he gets a tip on my location," I said. "I have some other properties we can use to set up a sting. I get the cameras up at each location, then you filter a different location back to each member of the previous team. That was five agents aside from Harrison, right?"

"Yes," Morrow said.

"Then wherever Ahmad sends his crew, that's our guy," Harrison said. "I love it."

"Won't all those tips on your location make Ahmad suspicious?"

"I don't see how," I said. "He's only going to get two—the fake one through the mole, and the real one."

"Are you sure you can handle the cameras?" Harrison asked. "I can send someone I trust. That way you're not exposed."

"The property owner has a security person on staff who can handle the cameras," I said. "I don't have to do it myself. And no one would think anything of him being on property since he works for the owners."

"If we're using the mole for the fake location, then how are we going to get the real location to him?" Harrison asked.

"I have a friend who's going to handle that," I said.

"What kind of friend?" Morrow asked.

"The same friend who owns the properties we're using and I'd appreciate it if you'd leave it at that."

They were completely silent for several seconds.

"You're keeping some interesting company down there, Redding," Morrow said.

"You have no idea," I mumbled, and hopefully, he never would.

"Is this friend of yours aware that he could sustain property damage?" Morrow asked. "And that since we were never there, I can't guarantee we could cover the cost?"

"I've already asked," I said. "That's not an issue."

"If Fortune's friend is okay with all of this and she trusts them, then I'm good," Harrison said. "I like the location and the plan to breach through the water. It eliminates the problem with infrared. We'll need to get a diver down there to check the tunnel, though."

"I've already done that. It's clear. Three feet in diameter. I sawed through the grate on the canal end but given the slow flow of water, I don't anticipate any chance of blockage as long as we don't take forever to do this. If you'd rather, I can remove the old grate completely and get a temp one in place."

"There's an occupied office building across the canal from the warehouse," Morrow said. "Won't a diver in that location look odd?"

"I'd go at night or dressed as a city employee. It's easy enough to put some stickers on a boat long enough to get the job done. People won't blink twice at a government vehicle."

"I still don't like it," Morrow said. "But then I haven't liked anything about this since we started going after this bastard years ago."

"Then let's get this one off your list," I said. "Heck, you might even think about retirement after this. Although with me resigning, your stress level might go down a notch or two."

"Ha," Morrow said. "We have to get you out alive first."

"What do you need from us?" Harrison asked.

I gave him a list of supplies—weapons, security equipment, and a replacement grate if they decided it was needed.

"I need that security equipment ASAP," I said.

"I'll get it overnighted," Harrison said. "What about the staged stuff? Cot, cooktop..."

"I'll handle those items here. It will look less odd for me to purchase them than to have a ton of shipping containers show up at my doorstep."

"Okay. We'll get this handled," Harrison said. "You let us know when the cameras are in place, and we'll filter back the bad location information and see if we can ferret out the mole."

"If we can get that guy out of the agency," Morrow said, "it would go a long way to my feeling better about this."

"Me too," I said. "But I'm only giving it a couple days once the info is filtered. If no one shows, then we move forward anyway. When can your team be ready?"

"I've got them here in DC awaiting assignment," Morrow said. "But I'm not going to be able to hold them here forever. There's a lot going down in the sandbox."

"You're not going to have to hold them long," I said. "Assuming the security equipment is all in working order, I'll have it ready to go tomorrow, depending on delivery time. Two days to ferret out the mole, takedown after that."

"Three to five days, then?" Morrow said. "You're sure you can be ready in that time?"

"I've been ready," I said. "And guys, if I don't get a chance to say it later on—thank you."

"I reject your thanks," Harrison said. "At minimum, you owe me a beer, and I plan to collect just as soon as this is over."

"Sounds good."

And it did. I just hoped we were both in drinking condition when it was over.

CHAPTER TWELVE

I STOOD at my kitchen window staring out at the bayou. Everything was in motion in DC and until I got the security cameras and passed them along to Mannie, I had nothing else to do. At least not for the takedown. Given everything that had transpired over the last couple days, and the fact that I'd spent an entire morning planning for a mission that might be my last one—one way or another—I couldn't manage to sit still. I was restless. Itchy. The way I always was before an assignment, but this time it was so much worse.

Because this time, it means everything.

And that was the crux of it. This mission wasn't my job. It was literally my life on the line. My future. And although I'd been trained to contain and control worry, this time none of the mental exercises I normally used were working. I checked my watch again and sighed when I saw it was only two minutes since the last time I'd checked it, which had been only one minute from the time before.

Finally, I picked up the phone and called Ida Belle and Gertie. Might as well chase that darn alligator or figure out a way to inspect more freezers. Something. Anything was better than sitting here and going over everything that could go wrong with the takedown. Mentally rehashing it wouldn't improve my odds.

Ida Belle and Gertie showed up in Ida Belle's SUV about ten minutes later, which meant they'd probably spent their day on standby, in case I called. I wasn't sure what I'd done to warrant such good friends, but boy did I appreciate them. More than they probably knew. I waved them in and they followed me to the kitchen where we all took a seat, no one saying a word.

They looked at each other, then back at me, and finally Gertie spoke. "I told you something was wrong," she said to Ida Belle. "You could hear it in her voice."

"Bring us up to speed," Ida Belle said.

"There's not much to say, really," I said. "I selected the location and sent the information to Harrison. Then he and Morrow called and we discussed the details of the mission."

Gertie's eyes widened. "So it's set? I mean, it's definitely going to happen?"

I nodded. "It's definitely going to happen."

"When?" Ida Belle asked.

This was the sticky part. I knew I couldn't leave them out entirely, but I also wasn't about to let them in harm's way. "Soon," I said. "Probably within a week."

"That fast?" Gertie asked. "Wow. I mean, we knew it was coming but now that it has a time frame on it, it seems so sudden."

"The operatives Morrow selected are being held in DC," I said. "They can't be forever. The agency has other things they could be addressing."

"Morrow and Harrison were good with your plan?" Ida Belle asked.

"'Good' is probably too strong a word, but no one threw

out anything better," I said. "The hard truth of the matter is our back is against the wall on this. Either I expose myself to get to Ahmad or I live looking over my shoulder for the rest of my life—and it probably wouldn't be a very long one."

Ida Belle nodded. "So what can we do? I sense an overwhelming need for distraction."

"Yes," I said, grateful for friends who actually got it.

"I remember that feeling before we went on a mission," Gertie said. "It was one part excitement, one part concentration, and one part wanting to get sick."

"The good ole days, right?" Ida Belle said and smiled.

I was one of the few people who knew about Ida Belle's and Gertie's real roles when they served in Vietnam. But even if they'd taken out a front-page ad, I doubted many would believe that the two seniors had been spies. Unless they knew them well, of course. Then so many things made sense. Still, they'd never talked much about their service, and I'd never asked. It was the same with Carter. I might technically be a civilian but I'd been in the middle of plenty of war games. I knew better than most the sort of things undercover operatives and Special Forces faced. Often, they weren't the sort of memories people wanted to revisit.

"I bet you both were pistols," I said and smiled, easily picturing a young Ida Belle and Gertie giving them hell overseas.

Gertie looked over at Ida Belle, and I could see the depth of their friendship in that single look. "We were something," Gertie said.

"Still are," Ida Belle said. "And still undercover. So what's on the agenda? We can take a boat ride and look for that wayward alligator or we can pursue this missing food thing."

"Did Ally find out who Clarissa is dating?" Gertie asked.

"I don't know," I said. "Let me check."

Any news on Clarissa's boyfriend?

I sent the text. I had put a bug in Ally's ear after our chat with Braxton, and she was going to ask Francine. If that didn't work, she would attempt to coax the information out of Clarissa.

My text alert went off and I checked the display.

Poot Lowery.

"What the heck is a Poot Lowery?" I asked.

Gertie shook her head. "The Lowery brothers are no good."

The name suddenly clicked and I remembered a pair of brothers that had almost capsized me and Ally shortly after my arrival in Sinful.

"One of them is named Poot?" I asked. "Do I dare ask what the other is called?"

"Zit," Ida Belle said, and grinned.

"Poot and Zit?" I stared. "You've got to be kidding me this time."

"Couldn't make that up even if I tried," Ida Belle said.

"Okay, give me the story."

Ida Belle gestured to Gertie.

"Poot was a gassy baby who became a gassy boy," Gertie said. "And since he was raised by mannerless people, he thought it was funny to pollute a classroom or Sunday school class. So 'Poot' because he was always pooting."

"And Zit? Acne problems?"

Gertie shook her head. "Short for 'Smells It.' People used to say one poots and the other smells it."

"I swear to God you are making that up."

"I'm not that creative," Gertie said. "Or that gross. That was the kids' doing."

"And they allow people to call them that?" I asked, still confused.

Gertie shrugged. "They don't seem to have a problem with it."

"So not only does Clarissa date a troubled man," I said, "but he's stinky too."

"Her choice in men and her mother's choice in tile are setting back the women's movement at least five decades," Ida Belle said.

"I can see how a guy like Braxton might end up with a woman like Destiny—young guy, kinda geeky, can get the hot girl, sort of thing," I said. "But what surprises me is that she married him and moved to Sinful. Doesn't seem like the life a party girl would be looking for."

Gertie nodded. "I asked her about it once. She told me he was the only one of her suitors who had a steady job and all his teeth."

"In Louisiana, that makes perfect sense," I said. "Okay, so now we know who Clarissa is seeing, but does that help us any as far as investigating goes? I don't suppose you could pass off a request for decorating tips with someone who gladly goes by the nickname Poot."

"No," Ida Belle said, "but I think I know a way." She pulled out her cell phone and dialed. "Shorty," she said. "This is Ida Belle. Say, do you still own that place off Bullet Bayou? Great. I know you were thinking about selling at one point...is that still in the cards? I have a friend in New Orleans looking for a weekend escape-the-wife sort of situation. He's wanting right on the water for the fishing. Uh-huh. Oh, I didn't realize. Well, if it's okay with you, he asked me to scout anything I came up with first as I had a good idea what he was looking for and how much work he's willing to do. I don't suppose now works? Good. See you in five minutes."

She shoved her phone back in her pocket and grinned. "We're all set."

"Was that Shorty the butcher?" I asked.

"Yep. He owns the cabin the Lowery brothers rent. He's been thinking about selling it forever, but it's wishful thinking as long as those two live there. The place is probably a pit. But he says the lease gives him permission to show the property, so we can pick up a set of keys and let ourselves in."

"One small thing," I said. "Didn't you tell me once that Bullet Bayou earned its name because the inhabitants tended to shoot first and ask questions later?"

"That's right."

"And you think it's a good idea to stroll into someone's house. Even with keys from the owner, that sounds risky. I get the impression that the Lowery brothers won't care about our legal standing."

"We'll knock on the door first," Ida Belle said. "I wasn't planning on strolling right in as if the place was vacant."

"Maybe we should stroll in with bulletproof vests," I suggested.

"But it's so hot," Gertie said. "I'm wearing a padded bra. That should do."

"Why are you wearing a padded bra?" Ida Belle asked.

"Because underwire hurts and gravity is not your friend. Besides, I can pull out some of the padding and have additional storage space."

Ida Belle looked over at me. "We're good. The Lowery brothers are mannerless, and I wouldn't put petty theft or poaching past them, but I don't think they'd shoot someone. That's not the sort of trouble they usually go looking for."

I shrugged. "You know them better than I do. I guess we've got a key to pick up then."

We headed out to Ida Belle's SUV and off to the butcher shop, where Gertie ran in and picked up the key. Then Ida Belle drove out of town and turned onto what passed as a road, which was in keeping with most of the roads in Sinful outside of the town limits. About a mile down, she made a turn off the "good road" and onto an even worse one. This one could charitably be called a trail for vehicles. Two strips designated the tire path. In between the tread-worn lines, weeds grew and the foliage pushed right up to the edge of the trail.

"If I remember correctly," Ida Belle said, "it should be just a little ways up."

"We've doubled back north far enough that we should be hitting water soon," Gertie agreed.

"Or maybe we've entered one of those gateways like in the movies and the next thing you know, we'll see dinosaurs," I said.

"Dinosaurs would be an improvement over the Lowery brothers," Ida Belle said. "And here we are."

The trail ended in a small clearing of dirt with just enough room to park without hitting the front porch of the house. No other vehicles were parked out front, so I hoped that meant the Lowery brothers were off polluting and smelling the air somewhere far, far away. I gave the structure a once-over and have to admit, was a bit surprised. I'd expected something from a Stephen King novel, but aside from the normal wear and tear one would expect of a place exposed to these elements, it was rather nice.

"This isn't bad," I said. "Not at all what I expected."

"You might want to withhold judgment until you get inside," Gertie said. "Shorty built the place himself and he did a good job, so I'm not surprised it's held up. But the outside walls aren't getting near the abuse that the inside is."

We climbed out of the SUV and headed up the porch. The paint was showing some wear in a couple places but there were no signs of rotted wood, and the grayish-blue paint color looked good against the green backdrop of the swamp. Ida

Belle knocked on the door and we waited for a bit, but there was no noise inside.

"Best give it a second round," she said, and this time, she pounded on the door like the police. "Anyone home?"

We waited again, but still heard nothing.

"Either they're not home or they're passed out drunk," Gertie said.

"This is my territory," I said. "Ida Belle, you're the breacher. Unlock the door and push it open, but stand aside. I'll enter and head for the nearest doorway to clear the room; you follow and clear the next doorway. Gertie, you back up Ida Belle. Continue until every room is clear."

Gertie raised an eyebrow. "One might think you did this for a living."

"Occasionally," I said. "If anyone spots a person, yell for backup and attempt to wake them, but not before checking for a weapon on nightstands or other places where they're easy to secure. Ready?"

Ida Belle nodded and stuck the key in the door. I pulled my pistol from my waist and got in the ready position. I glanced back and saw Gertie remove a Desert Eagle from her purse. "Absolutely not," I said. "That thing would blow out an entire wall of this place. Pick something smaller."

She sighed but put the cannon back in her purse and pulled out a nine-millimeter. "Boring enough?" she asked.

Ida Belle shook her head and turned the key, then she pushed the door open and I stepped inside, casing the room in a second. It was one large room with the living area in front and a kitchen along the back wall. A doorway to the right was the closest, so I headed that direction, stopping at the edge of the doorway to listen. Ida Belle had entered directly behind me and was mimicking my actions at a doorway on the opposite wall.

I didn't hear breathing inside, so I stepped around the corner, but it only took a second to ensure the tiny bedroom was clear. I headed out of the room and for the interior doorway on the back wall. I could see a pedestal sink, so I'd already figured it was the bathroom, and I was right. Ida Belle came out the other doorway, Gertie right behind her.

"This bedroom's clear," Ida Belle said. "I mean, it's filthy, but no one's inside."

"Same with the other bedroom," I said, "and you don't even want to look in the bathroom. Shorty might need to burn the place down and collect on insurance."

"As much as it pains me to do," Ida Belle said, "let's look in the refrigerator and get the hell out of here before we catch something."

Gertie headed for the kitchen and pulled open the top and bottom of the refrigerator. "Nothing in here but beer and moldy cheese."

"Would they have a deep freeze?" I asked. "I thought everyone in Sinful had frozen seafood somewhere in their house."

"Maybe on the back porch," Ida Belle said. "There's not really room for one in here."

We headed out the back door and onto the screened porch. Sure enough, there was a small deep freeze close to the door. I lifted it and stared inside in dismay. "This thing is packed."

"Start unloading it then," Gertie said. "The bacon boxes could be in there."

I started lifting out milk cartons with frozen shrimp and fish and stacking them on a table near the freezer. "At least they dated this stuff," I said.

"You plan on coming over for dinner?" Ida Belle asked.

"No. I just meant maybe they're not completely stupid."

"Oh, no one ever said they were stupid," Gertie said. "Just mannerless, shiftless, and lazy. They were both actually quite clever in school. Unfortunately, they tended to use that skill to steal from other students rather than apply it to their classwork."

"Should I even ask what they do for employment?" I asked.

"Last I heard, Zit was still working a commercial shrimp boat," Gertie said. "As a hand, mind you. He doesn't own it. And Poot works road construction when he bothers to work. The rent's not high, so my guess is they're working mostly for gas and beer money."

"Well, they're not scamming frozen goods from the café via Clarissa," I said as I pulled the last package of fish from the freezer. "No bacon, pot roast, or chickens."

"Maybe they already ate it," Gertie said.

"Two boxes of bacon?" Ida Belle asked. "Unless they were hosting a breakfast gathering every day, I don't see how."

"They could have used it as bait," Gertie said.

"That's true," Ida Belle said. "But that's still a lot to go through in a short amount of time, even as bait. Besides, I checked the trash at the side of the house while you two were emptying the freezer and there are no boxes or anything else to indicate the bacon was ever here."

"Then maybe Clarissa isn't our thief," I said. "Bummer. She seemed perfect. Guess we better get this put up and get out of here before someone returns home."

It had been one of the least dramatic investigative outings we'd ever had, and I was anxious to keep it that way. Gertie started feeding me the packages and I attempted to arrange them all somewhat as they were when I'd taken them out. We were down to our last ten packages when I heard the gunshot.

CHAPTER THIRTEEN

I DROPPED to the ground and yelled at Gertie and Ida Belle to take a dive, but by the time I got the words out, they were already flat on the deck with me. "Where did it come from?" I asked.

"The bayou," Ida Belle said as a second rifle shot ripped through side of the porch and lodged in the wall next to the freezer.

The porch was walled halfway up and screened on the top, but the wall was nothing more than a thin sheet of plywood. It was no protection from serious fire. We needed to get clear, but the door into the cabin was located directly behind the screen door off the porch, which meant exposing ourselves in order to get away. Three people crawling against the speed of a rifle shot wasn't very good odds.

I tucked behind an ice chest and inched up to peer over the half wall and spotted the Lowery brothers about twenty yards away in their bass boat. The one with the shaved head fit the description Gertie had given me on the way over of Zit. That meant the one with the New Orleans Saints hat and the rifle must be Poot.

"Did you hit 'em?" Zit asked. "They're stealing our fish. Make sure you hit 'em."

"Stop shooting!" Ida Belle yelled. "Shorty gave us permission to look at the property. We have a key."

"Shorty gave you permission to steal our food?" Zit yelled back. "I don't think so."

"They're never going to buy that," I said.

"We have to do something," Gertie said. "We're sitting ducks."

I pulled out my pistol and looked over at Ida Belle. "You're closest to the door. I'll draw them off with gunfire, and you make a dash for it and get the SUV running. Gertie and I will follow."

Ida Belle nodded and I popped up from behind the cooler, narrowed in on the brothers, and squeezed off three rounds in the water surrounding them. Ida Belle scrambled through the door and into the cabin. Poot did exactly what I'd expected and dropped into the bottom of the boat. Unfortunately, Zit was either drunk or feeling invincible. He bent over and came up with a pistol.

"Crap," I said. "Zit's got a pistol. Get ready to run."

"I got this," Gertie said, and pushed herself up on her hands and knees. "I'll lob a flare in their boat. That will keep them busy."

Before I could respond, she positioned a gun around the edge of the screen door and leaned over to fire. I got a glance at the gun and panicked.

"Wait!" I yelled. "That's not a flare gun."

The Desert Eagle sounded like a cannon when it fired. The recoil sent Gertie rolling over on her side. I bolted up, grabbed her shirt collar and the gun, and hauled butt inside the cabin.

"Keep going," I told Gertie, and I stopped on the back side of the kitchen wall and peered around. I could hear two voices yelling and hoped it was angry yelling and not "call 911" yelling. I let out a breath of relief when I saw both brothers standing in the boat, neither showing the signs that they'd taken a .50 cal bullet.

Unfortunately, their boat hadn't fared as well. It was tipped to one side and sinking fast. They weren't far from the bank, so I had no reason to think they were in danger, therefore I did what any rational human being would do in that situation.

I ran.

I didn't even get the passenger door shut before Ida Belle stomped her foot on the accelerator and sent the SUV flying backward. She slammed on her brakes as quickly as she'd stomped the gas, turned the wheel, and launched the vehicle back down the trail, sending a shower of dirt a good ten feet behind us.

"What happened?" Ida Belle asked.

"Pandora's purse happened," I said.

Ida Belle glanced at Gertie in her rearview mirror. "You didn't set off dynamite again, did you?"

"What?" Gertie yelled.

"She's deaf from the blast," I said. "Rambo decided to launch a flare into the brothers' boat, except she fired the Desert Eagle instead." I held up the gun.

"How did you get my gun?" Gertie yelled.

I slumped in my seat and put the gun on the floorboard. Ida Belle glanced back again and shook her head. "I swear to God, woman, you are going to kill us all one day. You have to get new glasses."

"That's right!" Gertie yelled. "I saved your asses."

"I'm going to kill her in her sleep," Ida Belle said. "Before she takes the two of us with her."

"I don't think you're going to have to," I said, and pointed to the vehicle that was coming straight at us. "Just turn her over to Carter."

Ida Belle groaned. "This is the last thing we need."

"Not the absolute last," I said, "but it ranks right up there."

Ida Belle slowed until she was a couple feet in front of Carter's truck, then stopped. When neither Ida Belle nor I moved, Carter climbed out of his truck and headed for Ida Belle's door. She pressed the button to lower the window.

"Send Carter to arrest those fools!" Gertie yelled.

Carter raised an eyebrow, then looked at Ida Belle and me. "When someone reported an explosion, I knew it was you."

"That's just playing the odds," Ida Belle said.

Gertie nodded. "Whole place has gone to the dogs!"

"Based on the guilty looks two of you are wearing," Carter said, "it would seem the odds are correct. And since the defiant one is apparently deaf, I'm going to assume she's the perp."

"You're not having to work very hard for this at all," Ida Belle said. "Here's what happened—a friend of mine is interested in buying Shorty's cabin. He's been renting it to the Lowery brothers but gave me a key and said it was all right for us to check it out. We knocked, no one was home, so we looked around. When we were standing on the back porch, the Lowery brothers arrived by boat and thought we were robbing them and started firing."

"Makes sense so far," Carter said. "Get to the part about explosives. Do I have to tell Shorty you blew up his cabin?"

"No," Ida Belle said. "You have to tell the Lowery brothers you don't know who sank their boat. Otherwise, they'll come after Gertie."

His eyes widened. "She threw dynamite at them?"

"No. Of course not," Ida Belle said. "Fortune returned fire —in the water only—to get Poot to stop firing long enough for us to get the heck out of there. I got out and Gertie was supposed to go next."

"So why didn't she?" he asked.

Ida Belle motioned to me. "This is where Fortune has to take over. I ran for the SUV to prepare for the getaway."

I sighed. "Poot stopped firing but Zit took it upon himself to pull a pistol and help out. Gertie decided she was going to provide me cover and fire what she thought was a flare at their boat."

"I take it the gun in question wasn't a flare gun?"

I lifted the Desert Eagle from the floorboard and passed it to him through the window. "We're all safer if you collect it as evidence," I said.

"It's a beauty, right?" Gertie yelled.

He looked at the gun, then at Gertie, then at me. "You knew she was carrying this and you let her in the vehicle with you?"

"We didn't know she had it," I said. "I mean, not exactly."

"We don't search her purse every time we go somewhere with her," Ida Belle said.

"Why the hell not?" Carter asked.

"Plausible deniability?" I said.

"What does it say about all of us that what you just said makes perfect sense?" Carter asked.

"That we're all intelligent," Ida Belle said, "and somewhat afraid of Gertie's purse."

"Did the brothers get a good look at you?" Carter asked.

"Through the tree limbs and the screen...I doubt it," I said.

"Good. Okay, I'm going to keep the gun for now," Carter said. "And I'll figure out something to tell the Lowerys, but I suggest you call Shorty and ask him to keep your names to himself. He can always claim an out-of-town buyer that he didn't know." He stared at us for several seconds. "I don't suppose you're going to tell me why you were really there?"

"See," Ida Belle said. "Intelligent."

He shook his head. "Let me back up so you can get out of here before someone sees you. And I highly suggest you make Gertie carry a wallet only."

"Wouldn't help," I said. "She has this whole padded bra thing going on."

He held up his hand. "That is all stuff I never need to know." He turned around and headed back to his truck.

"Where's he taking my gun?" Gertie yelled.

"Hopefully to the smelter," Ida Belle said.

"To the homeless shelter?" Gertie yelled. "What the hell for?"

I grinned. It was hard not to.

The great food caper had spent the pent-up energy I had acquired that afternoon, so we decided to call it quits for the day. I tried to limit being shot at to once in a twenty-four-hour period. That was harder than it should have been in Sinful, but I'd sorta come to expect it. When we got back to my house, we had some cobbler and discussed the remaining suspects on the food theft. Well, Ida Belle and I discussed it. Gertie continued to misunderstand everything and yell about Carter not returning her gun.

I agreed with Ida Belle that Marco was probably the next best suspect. Unfortunately, she didn't have a clever way to access his kitchen so unless we resorted to breaking and entering, we had to figure out another way to check him out. Finally, we'd settled on going through his trash to see if he'd discarded the bacon boxes in there. Trash pickup was the next morning, so tonight was our only chance. Marco's house was one block over from Ida Belle's so I told her I'd meet her there at midnight. That gave me time to have dinner with Carter and bring him up to date on what I wanted him to know about the takedown. He was grilling at his house, so I'd just claim being tired as an excuse to cut out for my place. It probably wouldn't be a lie. I had a feeling this entire day was going to catch up with me at some point.

"See you at midnight," Ida Belle said as she and Gertie walked out.

"The sun is shining," Gertie yelled. "That's not moonlight." She shook her head and stepped off the porch.

"If her hearing isn't back to normal by tonight," Ida Belle said, "she's not invited."

I nodded. "Probably a good idea. It's hard to be sneaky with someone yelling."

I gave them a wave and headed back inside. I only had an hour to kill until I headed over to Carter's house, and I could spend part of that with a long, hot shower. I decided to spend the rest of it giving the kitchen a good cleaning and throwing on some laundry. I'd never had a big wardrobe at all and had even less to speak of in Sinful. Combine that with the frequent need to change outfits more than once a day and it easily led to a clean clothes crisis.

What I needed to do was order some more stuff. It wasn't as if I was shopping for evening gowns. Yoga pants and T-shirts were easy enough to get in bulk and didn't require trying on. You just got more of what you already had in different colors. And Walter was happy to order anything I wanted that he had access to, which was great because I preferred to give my business to locals. But every time I'd sat down with my laptop to put together an order list, something stopped me.

At first I thought it was because my mind wasn't really

made up about staying in Sinful, and maybe that was the case. But now I think I was avoiding it because I was afraid something would go wrong and I wouldn't be able to stay in Sinful even though I wanted to. I don't know why it mattered. I would need clothes wherever I went, but somehow, the thought of packing up a bunch of garments meant to wear here seemed more depressing than packing up the stuff I'd worn a bunch of times. It was a stupid, sentimental, completely girlie sort of thought, and I blamed Sinful for all of it.

I threw a load of clothes in to wash and turned on the dishwasher, then stared at my laptop. To heck with it. I sat down at the kitchen table and put together a list of tanks, tees, shorts, yoga pants, and socks and sent the whole list to Walter, asking him to process it whenever he had time. It would probably take a week or better for him to get it in. This was my leap of faith. I was placing that order determined to be here to collect and wear every single item in the mix.

I closed my laptop, ready to head upstairs for my shower, and heard yelling outside. Worried that Godzilla had come back and chased someone into my yard, I pulled my pistol out of my waistband and ran out the back door. At first I didn't see anything, but then the yelling started again and I realized I'd been looking too high.

All the noise was coming from the cage. But it wasn't Godzilla in it. It looked like...well, a zebra.

Then the zebra raised its head. My neighbor, Ronald, was hunched in the cage on all fours and wearing what looked to be a white-and-black-striped onesie. He caught sight of me and started up with the yelling again.

"Get me out of here, you barbarian!"

I hurried over to the cage, completely confused. With every step I took, I tried to come up with a logical reason for the scene in front of me, but even an illogical reason wouldn't form.

"What are you doing in there?" I asked as I stepped up next to him.

"I'm getting a back cramp! Open the door and get me out."

I went over to the door that had apparently tripped when he'd entered the cage and tried to lift it, but it wouldn't move. I checked the perimeter, looking for a lever or release, but couldn't locate one.

"What the hell are you waiting for?" Ronald yelled, his face so red, I thought he'd have a heart attack.

"I don't know how to open it. Give me a minute. I need to call someone."

"I don't have a minute." He sank down onto his elbows and started punching the display on his cell phone.

"I don't think this is the sort of thing you call the police about," I said, trying to save Carter the hassle of another round with Ronald the Idiot. I had no idea why he was in the alligator cage, but there was no possible way he had a good reason.

"I've already called the police and everyone else," Ronald said. "Now I'm calling my attorney."

"Your attorney knows how to open the cage?"

"No. But he does know how to file a lawsuit. I'm going to sue you and that insane Gertie Hebert. Everyone thinks the two of you are ruining this town."

"Anyone who's seen how you dress probably has different ideas."

I pulled my cell phone out of my pocket to dial Ida Belle, hoping I could get the cage open and Ronald out of my yard before Carter and "everyone else" showed up. I was just about to dial when I heard voices behind me. I turned around to see Carter, a fireman, a paramedic, and Father Michael hurrying across my lawn. Good Lord, Ronald hadn't been joking.

They all stepped up to the cage, looked down at Ronald, who hadn't stopped complaining since he'd set eyes on them, then looked over at me, as if I had a good explanation for this.

"I got nothing," I said. "I came out here and found him this way."

"I think it's against the law to trap wild animals on your property," the paramedic said, clearly trying not to laugh.

"Actually," the fireman said, "you have the right to trap and relocate if the animal is a public nuisance."

"He's definitely that," I said.

Ronald's face turned even darker red. "Nuisance? This woman and those two old bats she cavorts with are the public nuisance. Now get me out of here!"

"Why didn't you let him out?" Carter asked.

"I tried but I don't know how to open it."

Carter shook his head and went to the end of the cage and lifted some latch on the bottom that had been hidden in the grass, then swung the door open. Ronald scrambled out and the paramedic reached down to help him to his feet.

"I want her arrested," Ronald said to Carter. "She's not getting away with it this time."

"Getting away with what?" I asked. "Once again, you're on my property. Something you still haven't explained."

"I was chasing my ferret," Ronald said.

I looked at the other men. "That sounds dirty. Is it dirty?"

Carter glanced at Father Michael, who shrugged.

"I have a pet ferret," Ronald said. "He got out and I found him in this cage eating something that will probably give him digestive issues. I crawled in to get him out and the door closed. Now will you arrest this woman?"

"For what?" I asked. "You and your ferret were trespassing.

I want this man arrested for letting his ferret eat my bait. Not that I believe that story for a minute."

"I would *never* lie," Ronald said. "Unlike some people."

"Then produce the ferret," I said. "Or did he run away from you again? No one would blame him, mind you."

"Um." The paramedic pointed to Ronald's rear. "Do you need medical attention?"

I peered around and saw Ronald's backside moving, then suddenly, a gray-and-white head pushed its way out of the trapdoor on the onesie, took one look at us, and bolted. Ronald emitted a strangled cry and took off after the escaping creature.

"Well, gentlemen, now that the ferret has appeared, it looks like the show is over," Carter said.

The paramedic grinned. "I'll be telling this one for weeks."

The fireman looked over at Father Michael. "Why did he call you?"

"He said he might die and needed last rites," Father Michael said.

"And you believed him?" I asked.

Father Michael shrugged. "Of course not, but I figured whatever was going on would be more interesting than the christening I was preparing for."

"Tell us the truth," I said. "Ronald is a serial killer, right? One of those creepy guys who has bodies buried in his basement? I know that confessions are confidential but I live next door, so I feel I have a right to know."

I didn't figure he'd tell me, but I'd always wondered about what interesting things priests heard about during confessions. Now, there was a reality show if anyone could get some priests to do it. So much more interesting than that crap Gertie watched.

"I think you're safe, Ms. Morrow," Father Michael said. "Mr. Franklin is a bit odd, but essentially harmless."

"Tell that to the ferret he had trapped in his pants," I said.

The paramedic laughed, and he and the fireman set off across the lawn. Father Michael gave us a nod, then followed behind them. Carter looked at me and shook his head.

"What?" I asked. "This one is totally not on me. Ronald and his ferret are on the hook for this one. You should start billing him for abuse of the town's resources."

"I'm going to take that under consideration. Do you have more bait?"

"I think Gertie left some chicken necks."

"Then let me get this set back up."

"Cool. Maybe next time I'll catch something more dangerous than Ronald and his ferret."

"Never underestimate a man who's willing to wear a onesie in public."

I shook my head. "There are so many things in this town that I can never unsee."

Carter sobered. "Hopefully, you'll be around long enough for them to wear off. Have you heard anything?"

"Yeah. I wanted to go over what I know with you tonight."

"So it's set?"

"Not yet, but it's in motion."

He blew out a breath. "This is really happening, isn't it?"

I nodded.

He looked at me several seconds without speaking, then finally asked, "Are you ready?"

"Yes."

He wrapped his arms around me and pulled me close. "I wish I were."

CHAPTER FOURTEEN

It was close to midnight when I left the house and hopped into Ida Belle's SUV. I was somewhat surprised to see Gertie in the back seat.

"How's your hearing?" I asked, keeping my voice level.

"Back to normal," Gertie said. "I'm still miffed that Carter has my gun, though. He's refusing to return it until he closes the file on his investigation. What investigation? If anyone needs to be investigated, it's the Lowery brothers for shooting at people."

"We *were* in their house," Ida Belle said. "I've shot at people for less." She looked over at me. "I heard you caught a zebra and a ferret in the gator trap."

I laughed. "It was a busy afternoon."

"Everyone's been talking about it," Gertie said. "Was Ronald really wearing a zebra-striped onesie?"

"Like you're always telling me," I said, "I couldn't make that up."

Ida Belle laughed. "My favorite part is when the ferret crawled out of his butt."

"Do you blame him?" Gertie said. "That poor animal was

probably trying to escape, then got distracted by some good dinner and went right back into captivity. I can't think of any place worse to live than Ronald's pants."

"Do people know about him?" I asked. "I mean, no one appeared to be fazed by the situation but I didn't know if that was because everyone knows Ronald is driving the crazy train or because it's Sinful and nothing surprises anyone anymore."

"Probably a bit of both," Ida Belle said. "We've always known Ronald was eccentric. Marge saw a couple of things that were unique, even by Sinful standards, but I think he's managed to keep the worst of his oddities hidden."

"Until now," Gertie said, and giggled. "Fortune has made him so mad, he's marching around with all his crazy on display."

"How come everything is always my fault?" I asked.

"Convenient scapegoat," Ida Belle said. "I heard through the Sinful Ladies grapevine that Celia Arceneaux is trying to get Father Michael to give evidence that you've driven Ronald to a state of mental breakdown and that living next door to you is a life-threatening matter."

"I *did* want to shoot him the other day when he suggested I use Merlin for gator food," I said. "But I fail to see what getting a priest to lie about me would accomplish. Father Michael didn't appear even remotely fazed by anything he saw. I'm guessing it didn't measure up to what he's heard in confession."

"Not to mention, I have no idea what she hopes to accomplish," Gertie said.

"She thinks public pressure could force Fortune to move," Ida Belle contended.

Gertie nodded. "She's grasping at straws."

"That's pretty much all she has left," I pointed out.

"That's all she's ever had," Ida Belle corrected, "but it hasn't stopped her from waging a personal war for three decades now, and it's not likely to deter her in the future."

"Well, she better ramp up her game," I said, "because when I'm officially a free agent, things are only going to get worse for her."

"I'm sure she's banking on you leaving soon since the summer is almost over," Gertie said. "Boy, is she in for a rude awakening when she finds out you're staying. You are staying, right? You haven't changed your mind?"

The anxiety in her voice when she asked those questions made my heart tug a little. I'd never had people who cared about me this way. Who deliberately sought out my company and didn't want it to end. It was really nice and something I never thought I'd be happy about.

"I haven't changed my mind," I said. "I mean, there's a ton of things I have to figure out, but I'm not leaving unless I don't have any other options."

"Did you tell Carter about the plan?" Ida Belle asked.

I nodded. "We had dinner tonight and I filled him in. At least, on the things I could fill him in on."

"He didn't ask about the warehouse?" Ida Belle asked.

"No. I'm sure he assumes it's something the CIA came up with. He was momentarily miffed that I didn't ask him to check out the location with us this morning, but we both know he had things to handle here."

"And you didn't want him thinking too hard about who owned the properties," Ida Belle said.

"There's that too," I agreed.

"Have you talked to Big and Little?" Gertie asked.

"Yeah. I talked to them before I called Harrison and Morrow with the location and again afterward, when it was a go. They're on standby to deliver the tip just as soon as I give them the green light. They also know I plan to use the other locations to try to ferret out the mole. The cameras should be here tomorrow, and Mannie will get them installed right away."

"I really like him," Gertie said. "If I were ten years younger, I'd totally take a run at him."

"If you were ten years younger, you'd still be old enough to be his grandmother," Ida Belle said.

"I could have handled him," Gertie said.

"You couldn't have handled that man when you were twenty," Ida Belle said. "Lara Croft couldn't handle that man."

"I bet Fortune could handle him," Gertie said.

"Fortune might be able to," Ida Belle agreed, "but she's already got enough man to drive her crazy. No one needs more than that."

"I wonder if Little is single," Gertie mused. "He looks nice in a suit and would probably be more manageable."

"Good Lord, woman, would you give it a rest?" Ida Belle said. "You're not going to start dating mobsters."

"You know," I said, "now that you mention it, I don't know anything about their personal lives. I've never heard them talk about wives or girlfriends, and they don't have anything personal on display in their office. But men in their line of work usually keep that sort of thing very private."

"That's true," Gertie said. "For all we know, Mannie could be married, have six kids, and host a barbecue every Sunday."

"If Mannie has six kids," Ida Belle said, "they are probably capable of staging a hostile takeover of a small country."

"Fine," Gertie said, "they're off the table as potential dating material, but there's a serious shortage of eligible men in Sinful. When this is over, you have to promise me we're going to take that vacation we keep talking about. I'm overdue for a little romance."

"Looks like we'll be headed to Florida then," Ida Belle said.

"Why do you say that?" I asked.

"Florida is God's Waiting Room," Ida Belle said. "Gertie will have a buffet to choose from."

Ida Belle pulled her SUV to the curb and pointed at a house behind us. "The one with the lawn that needs mowing is Marco's. Should I park down the street so no one can ID my vehicle if we have to get away fast?"

"If we have to get away fast," Gertie said, "I doubt anyone will be able to see your vehicle at warp speed."

"She has a point," I said. "And we stand a better chance at driving away than running if things go south." I rolled my eyes toward the back seat.

Ida Belle put the SUV in gear. "You're probably right. Besides, the lighting on this street is crap anyway. Not like anyone can see much. How about I just pull up to the curb in front of the cans, we do our search, and we get the heck out of here?"

"Sounds good to me," I said.

Ida Belle rounded the block and pulled up in front of Marco's house, positioning her SUV in front of the cans. "I was rather hoping he only had one can. He lives alone. How much trash can one man produce?"

"He probably doesn't put it out until everything is overflowing," Gertie said. "Typical male."

As I was guilty of the same thing, I kept silent and hoped the trash wasn't too old and didn't contain chicken parts. Aged chicken in Louisiana summer heat was a bad deal all the way around. The chicken necks in the gator trap were already starting to reek and they had only been there one evening. I pulled headlamps and latex gloves from my pocket and handed everyone their set, then we climbed out of the SUV and headed over to the trash cans. I opened the lid on the first one and blanched.

"Yuck," Gertie said. "Stale beer."

"Smells like Bourbon Street on a Monday morning," Ida Belle said.

"It's all bagged at least," I said as I started pulling the bags out of the can. "Everyone take one and let's get this over with."

As soon as we opened the bags, I wished I had brought gas masks. Marge had one in her fishing tackle. When I'd first seen it, I wondered why it was stored there rather than in her super-secret closet with all her other cool stuff. But then I'd had a trip to the best fishing place in Sinful, an island named Number Two because of its stench, and everything made sense. I didn't plan on doing much fishing and definitely not on Number Two, but if I was going to stick around Sinful, I might need to order a couple more masks. There were all sorts of smelly things one could accidentally get into, and my chance of getting into them with Ida Belle and Gertie was probably high.

I held my breath and plowed through milk cartons, pizza boxes, and a pile of fish heads until I reached the bottom, then I drew in a breath from my mouth. "Nothing in this one."

"Clear here as well," Ida Belle said, and Gertie nodded.

We tied up the bags and put them back in the can, then moved on to can number two. This one had three bags as well, so I divvied up the fun and we started the stinky search all over again. I had made it about halfway through when Gertie perked up.

"I have something here," she said. "It's bacon boxes!"

Either excitement got the best of her, or her hearing still wasn't quite up to par, but she'd uttered that last phrase just a little too loudly. I froze and a couple seconds later, lights flipped on in Marco's house and I heard yelling inside and then, even more troubling, barking.

"Does Marco have a dog?"

"Two," Gertie said. "Big ones."

"Retreat!" I yelled and ran for the SUV. I heard footsteps behind me and as I jumped into the passenger's seat, turned and saw Gertie heft her bag of garbage over the back seat and into the rear of Ida Belle's SUV. I thought Ida Belle was going to take the time to shoot her on the spot or at the least, drive off and leave her there. Then the front door to the house opened and two pit bulls ran straight at the SUV. Gertie jumped in and slammed her door and Ida Belle took off down the street.

I lowered the window and a wave of humid, hot, August Louisiana air hit my face. Ida Belle managed to make it around the end of the block before cursing Gertie nine ways to Sunday.

"You threw bachelor garbage in my vehicle," Ida Belle ranted. "It smells like a sewer. What the hell were you thinking?"

"We couldn't leave without the evidence," Gertie said. "You should be thanking me. We caught him red-handed."

"You can hold your breath waiting for that thanks," Ida Belle said.

"I'm holding my breath now," I said, and stuck my head out the window. "I might hold my breath until next year."

Ida Belle rounded a corner, the vehicle's tires squealing.

"This isn't the way to your house," Gertie said.

"I know," Ida Belle said. "It's the way to *your* house. Until this SUV is one hundred percent stench-free, it's going to reside in your garage."

"What about my Cadillac?" Gertie said.

"Stop pretending you take care of that car," Ida Belle said. "I'm not having this thing stink up my garage and waft into my kitchen. You can clean it and live with it until there's no more smell of garbage."

"Fine," Gertie said. "But you're going to be sorry when my quick thinking solves the mystery."

Ida Belle shot a dirty look at Gertie in the rearview mirror, and I was pretty sure she didn't care if Gertie had found the fountain of youth in the bottom of that garbage bag. I drew in another breath of hot, humid air and counted the seconds until we reached Gertie's garage. We pulled up to the curb and Gertie stomped inside to get the keys to her Cadillac. I jumped out of the SUV and went to stand in the flower bed. It had been recently fertilized, and I swear to God, it smelled better than the SUV.

Ida Belle paced in front of her vehicle, giving it worried looks and occasionally patting the hood as though she were comforting an injured child. Finally, the garage door came up and Gertie backed out her Cadillac. Ida Belle pulled into the garage and Gertie parked in the drive, then we hurried inside where Ida Belle was already lifting the back hatch on her SUV.

"Close the garage door," Ida Belle said.

"Are you sure?" I asked.

"Unfortunately, yes," she said. "If Marco comes looking for us, we'd be easy to spot with the door open."

She had a point. There probably weren't many black SUVs with Marco's garbage inside them. He might catch on that we were the ones going through his trash. I punched the button and the door began to lower, then I hurried to the back door and opened it. I wasn't sure it helped, but at this point, it couldn't hurt. I scooted to the back of the SUV to find Ida Belle staring at the inside, the expression on her face somewhere between terrorist and serial killer.

I knew the bag had been open when Gertie tossed it into the vehicle, and I figured some stuff had spilled out, but this was way worse than I'd imagined. The bag looked as if it had met up with something in Gertie's purse.

It had exploded in the back of the SUV, leaving only shards of plastic and the rest of it random garbage. Shrimp heads, banana peels, milk cartoons, beer cans, and a lot of stuff I couldn't readily identify covered the once-pristine liner. I immediately launched into action.

"The liner is rubber, right?" I said. "So we'll make sure everything is on it and pull it out. The carpet beneath should be fine. Maybe just some spot cleaning."

"The hell you say, spot cleaning," Ida Belle grumbled.

I reached in to knock a couple of beer cans onto the liner, then moved to one side and motioned for Ida Belle to do the same. Carefully, we pulled the liner out and laid it on the garage floor.

"Okay," I said, looking at the mess. "Where are the bacon boxes? We need to find the stamp for the café on them to be sure."

Gertie gave me a look like I'd lost my mind and pointed to two white boxes with red lettering that were torn and rumpled. "Right there in front of you."

I glanced at Ida Belle to make sure she wasn't pulling a gun out, then sighed. "Those say *bagels*, not bacon."

Gertie leaned over to inspect the boxes then raised back up. "Oops."

"Give me your keys," Ida Belle said, and stuck her hand out to Gertie. "I'm taking your car. I'll drop Fortune off."

"What about all this trash in my garage?" Gertie asked.

"You can clean it up," Ida Belle said, "and bleach my liner, and shampoo my carpets. Tomorrow morning, you can make an appointment for the eye doctor."

"When are you bringing my car back?" Gertie asked.

"When mine no longer stinks," Ida Belle said. "Come on, Fortune."

I considered jogging home, as it looked like the safer alternative, but when we got to the front drive, I hopped in the passenger seat of Gertie's car and watched as Ida Belle silently started the car and backed out of the driveway. I'd seen her mad before, but not like this. I made a mental note to never, ever do something to harm Ida Belle's car. It was apparently like injuring a firstborn.

She turned the corner but instead of heading for my house, went back in the direction of Marco's. "I wanted to see what was going on," she said.

As she drew up to the corner, I practically vaulted over her and switched off the headlights. "Keep going!"

She stared at me a second as if I'd lost my mind, then looked past me and saw Deputy Breaux's truck parked in front of Marco's house. Ida Belle pressed the gas evenly but guided the car quickly across the intersection and headed for my house.

"I swear that woman is going to make me crazy," Ida Belle said. "I know she's my best friend, and now she's your friend, but if you move forward with this whole PI thing, you should tell her she can't help unless she gets new glasses."

When I thought about the trash cleanup, and the liner bleaching, and the carpet cleaning that were all in Gertie's immediate future, I figured the problem might rectify itself. Not to mention that Gertie probably knew she'd finally crossed Ida Belle's line in the sand. Blowing up purses and shooting holes in boats was one thing. It was completely another to soil Ida Belle's SUV.

"I have a feeling she's going to get on that one," I said. "But in other news, we're back to square one again on the food thief."

"Yeah, I know. I wish I had a clue as to where to look next but I have to be honest with you, none of the remaining people look good for it."

"Based on what I've gathered from you guys and Ally, they don't to me, either. But that food's not walking out of the café on its own."

"No. And I agree that it's most likely an employee. A friend or relative getting the key and going in at night is one thing, but taking food out during the day would take some serious cojones."

I nodded. "No one would look twice at an employee carrying a frozen chicken, but if their cousin dropped by to visit and then walked around with one, it would probably look strange."

"Unless they have one of Gertie's bottomless purses of fun."

"There is always that angle."

Ida Belle pulled into my drive, and I looked over at her. "Don't worry about it," I said. "Worst case, Francine gets her security cameras set up and she knows who it is by next week anyway. This was just an exercise."

"I know, but I wanted it to be a successful one."

Something in her tone made me pause. Maybe a sense of urgency that I didn't expect. "Why is it so important to you?" I asked.

She sighed. "Because I was thinking that if you were successful at solving this, it would help cement your decision to stay. And I really want you to. Not if you're still in danger, of course. But if you have the option of anywhere, I really want it to be here."

"Even if it means never knowing what Gertie has in her purse?"

She looked over at me and smiled. "Even if it means having trash thrown in my vehicle. You're important to me, Fortune. And I don't say that about a lot of people. You're important to a lot of good people in this town, and we'd all lose something special if you left."

"Thank you," I managed, feeling a little choked up. "That goes the same for me. So please don't worry. On that one thing, my mind is made up. As long as it's an option, you're stuck with me. Besides, no way would I leave and let Celia off that easy."

"Got that right. Go on inside and get some sleep. You need to be in top shape for the days coming."

It occurred to me that if this exchange had happened between two normal women, they probably would have hugged, maybe even cried. But Ida Belle and I weren't exactly normal women. I climbed out of the car, then leaned over and looked at her.

"Have a good night," I said.

It sounded like one thing, but from the look she gave me before pulling away, I knew she got it.

CHAPTER FIFTEEN

My phone went off the next morning, jolting me out of sleep. I bolted up and grabbed my pistol, scanning the room as my feet hit the ground. It took a second for me to register that it was my phone and not something nefarious, and I tossed the gun on the bed and lifted the phone from the nightstand. Six friggin' a.m. This better be good.

It was a text from Gertie.

NEED HELP NOW!

That was all it said. I sent a text back that consisted of only question marks, but no reply was forthcoming. I tried calling but no one answered. Now worried, I grabbed a couple spare weapons and ran out of the house. I made the drive to Gertie's house in half the time it should have taken and almost clipped Ida Belle as we turned onto the street from two different directions. We both flew into the drive and jumped out of our vehicles, guns blazing.

The garage door was open, so we made a beeline for it. And just as we got to the entry, Carter stepped out. We drew up short and he stared at both of us, his mouth partially open. Finally, he shook his head.

"You two are frightening," he said.

I looked over at Ida Belle. She was wearing a camouflage bathrobe and had a head full of curlers and some kind of brown mask on her face. In her right hand, she held a shotgun. In her left, a nine-millimeter. The hilt of a hunting knife stuck out of her pocket. Now concerned, I glanced down as I couldn't remember what I'd worn to bed and hadn't taken the time to dress before running out.

I breathed a sigh of relief when I saw that all the important things were covered by shorts and a tank top, but just barely. I had my nine in my right hand and a .45 in my left. Neither of us wore shoes.

"The knife is a nice touch," I said to Ida Belle. "I only had time to grab another gun."

"I keep the knife in the robe," Ida Belle said.

"If this meeting of the two scariest women in Sinful is over," Carter said, "I'd like to address the situation inside."

Gertie!

"Is Gertie okay?" I asked. "I got a text."

"Me too," Ida Belle said. "But she wouldn't answer."

Carter nodded. "I got the same text. I just got here faster and even managed shoes. Gertie is fine, but she's got a situation. Not a police situation, so I'm tempted to leave you two to deal with it and go back to bed for another hour. But since I suspect there's more to the story than what I've heard, I'm going to stick around for a bit and see how things shake out."

Uh-oh.

I glanced over at Ida Belle, who wore her signature blank look. The woman really was a pro. "So what's going on?" I asked.

"Come see for yourself," he said and motioned us inside the garage toward the door to the house, which was propped open.

When we got within a couple feet of the door, two cats shot out of the house, almost tripping Carter as they went.

"What the heck?" Ida Belle asked, clearly as confused as I was.

Gertie scrambled to the door, her hair sticking out in every direction, her face flushed. But that wasn't even the interesting part. I'd seen the nun costume before when we did one of our undercover adventures, but I couldn't fathom a reason why she would wear it to sleep in or why she would put it on after waking up. I knew that a crisis often brought people closer to God, but Gertie wasn't even Catholic, so this was taking things a bit too far.

"Why are you dressed like a nun?" Ida Belle asked.

"It covered the most of me," Gertie said. "They're relentless. You have to help me get them out."

I heard glass breaking and caught a whiff of fish. I peered behind Gertie, and that's when everything made sense. Well, more sense than it had before.

At least twenty cats raced through her house, running up curtains, jumping from counter to table to chair then windowsill, all in a frenzy, and they only stopped running long enough to fight with each other. Ida Belle pushed past me, took one look at the chaos, and began to bark orders.

"Get as many aerosol cans as you have—hair spray, deodorant, air freshener—doesn't matter," she said. "Fortune and I will look in the kitchen. Carter, check the garage. And no bug spray."

Gertie didn't even hesitate before running off toward the guest room. I cast a glance at Carter, who shrugged, and then I hurried into the kitchen after Ida Belle and started searching cabinets and drawers for spray, pulling out cans and plopping them on the counter as I went. Gertie sped back into the kitchen with the nun robe pulled up and a load of cans in it and dumped them all in the kitchen sink.

"Cats hate the sound of aerosol spray," Ida Belle said. "So Fortune and I will take some cans and head upstairs. Gertie, take the guest bedroom. Scare the cats out of the rooms with the spray and close the door afterward. We'll head downstairs, forcing them all toward the kitchen. Gertie, you get them down the hall and into the kitchen. Carter, make sure when they run out, they don't come back in the house."

"I think I have something to handle that," he said, and headed back into the garage.

I hurried upstairs with Ida Belle and into a spare bedroom. Two cats were fighting on the bed, so I stepped up, positioning myself behind the cats, and sprayed. The cats immediately broke apart and ran for the door. I chased after them, following up with another spray for good measure. Then I looked under the bed to make sure there weren't any lurking underneath and hurried out of the room, closing the door behind me. I gave the hall bath a quick once-over, then moved out into the hallway, where Ida Belle was pulling the door to the master bedroom closed behind her. Five more cats were headed for the stairs.

We ran downstairs behind a wave of cats, dodging even more at the bottom of the stairs as Gertie herded them down the hallway from the guest room. With a lot of effort, we managed to get them from the living room into the kitchen, and that's when things got more difficult. Whatever Gertie was cooking—and I assumed it was a stinky fish casserole for Godzilla—was too attractive for the cats to leave. They had allowed themselves to be pushed into the kitchen but that's where they dug in, refusing to go out the back door, no matter how much we sprayed.

"Move!" Carter yelled, and waded in from the garage with

an air compressor, closing the garage door behind him. He stood in the entryway between the living room and kitchen and ordered us to stand behind him and block the opening. We took our position, and he let loose with the compressor.

The compressor was easily ten times louder than the aerosol cans and sent the cats into a frenzy. They must have thought a lion was in the room hissing at them because they ran over everything in the room and one another trying to get out the door. As the last one exited, I heard Gertie yell, and then she shoved me in the back and ran past all of us and out the back door. We hurried behind her as she ran into the yard, thrashing about, the nun suit flapping around her.

"Straggler!" she yelled.

I knew we should do something but since I had no idea what was going on, I had even less of an idea what to do about it. I glanced over at Carter and Ida Belle, but they didn't look any more enlightened than me. Finally, Gertie tripped over the leg of a lawn chair and went sprawling onto the lawn. A cat shot out of the robe and took off across the lawn, clearing the six-foot fence in the back like an Olympic athlete.

Gertie flopped back on the lawn, arms and legs splayed out, and I could see her chest heaving with the effort to breathe. We hurried down the steps and leaned over her.

"Are you all right?" Ida Belle said.

"I need a drink," she said.

"I need an explanation," Carter said. "So heft her up, and let's get inside and close the doors before we have a repeat visit. Then you can explain why you've suddenly become the Pied Piper of cats."

I glanced over at Ida Belle as we helped Gertie up, and she raised an eyebrow, which let me know she had the same concern I did—that Carter was onto our trash thieving. I just hoped she had a good story for this one, because I didn't have anything. We headed back inside, making sure the door was closed and locked for good measure, and Ida Belle poured us all a shot of whiskey and put on a pot of coffee.

Carter waited for Gertie to get her breath back, then held out his hands. "So? Why the cat invasion? And before you attempt to go with whatever stinky thing you're cooking in your oven right now, I'd like to point out that your garage smells of bleach and carpet cleaner and Ida Belle's SUV is parked inside, not your Cadillac."

"A package of chicken necks I took to Fortune's for bait leaked in the back of Ida Belle's vehicle," Gertie said. "She went totally mad cow on me and insisted that I clean the thing and that it stay here until the smell was gone. So I bleached and shampooed it yesterday and was hoping it was aired out by today, which is why the back door of the garage was open. I forgot about the doggy flap on the door from the garage and into the house."

"You don't have a dog," I said. "And if you did, why would he need to go into the garage?"

"I did at one time," Gertie said, "and he peed every five minutes when he got old. So I put a doggy door on the back door in the kitchen, but then last year, I replaced that door with the glass insert one for a better view and moved the old one to the garage since it was heavier-duty than the one that was there. I had no idea the flap was open. It's plexiglass. I couldn't tell."

"You could if you got new glasses," Ida Belle grumbled.

Gertie shot her a dirty look, then directed an innocent gaze at Carter.

Surprisingly, it all sounded completely reasonable. At least to me. I looked over at Carter to see if he was buying it, but his expression hadn't changed. Which meant Gertie hadn't sold it well enough, or he had more information that he hadn't hit us with yet. I was betting on the latter.

"So the smell in Ida Belle's SUV had nothing to do with a report of someone in a dark-colored SUV stealing garbage last night?" Carter asked.

The three of us immediately shifted to our confused and slightly disgusted expressions. It was easy enough. I just thought about how bad the SUV smelled the night before and everything fell into place.

"Why would someone steal garbage?" I asked.

"That's a great question," Carter said. "And I was really hoping to get an answer to it."

We all looked at one another and shrugged.

"Paparazzi?" Gertie suggested. "They steal garbage. I've seen it on TV."

"In Sinful?" Carter asked. "Whose garbage would be of interest to them here?"

"There are plenty of interesting people doing fascinating things in Sinful," Gertie said.

"Uh-huh," Carter said. "And I'm looking at three of them. So if I check your trash cans, I won't find anything in them that belongs to Marco Gilley?"

Gertie frowned. "I don't think the paparazzi would be interested in Marco's trash, and I'm certainly not. Feel free to check my cans but all you're going to find is a mess of junk mail, some empty milk cartons and a couple of cans."

Carter stared at her for several seconds and I could see the indecision on his face. I knew he wanted to call her bluff, but the thought of digging through garbage made the whole idea less desirable.

"Oh hell," Ida Belle said, "give the man some gloves and send him out to the curb before trash pickup comes by."

I struggled to maintain a straight face. What was she

doing? I looked over at her and she gave me a barely imperceptible shake of her head. I had to assume she'd clued in to something that I hadn't. Gertie grabbed a pair of latex gloves from a drawer and handed them to Carter.

"There's only one bag," Gertie said. "I cooked mostly from frozen stuff this week, so not a lot of trash."

Carter hesitated a second, then took the gloves and headed out the front door. I waited until the door had closed behind him to speak.

"I hope you have a good explanation for having Marco's trash," I said, "because my imagination is shot."

"Don't be silly," Gertie said. "I didn't put Marco's trash in my can. It smelled to high heaven for one, and you never know when someone might come by and dig through your garbage."

"Like the paparazzi?" Ida Belle asked, and grinned.

Relief flooded through me. "So where did you put it?"

"Celia's can," Gertie said. "It will stink so bad, she'll have to bleach her can."

"Was Marco's name on anything?" I asked.

"Doesn't matter," Gertie said. "Her trash was already at the curb, and she won't notice the stench until she brings in the empty can after pickup."

We looked out the front window and watched as Carter opened the lone garbage bag and dug through it. It didn't take long before he pulled off the gloves, added them to the bag, then retied it and put the entire thing back in the can. Gertie opened the front door as he approached.

"Well?" she asked.

"It was just what you claimed," he said.

"So you have incorrectly accused us of something we didn't do," Gertie said. "Don't you think you should apologize?"

Carter gave her a look that clearly said "hold your breath."

"I accused you of something I'm still pretty sure you did,"

he said. "I just don't know why or where you hid the evidence. But since it's low on my priority list and breakfast is high, I'm going to head home for a shower and then to the café. If you three could manage to stay out of trouble long enough for me to get my day started, it would be highly appreciated."

We watched as he pulled away, then headed back to the kitchen for coffee.

"Spill it," Ida Belle said. "What the hell happened?"

"Mostly like I told Carter," Gertie said, "except I left out the part about how the garage reeked of fish even after I was done cleaning. I cracked the garage door at the bottom and left the back door open to draw some air through there but it must have attracted the cats. Then they got inside the garage and smelled what I was cooking for Godzilla and all hell broke loose."

"So many cats," I said. "Where did they all come from?"

"All around," Gertie said. "I recognized a few from the neighborhood. Others were probably feral. I hope no one peed."

"If they peed in here, you might as well burn the house down," Ida Belle said.

Her phone signaled an incoming text, and she pulled it from her pocket and grinned. "Marie says a gang of cats attacked Celia when she was taking a bag of garbage out ten minutes ago."

"Don't tell me she's up a lamppost again," I said.

"Nope. A tree."

I stared. "If someone calls Carter about this, he's going to dig through her trash."

CHAPTER SIXTEEN

"HURRY!" Ida Belle said, and ran out the front door. Gertie and I scrambled behind as she jumped into Gertie's ancient Cadillac. We barely got the doors closed before she took off down the block. Two streets over, she turned and I saw the garbage truck ahead of us.

Ida Belle pulled up behind the truck and ran over to the driver. I saw her gesturing toward Celia's street and then hand the driver some money. He leaned out the window and gave Ida Belle a high five before pulling away.

"What did you tell him?" I asked as she got back into the car.

"I told him we'd played a prank on Celia and put fish heads in her trash. But I needed him to break route and pick up her street now or we'd get busted. I gave him a twenty for the trouble. He gave me a high five because he can't stand Celia."

"I know we should stay away," I said, "but I have to see Celia up the tree."

Ida Belle grinned and directed the car toward Celia's house.

The trash truck was picking up her can as we rounded the corner, the strong winds lifting some of the paper and cardboard and blowing it out into the street. A dozen cats milled around her front lawn, hissing at the truck as it took away their prize while some chased the flying fragments. When the truck set the can back on the ground, the cats swarmed it, knocking it over and scrambling in and out, fighting over the tiny space. I scanned the yard and spotted Celia sitting on a branch in an apple tree about twenty feet away.

For a woman who'd had her undergarments on display way more times than I could count, I'd have thought Celia would have learned to never leave the house unless fully clothed, maybe even wearing two pairs of underwear and a pair of overalls on top of a whole other outfit. But no. Instead, she'd elected to take out the trash in her bathrobe. Now she sat on the branch, looking like a chubby wildcat in her leopard-printed robe.

As soon as she spotted us, she started yelling.

"Maybe we should leave," I said.

"Too late," Gertie said, and pointed at Carter's truck rounding the corner.

"Might as well get out and video it then," Ida Belle said. "You never know what might be useful later on."

We climbed out of the car and started up the sidewalk. Carter pulled to the curb, got out of his truck, and stared at us. "And what, exactly, are the three of you doing here?" he asked.

"We heard Celia was up a tree," Ida Belle said, "and I want video in case I need to blackmail her at some point."

"And you knew she was up a tree how, exactly?" he asked.

"Marie," Ida Belle said.

"She said Celia was attacked by a roving gang of cats," Gertie said. "I bet it's the same ones that tore up my house."

"You think the cats have formed a gang?" Carter asked.

I pointed to a pack of them fighting in and around the trash can. "They *are* acting like a bunch of thugs."

Carter looked at the empty trash can, then back at us. "Gee. I wonder what attracted those cats to Celia's trash?"

We all shrugged.

"Stop your gum flapping and get me out of this tree," Celia yelled.

"And I want them arrested," Gertie grumbled. "You know it's coming."

"She's waiting to see if she makes it out of the tree fully clothed," I said.

Gertie nodded. "It's harder to be taken seriously when your bare butt is showing."

Ida Belle whipped out her phone and started to record as Carter approached the tree. "Why don't you just climb down?" he asked.

Celia glared at him. "What do you think I am? A monkey?"

Ida Belle reached over with her free hand and clamped it over Gertie's mouth. "Don't answer that."

"I know you three are responsible," Celia continued to rant.

"Sorry," I said, "we're not capable of herding cats. Carter can attest to that. This roving band of trouble attacked Gertie before they attacked you. Why do you think we're all out here this early in our pajamas?" I looked over at Gertie. "And dressed as a nun?"

Celia glared at Gertie. "Bad enough you make a mockery of women everywhere, but now you're mocking my faith. God is going to send lightning down on you."

"Maybe if I stood under that tree," Gertie said, "he'd take out that branch you're sitting on and solve two problems at once."

"Deputy LeBlanc?" A man's voice sounded from next door and I looked up to see him step through the shrubs and into Celia's yard.

Fiftyish. Five foot eleven. Two hundred pounds. Decent muscle at one time but had gotten lax. Based on the dirty look he shot at Celia, she was the only one of us at risk.

"Carl," Carter acknowledged. "Got a bit of an issue here. I don't suppose you have a ladder I could borrow?"

"If it means she'll go inside and stop her yelling, I'll climb up it and carry her down myself," he said.

I heard a crack—not a loud one, but definitely not something occurring in nature—and looked up at Celia just as an apple above her head dropped. She'd glanced up at the sound herself and the apple hit her right in the middle of her eyes. She yelled and let go of the limb, pitching forward onto the lawn. I saw movement at the shrubs and glanced over just in time to see a teenage boy, who looked familiar, slip a BB gun in the bushes before stepping forward.

"Maybe she died," he said.

Celia scrambled up from the ground, covered in dirt and leaves, and glared at the teen. "Your uncle should teach you some manners."

"I have manners," he said. "I just don't waste them on people like you."

"Now, Jordan," Carl said, although I could tell he didn't exactly disagree with the teen's sentiment.

Jordan. Carl. That's why the teen looked familiar. He was the busboy at the café that Celia had accused of stealing her purse during the alligator incident.

Jordan threw his hands in the air. "What? You want me to feel bad that the old biddy fell? She shouldn't climb things if she can't get down, and I think everyone in town knows how that turns out. If she could keep her clothes on and her mouth shut, you might be able to sell the house. But no, everyone finds out who lives next door and the offers leave the table."

He whirled around and headed back into the bushes,

snatching the BB gun on his way. Carl gave Carter an apologetic look. "He's a little frustrated. I have to sell the house in order to get money for his college. Can't afford a place in New Orleans and here and tuition."

"He's a hoodlum is what he is," Celia said.

"My nephew is a good kid," Carl said. "He just doesn't like you and I can't say that I blame him. Maybe if you cleaned up around your place more often, it wouldn't attract animals. The place has smelled of something rotten for days."

"Something died under my house," Celia said.

"Shame it wasn't something inside," Gertie mumbled.

Celia glared at her, then trained her stare on Carter. "Well, are you just going to stand there or are you going to arrest these people?"

Carter's jaw twitched and I knew he was already maxed out on nonsense. Not a good sign as it was barely 7:00 a.m.

"No!" he said, so loudly Celia's eyes widened. "I'm not arresting anyone, including you. I want all of you people to go home, get dressed, and I don't want a single 911 call because of you again today. Not even if you're being murdered. Am I clear?"

Celia was pissed but smart enough to know when to keep her mouth shut. She whirled around and stomped off to her house. Carter looked at the three of us. "I mean it," he said, and nodded to Carl before walking off. Carl gave us a weak wave, then headed back through the bushes.

"Well, I guess the show is over," Gertie said. "Let's get the heck out of here."

We headed back to the car and as I started to climb in, I saw a piece of white cardboard lodged under the wheel. I reached over and pulled it out, then hopped inside the car.

"Look at this," I said and pointed to the red stamp on the cardboard.

"It's says Francine's Café," Gertie said. "That's a bacon box."

"What's it doing under the wheel?" Ida Belle said.

I pointed down the street at the pieces of trash blowing around. "I noticed paper flying out of the truck when he picked up Celia's garbage."

"Did we miss it when we searched Marco's garbage?" Ida Belle asked.

"I don't think so," I said. "If we were just depending on Gertie's sketchy eyesight, it would be one thing, but we all looked at the stuff from the back of your SUV."

"Then where did it come from?" Gertie asked.

"With this wind, it could have come from anywhere on this street and maybe even the next," Ida Belle said.

I shook my head. "But you diverted the truck to this street, which means he hadn't done the ones on either side before he got here. I don't think the box would have traveled two blocks, even in this wind."

"That's true," Ida Belle said.

"I hate to say it, but Jordan lives right next door to Celia," I said.

"True," Gertie said, "but Cora lives on this street too. And I heard yesterday that she brought two dozen bacon-wrapped shrimp to the Catholic church dinner on Sunday. Besides, whoever stole the food could have put the containers in someone else's trash just like we did."

I nodded. "Maybe we should take a closer look at Cora and Jordan."

"Breakfast first," Gertie said. "I'm starving."

"*First*, we change clothes," Ida Belle said.

"Oh yeah." Despite the fact that I was seated in a car with a woman wearing a bathrobe and curlers and another dressed like a nun, I'd completely missed that. I wasn't sure what that said about me, but it probably wasn't anything good.

"Okay, so we change clothes and meet at the café in twenty," I said, wondering if a day in Sinful would ever start normally.

I smiled. I was sorta hoping it wouldn't.

THE CAFÉ WAS FAIRLY quiet but it was early. Ally had the day off but I saw Cora carrying a tray and gave Ida Belle a nod. It was as good a time as any to chat her up. I didn't expect her to fess up to stealing, especially while she was on shift from the place with the missing merchandise, but people often revealed things in random conversation that they didn't think about.

"Good morning, Cora," Ida Belle said as she stepped up to our table.

"Morning, ladies," Cora said with a smile. "I heard there was a fuss down at Celia's this morning."

"Good news travels fast," Gertie said.

"Well, when you live down the street and your husband mostly works from home," Cora said, "you tend to hear about things. Especially when they're odd. Did she really get attacked by cats?"

"That's what she said," Ida Belle said. "By the time we got there, she was already up the tree. There were cats fighting in her garbage though."

"I've never seen cats do that," Cora said. "I mean, not a bunch at one time."

"They seemed to be fighting over a bacon box," I said. "You'd think at her age and with her physical condition, Celia would be watching what she ate a little more."

The smile faded from Cora's face and she glanced back at

the kitchen, then looked back at us, but I noticed she didn't meet my eyes. "I better get moving," she said. "What can I get you ladies to drink?"

We gave our drink orders and Cora hurried away. "That was interesting," I said.

Ida Belle nodded. "Definitely. But why would Cora steal food? It doesn't make sense."

"There's a lot of pressure over at the Catholic church," Gertie said, "especially on the wives of employees. They pay them squat but judge everything they contribute. If it doesn't meet the grade, then people start talking."

"Over what you bring to church dinner?" I asked.

"Oh yeah," Gertie said. "They once fired a piano player for bringing store-bought rolls."

I stared. "You're kidding."

"She only brought one pack, you see. It's not enough to just make something good. If you're getting money from the church in any form, the parishioners expect you to bring a lot of it as well."

Ida Belle frowned. "I can see where that might be a problem. A music director's position can't possibly pay that much. And Celia serves on the church board."

"Of course she does," I said. "But bacon is only half the problem. Isn't shrimp more expensive?"

Gertie nodded. "But I happen to know that Cora's husband played the piano down at the shrimp house for the mother of the owner. It was her eighty-fifth birthday."

"What the heck does that have to do with anything?" Ida Belle asked.

"If you'd let me finish," Gertie said, "I know about it because Cora was excited that they traded shrimp for his time."

"Heads up," I said.

Cora headed our way with a tray and placed our drinks on the table. "Do you ladies know what you want to order?" she asked, seeming a bit hurried even though only three tables were occupied.

We gave our orders and before she could rush off, I stopped her. "Cora, I was wondering," I said. "Someone told me you made bacon-wrapped shrimp for the last church dinner. Is that hard to do in bulk? I'm thinking of hosting a party and would like to try it."

Cora froze and for a second, looked like a deer caught in the headlights. "It's not that hard," she said. "I'll get you the recipe."

She whirled around and hurried off. I looked at Ida Belle and Gertie. "Well?"

"It doesn't look good," Ida Belle said. "She's too nervous over a simple conversation."

"Well, the bacon boxes are long gone," I said, "so there's no way to pin it on her. And even if we broke into her house and found chickens and pot roast, there's no way to prove it came from the café."

"The chip box might be stamped," Gertie said.

"Yeah, but don't you think she'd have gotten rid of the evidence before her husband saw it?" I asked.

"True," Gertie said. "So what do we do now?"

"I don't think there's anything we can do but let Francine put up the cameras and see what happens," I said.

"Maybe we scared her enough to stop," Ida Belle said.

"Maybe," I agreed.

I watched as Cora served a table on the other side of the café. She glanced over at us, but when she saw me looking, immediately redirected her gaze. Something was definitely up with her. But was she a thief?

She seemed an unlikely choice, but if living in Sinful had

taught me anything, it was that things were often not what they seemed.

THE REST of the day was a slow grind, but I have to admit, I was okay with it for a change. The security cameras were delivered at eleven, and Ida Belle, Gertie, and I hauled them all to Big and Little's warehouse, where Mannie loaded them into the back of his truck. He'd also offered to stage my hideout room at the takedown location and showed us the cot, blankets, and ice chest and cooktop that he planned to use. It was exactly the sort of thing Ahmad would expect me to have and made me wonder, once again, just what Mannie's past included.

We spent the rest of the day hanging out at my house, watching movies. No investigating. No chasing alligators. No crazy cat escapades. And most importantly, no 911 calls.

Mannie checked in midafternoon to tell me everything was in place, and I called Harrison to let him know the cameras were ready for monitoring. He was going to filter the fake intel to the Miami team that afternoon, and then all we had to do was sit back and wait. I just hoped this exercise gave us what we wanted. Even though I was leaving the agency when this was over, the good men and women still working there were in jeopardy as long as someone who could be bought was working beside them.

Carter and I were supposed to have dinner, but he got a burglary call from the hospital right before quitting time. Since it involved the theft of pharmaceuticals, he needed to work the scene himself. Deputy Breaux was learning, but he was still too green to handle something of that magnitude. Given the number of people that traversed the hospital every day, Carter knew it would take a while, so he'd told me to go ahead and eat without him. If he got out at a decent time, he said he'd come by, but when 11:00 p.m. came and went with no word, I headed up to bed.

I stared at the ceiling for a long time, wondering if I should pick up a book and try to read. Then Merlin jumped onto the bed and curled up next to me, purring, and I finally drifted off to sleep.

I got the call at 8:00 a.m. the next morning.

Without even checking the display, I somehow knew it was Harrison. The ring just sounded different even though I hadn't changed it since I'd owned the phone. I drew in a deep breath and slowly blew it out, then answered.

"I have awesome news, Redding," Harrison said.

I already knew what he was going to say. "You caught the mole."

"Oh yeah. Last night one of the operatives from the Florida job took a red-eye to New Orleans and went straight to that old motel."

"Which agent?"

"Summerfield."

"I don't think I've ever met him. Young guy, right?"

"Yeah. He's been with the agency for three years. Picked up right after a four-year stint in the navy."

"So what's the plan?"

"Morrow's already got the forensic accountants on it. He won't be able to hide money from them. They make the IRS look friendly."

"How long?"

"A day, maybe two, but it doesn't matter. Morrow arranged to have him sent on a job in California. He won't be anywhere near New Orleans when the takedown happens."

"Any word on that?"

"Yeah, the cameras are all working fine. Your guy did a bang-up job with placement. We have a green light."

My hand tightened on the phone. "Now?"

"Whenever you're ready to pull the trigger. I need ten hours to get my team in place. I'll brief them with the fake mission on the plane ride down, just in case our friend Summerfield has a partner."

This was it. The moment I'd spent the entire summer waiting for. The moment that would set off the thing that would change the rest of my life. Or end it.

"Tomorrow," I said.

"You're sure?"

"I've never been more sure about anything in my life."

"I'll get them on a plane tonight. You get the word back to Ahmad through your people. We'll be set to roll tomorrow."

"If Ahmad shows. He may be back in the Middle East."

"Our last intel placed him in Houston. We couldn't verify, but it makes sense. Big port. Either way, he'll show. Even if it takes a day. I'll hold the team in place until he does."

"What will you tell them if you're delayed?"

"Don't worry about that. I'll come up with something. Besides, I'm senior. Their job is to follow orders, not question them."

"Okay then. I'll talk to my people. And Harrison, thanks for pushing this through. I really appreciate it."

"You'd do the same for me," he said before disconnecting.

I put the phone on the table and blew out a breath.

This was it.

Now I just had to tell Carter.

CHAPTER SEVENTEEN

"TOMORROW?" Carter's eyes widened and he rose from my kitchen table to face me.

I'd gotten off the phone with Harrison that morning and driven straight to see Big and Little. I could have just called but with something this important, I felt that it should be done in person. They were happy to hear that the mole had been exposed but were somber when I told them it was time to put the rest of my plan into motion.

We discussed the exact details of the intel they would pass on, and I assured them that I had the best operatives at the CIA at my back on this one. They didn't look completely convinced, but I couldn't blame them. We all knew it could be the last time I sat in that office, and it showed on our faces. You could hear it when we spoke.

They both shook my hand before leaving, and Big kissed my cheeks again. Little surprised me by saying he'd light a candle for me at church that night, but I supposed the Mafia and the Catholic Church had always gone together. At least, that's how they showed it in the movies. The grin that Mannie usually had for me was nowhere in sight, replaced instead with a focus that I recognized from the men and women I'd worked alongside. He clasped my shoulder before I left and reminded me that he was available for anything—absolutely anything.

That had been hard, and telling Ida Belle and Gertie that everything had been set in motion had been even harder. But standing there in my kitchen and telling Carter was the worst of all.

"I mean, I knew the CIA was getting everything ready and the time was coming but I didn't think..." His voice trailed off.

"It's time," I said. "I need this to happen, no matter how it goes down."

"I need this to happen too, but it definitely matters how it goes down."

He pulled me into his arms and held me tight. I wrapped my arms around him and prayed that this wouldn't be one of the last times we did this. I buried my face in his neck and could feel his heart pounding against my chest. I'd pushed to expedite this, but standing here, holding him, I almost wished I had put it off another day.

"I want in," he said.

I moved back and looked up at him. "I know. Harrison has arranged a suite for the four of us at the hotel across the street from where the operatives are staying."

"The four of us? Ida Belle and Gertie?"

I nodded. "I couldn't just leave without telling them."

"It wouldn't have worked anyway. They'd burn the city down trying to find you if you disappeared."

I smiled. "Yeah, probably. Anyway, you're in but I don't know to what extent. It's Harrison's call and I trust him."

"And the troublesome twosome?"

"I'm pretty sure their role is to wait and pray. Heavy, heavy praying. Begging if necessary."

"I don't think I've heard those two beg for anything my

entire life. But I bet they would now." He bent down to kiss me. "You're the most important thing that's happened to us in a long time. And if Harrison says I have to stay behind, I won't like it, but I'm not about to question his judgment." He smiled. "I'll just grab a Bible and add my two cents to the begging end of things."

I gave him a squeeze. "So, no pressure or anything, but what do you want to do tonight? I've freed it all up for you."

He was silent for a bit, then smiled. "I think I'd like to grab a bottle of wine and head out in my boat to watch the sunset over the bayou."

"Perfect."

I RODE into New Orleans the next morning with Ida Belle and Gertie. Carter was fixing things at work so he could be away for a while—his excuse being a last-minute law enforcement conference—and would meet us there later. Harrison had already sent me the hotel reservation and we were set to go with a three-bedroom suite. Ida Belle and Gertie had passed around that we were headed to New Orleans for a gambling bout and would be back when we ran out of money. That way, no one was looking for us at a set time. I had no way of knowing how soon Ahmad would act on the information, but I figured it would be quick. He wouldn't want to run the risk of my getting suspicious and changing locations before he could get to me.

We were quiet a lot of the way, and I knew we were all lost in our own worries and fears about the takedown. When we did talk, it was about unrelated stuff, like the stolen food and Celia's butt-showing adventures. Godzilla hadn't been sighted since the incident in my backyard, and the only things that had taken the bait in the trap were feral cats, a raccoon, and a skunk. Fortunately, none of them weighed enough to trip the door. I'd already told Gertie that if a skunk got trapped in there, she was on her own. I'd removed the bait and closed the door on the trap before we left. The last thing we needed was for Godzilla to pay a visit while we were in New Orleans. I hoped he stayed away for a while.

"Did Big and Little put the word out?" Ida Belle asked, finally broaching the subject we'd all been avoiding.

I nodded. "I told them yesterday morning that they were clear to talk. They passed along the information through a mutual contact yesterday afternoon."

"What if he comes looking for you before you're there?" Gertie asked.

"Then he'll find an empty warehouse with my quarters set up and he'll wait nearby for me to return," I said. "He'll want to make sure it's me before he moves in, so he'll watch for a bit before he makes his move. Probably from a rooftop blocks away. That's his usual MO."

"So you'll give him something to see and that sets everything in motion?" Ida Belle asked.

"Exactly. I'll drive to the warehouse and go inside. If he's watching, he'll know I'm there and can see I'm alone."

"And he'll come after you," Gertie said. "Will he be alone?"

"I doubt it," I said. "He'll have men around somewhere to back him up, but he'll come after me alone. He's gone off the deep end and thinks he has to do it himself or the debt won't be paid."

Gertie shook her head. "What a nutter. Makes Celia look harmless."

"In so many ways, the Celias of the world are nothing more than a pesky insect," I said. "I know you guys have seen some of the evil that the average joe never hears about, and with global communication, there's far more information out there for people to read. But there's still so much that only a small circle of people know about. Things that would cause worldwide panic if they were public knowledge."

"I'm sure that's the case," Ida Belle said. "We live under a veil of protection that most are completely unaware of. I'm just praying that soon, there's one less for those in the know to worry about."

"Me too," I said. "Don't get me wrong, someone will step right in and take his place. This underground war of ours is never-ending, but the next guy won't be gunning for me. And maybe he won't have a side business trafficking kids."

The hotel was located in the French Quarter, and our suite had one huge living room, dining area, and kitchen, then three separate bedrooms and baths. We carried our bags into the bedrooms, then wandered back into the living room, all looking a little lost.

I was totally antsy. I knew Harrison had arrived with the team early this morning, but we had to stay put until he made contact. He'd get the team ready to mobilize, then head out to meet up with us. Morrow had remained in DC because he was afraid his presence would tip others off that something more than what Harrison had conveyed was afoot. The agency had eyes on the mole, but he still had the ability to contact Ahmad if he suspected something was going on. Morrow's leaving DC would set off alarms among the other operatives, and we couldn't afford for the mole to make the connection between Harrison's deployment with a team and me.

Gertie wandered into the kitchen and checked the refrigerator because food was where Gertie always headed when she was stressed or bored. This definitely fell into the first slot.

"Hey," she said, "this thing is fully stocked." She opened the pantry. "This too. There's MoonPies. And Wheat Thins. I saw sliced cheese in the fridge. Anyone want a snack?"

I wasn't hungry, but I knew I needed to eat. I hadn't managed anything so far that morning but coffee, and I couldn't afford for my strength to wane.

"Sounds good to me," I said. "There should be some protein shakes as well."

Gertie looked in the refrigerator again and nodded. "Chocolate or vanilla?"

"Chocolate," I said. "Ida Belle?"

"None for me," Ida Belle said. "I'll load up on cheese."

"There's bread and peanut butter," Gertie said. "I could make you a sandwich."

"That would be great," Ida Belle said, and we headed to the bar to sit.

Gertie moved around the kitchen, fussing with the food and plates as Ida Belle and I watched. We could have helped, but we both knew that this was what Gertie did to take the edge off. I wasn't sure what Ida Belle did, but then I also figured her nerve control was a lot better than Gertie's. At least, that's the way it seemed.

Gertie put the sandwich and a plate of cheese, crackers, and fruit on the counter along with drinks and my protein shake. Then she took a seat on another barstool and we all started to graze. The only sound in the suite was of us eating. A couple minutes into the snack, Gertie jumped off her stool and turned on the television.

"We need some background noise," she said. "This place sounds too much like a, uh...library."

I figured she was about to say "funeral" and caught herself. But she was right. The three of us sitting here, probably imagining the worst that could happen, had created a tense, somewhat depressing atmosphere in the room.

"What do you usually do before missions?" Gertie asked.

"They all sit around cleaning their guns," Ida Belle said.

I laughed. "We do that and go over the plans until we could recite them in our sleep. And then we play poker."

"Really?" Gertie asked.

I nodded. "Even pros need to take the edge off. Poker gives us something to do that requires a bit of concentration and appeals to our competitive spirit. We always play for money, so that doesn't hurt either."

"I bet we could get a pack of cards at that convenience store across the street," Gertie said.

"We don't need to," I said. "I brought some. And chips. I figured I shouldn't break tradition. Even though this is a departure from my normal arrangements, I should maintain everything that I can the same."

Ida Belle nodded. "That's smart. Puts you mentally into that place you used to go when things were about to happen. Heightens your senses because your body knows you're about to need them all."

We finished up our snack, and I retrieved the cards and chips and we set up at the dining table. "Regular five-card draw," I said as I shuffled. "None of that new crap."

"Sounds good to me," Gertie said. "I can't keep up with all the variations anyway."

I dealt the cards, and we started our game. With every hand, we got more relaxed and we started to talk about Celia and her absurdity, laughing about what she must have looked like running from the cats. We were an hour into the game when Carter arrived.

"Poker?" he asked, looking at the table.

"Yep," Ida Belle said. "Gertie is up—I have no idea how—but I'm going to get her in this next round."

"The only way you're going to beat me is if I stop playing,"

Gertie said. She rose from the table and motioned for Carter to sit. "You must be hungry. Let me put you together a sandwich."

Carter hesitated, but when he looked at us, Ida Belle nodded toward the chair next to her. He caught on that Gertie needed to do her thing and took a seat. "Deal me in," he said.

"Pony up money first," I said. "Buy-in is twenty bucks. Ida Belle's holding the kitty."

"You're playing for money?" he asked.

"What's the point otherwise?" Ida Belle asked.

He smiled and pulled a twenty from his wallet and handed it to her. "There is none. Just happy to see you guys observing the real rules of the game."

We played a couple hands while Gertie fixed Carter some lunch, then more as he ate, reverting back to our Celia discussion.

"She's really on a rampage," Carter said. "I got a call from the governor's office asking if she was a mental patient."

"She complained to the governor?" I asked.

"Not exactly," Carter said. "He has staff that prevent people like Celia from ever getting his ear, but apparently, she's worn them out to the point that they thought they'd call and ask if she was off her rocker."

"What did you tell them?" I asked.

"I said she was your basic southern Louisiana crazy, with a whole load of butthole thrown in," Carter said.

Ida Belle nodded her approval.

"They laughed and thanked me for letting them know," Carter said. "I have a feeling Celia won't be getting a return call."

"She'll show up at his office if she doesn't," Gertie said. "She's that pushy."

"Then she'll have to deal with the governor's security," Carter said. "My money's on the security detail."

We played for about an hour and finally, the knock at the door that I'd been waiting for came. I let Harrison in and we all huddled in the living room, staring at him as if he were personally delivering an atomic bomb. In a way, he was.

"I know you guys have been waiting and I know how much that sucks," he said, "so I'll get right to what you want to know. Everyone take a seat."

Carter and I sat on a love seat and Ida Belle and Gertie on a couch. Harrison perched on the end of a coffee table where he could easily see all of us. "First," he said, "I want to thank all of you for being here. I know you're aware of what we're up against, and I respect and admire your desire to be involved, despite knowing how dangerous this is.

"I debriefed the team on the flight here," Harrison said. "They were told that a foreign dignitary's daughter was kidnapped and we have intel that places her inside the warehouse. They've been instructed to infiltrate through the water tunnel and rescue the daughter. I'll be taking point. Once inside, comm will instruct us that he's spotted Ahmad inside the building and he is now our first priority."

Carter nodded. "That way, on the off chance that anyone on the team has been leaking information, he won't have the opportunity to do so."

"Exactly," Harrison said. "If someone is taking pay on the side, he won't risk exposing himself in the middle of a mission, and especially not in front of other men equally capable of killing him. Ahmad is just another paycheck to someone selling intel. When he's gone, someone will replace him."

"So you don't think there's any loyalty?" Carter asked.

"No," Harrison said. "Ahmad's not in business for a cause. His claims of being a terrorist are simply his form of advertising. He's in business for himself. He doesn't have followers. He has employees. If there's another mole, he won't show himself, and while I'd love to expose any traitors, the only goal here is to eliminate Ahmad. The agency will deal with anything else later. Mind you, all this precaution is strictly that—precaution. Neither Morrow nor I believe there is more than one insider, and the one we know about is going to go down."

Harrison pulled some papers out of his pocket and unfolded them, showing us a diagram of the warehouse. Then he went over the exact setup, from my location to the entry point for the team, to the expected point of ambush. It was all stuff I'd covered with them already, but I think it helped them to hear Harrison lay it all out in professional speak.

When he was done, he looked at them. "Any questions? I'll answer anything that I'm authorized to."

"What can I do?" Carter asked.

"I know you've got training," Harrison said, "but I can't put you on the insertion team. We work with a certain rhythm and you're not up to speed on our methods."

"I understand, but surely there's something."

"I'll have two men on the ground. I'd like you with them. If that's all right with you, of course."

"I'll go wherever I can help," Carter said.

"Great. The ground team will hang back until they get signal that Ahmad's men are on the property. We anticipate Ahmad will attempt the assassination alone but will have his men on the perimeter."

"And the goal is?"

"To eliminate the threat," Harrison said. "And as far as the CIA is concerned, you were never there. I'll introduce you to the team as a local contractor that we've been using for intel. We do it a lot, so they won't even blink. When I leave, I'll take you back with me and get you outfitted and give you a rundown on your route."

Carter nodded, and I could tell he was relieved to be included but still wishing he would be on the inside with me. He reached over and took my hand in his, and I could feel the sweat on his palm against mine, belying his otherwise calm demeanor.

"I don't mean to question you," Carter said, "but are you sure Fortune is okay in there alone? There's no way to have someone else with her without creating a heat signature?"

"Not that we can readily accomplish," Harrison said. He studied Carter for several seconds, then glanced at me before speaking again. "I know you're aware of what Fortune's work for the agency comprised, but I also know Fortune, and I doubt she's gone into much detail. So I'm going to share something with you."

Harrison leaned forward and looked directly at Carter. "The woman sitting next to you is one of the best we have and have had for well over a decade. She's an awesome human being, but she's also the deadliest person I've ever known. If anyone can handle Ahmad, it's Fortune."

Carter squeezed my hand. "Are you telling me I should be afraid to date her?"

Harrison smiled. "Only if you plan on pissing her off."

"So what can we do?" Gertie asked.

Harrison looked at the two women. "While I appreciate your service and am aware of exactly what it entailed, I'm afraid this mission isn't the place for you."

"You can't expect us to just sit here staring at each other," Ida Belle said.

"I don't," Harrison said. "When we're done here, you'll go next door and join the communications agent. I'll inform him of the real purpose of the mission right before I deploy with the team."

"What if the comm agent is compromised?" Ida Belle asked. "He'd have time to warn Ahmad off."

"I'd trust the comm agent with my life," Harrison said. "In fact, I do on a regular basis. He also happens to be my brother. But if the unthinkable happens, and he's turned, you have the CIA's permission to put a bullet in him."

One look at his face let Ida Belle and Gertie know that he was totally serious about every single word.

"You'll be able to see the video feed and hear all communication," Harrison continued. "I know it's not the same as being there, but it's what I can do."

They both nodded, and I could see they were somewhat relieved that they wouldn't have to just sit here and wait.

"Thank you," Ida Belle said. "Doing nothing isn't our strong point, but we want Fortune to have the best chance of success. Regardless of how we wish things were, our being there would weaken that chance. But we appreciate being allowed in the hub. Sitting here, knowing nothing, would have driven us both crazy."

"So when does this happen?" Gertie asked.

Harrison rose from the table. "Now."

I jumped up. "Now? Ahmad's in New Orleans?"

"We're pretty sure. Our intel reported a private jet leaving Houston and landing in New Orleans. The names on the manifest don't match, of course, but the descriptions match Ahmad and some of his men. The plane landed three hours ago. Enough time for Ahmad to get a scout en route to the warehouse and for him to find a position to monitor it."

Everyone else had jumped up along with me, and now we all looked at one another, none of us knowing how to act now that the actual moment was here.

"So what now?" Gertie asked.

"Now, Carter comes with me," Harrison said, "and Fortune gears up and heads to the warehouse."

"Don't you need to wire her?" Carter asked.

Harrison shook his head. "She'll have a small earpiece so she can hear our communications and comm will be able to communicate solely to her when needed, but we can't risk her talking once she's inside. Ahmad's scout could easily drop an audio sensor. She'll have a sat radio, but it's only for an emergency. Use of it otherwise would give away our involvement."

"Can she take her cell phone?" Ida Belle asked.

"Yes, but I doubt the signal will be reliable where she'll be," Harrison said.

"The farthest corner in a basement of cement," Ida Belle said. "Probably not."

Harrison put a hand on each of their shoulders. "I know you're worried, and I wish I could tell you that everything will be fine, but I'm not that guy. What we're doing is dangerous and we're playing with a target who is unpredictable and willing to die. The risk is incalculable. But also necessary. Sooner or later, this day has to happen. Better for it to come when we have some control over the circumstances."

Harrison pulled an earpiece out of his bag and handed it to me along with a booster. "Make sure you boost the signal when you're inside. When I go silent, you'll know we've gone under. Communication may be sketchy on the inside of the warehouse, even with the boost, so you might not hear everything. I'll signal comm with a blip so he knows we're in, but at that point, all communication will probably become one-way, with comm relaying intel as he receives it from the outside."

I nodded. It was exactly the way I would have handled it.

"I'll step out," Harrison said, "and let you guys say goodbye."

He stood in front of me and put his hand up for our ceremonial high five. "Kick serious ass," he said.

"Always," I replied.

I looked at Ida Belle and Gertie. "Thank you for being here. I know you think you're not doing much, but your presence here with me today and knowing you'll be with comm makes me feel better. It gives me even more strength and determination."

They both moved forward and hugged me, and we stood there, clinging to one another, until my arms started to ache. When they stepped back, Gertie was already crying and I could see Ida Belle's eyes growing red.

"Don't you dare die on us," Gertie said.

"Not planning on it," I said.

"Come on," Ida Belle said to Gertie. "Let's give them some privacy."

They headed into one of the bedrooms and closed the door behind them. I looked at Carter, excitement, fear, dread, and anticipation all coursing through me. I hoped for the best, but I was a professional. I knew the odds. And the odds meant this might be the last time I ever spoke to Carter. The last time I ever saw him.

"Promise me you'll walk out of that warehouse," he said. "You've changed my life, Fortune. I can't say it's always been for the better, but it's never been dull. A big part of me had stopped living. You changed that, and now that I know how life can be, I don't want to let it go."

I felt the tears form in my eyes. "After coming to Sinful, I realized that a big part of me had never started living. The one thing I want more than anything is to step over Ahmad's lifeless body and see you and Ida Belle and Gertie smiling. It's the image I've had in my mind for days, and I'm going to make it happen."

He pulled me into his arms and kissed me long and slow. I could feel his heart beating against my chest, and his arms trembled slightly as he squeezed me even harder. He'd lost someone he loved in the past. Someone whose job it was to take risks. And he'd promised himself that he'd never get involved with someone who took those risks again. So I knew what it would cost him to hug me and then let me go. My heart clenched so hard it made my chest ache. Carter might not be perfect, but he was perfect for me.

When he finally released me, his expression was serious, and I could see him already shifting into military mode. "Watch your back," I said. "The men you're with are some of the best the agency has. Depend on your team. Don't be a hero."

He smiled. "You sound like my old commander."

"He must have been a genius."

"Good luck, Fortune. I'll see you soon."

I nodded. "Soon."

He gave me one final kiss, and I could see the fear and uncertainty in his eyes as he looked back at me before closing the door behind him. I went into the bedroom and gave Ida Belle and Gertie one final hug, then grabbed my bag of gear and headed out of the hotel.

It was time to get my life back.

CHAPTER EIGHTEEN

IT WAS midafternoon when I pulled up at the warehouse. It was quiet, but that was expected. I knew the well-hidden cameras were watching my every move. I climbed out of the unregistered car the agency had provided and pulled my bag of supplies from the back seat. I glanced around, as I normally would, casing my surroundings. Everything about my behavior needed to appear as if I were a trained agent hiding out. A bag of supplies would be normal. Constantly checking my surroundings would be normal.

I hefted the bag on my shoulder, pulled my pistol out of my waistband, and hurried inside. I couldn't see Ahmad, but I could feel someone watching. Every good agent seemed to have that sixth sense built in. It had saved my life on more than one occasion.

Once inside, I did a quick visual sweep of the room, noting a new set of footprints in the dust. Someone had been here checking things out. It wasn't Harrison's team because they'd avoided the entry for exactly this reason—so that I could tell if someone else had entered—and because we wanted my footprints to be the only sign of occupancy left behind. The footprint was probably one of Ahmad's men, doing some reconnaissance for his boss.

I motioned toward the camera that I knew was in the upper-left corner and pointed to the ground. There was a bit of static in my earpiece for a second, then I heard the clear, calm voice of the communications operative.

"One of Ahmad's men doing recon," he said. "He entered while you were driving over and was inside about ten minutes before leaving. We got him on film going to the basement, but the cameras down there are only connecting in small blips, so I can't verify that he entered your room."

I held up my thumb and headed downstairs. I'd figured the cameras might be sketchy with all the cement. I worried that my earpiece might be as well. I had the booster for it and its signal was much stronger than the cameras, but I knew there was still a chance I'd be sitting blind.

The tunnel room was clear, of course, and the tunnel uncovered. Harrison and his team would be upriver, waiting for Ahmad to show before they swam downstream and entered the tunnel under the cover of the muddy canal water. We had no way of knowing when Ahmad would appear or where, but regardless, Harrison's team had to be ready to move in a second and move fast or they wouldn't breach the warehouse in time to ambush Ahmad.

I continued down the concrete hallway to the last room, the one that had been designated as my hideout, noting the extra set of footprints as I went. Ahmad's man had attempted to step inside my prints when he walked, but he couldn't disguise his larger foot. Not from an expert. I headed inside the room and pulled the door closed behind me. It had a lock, but it was one that Ahmad could easily bypass as his man had apparently done before. We didn't want to create obstacles too large, or they might delay entry or wait for me to leave the building again to make an attempt.

I had used a penlight to traverse the dark hallway, but Mannie had provided me with a lamp. I turned it on and let a dim glow penetrate the room. It gave me enough clarity to operate but didn't illuminate the room so that everything was easy to pinpoint. I pulled the signal booster for the earpiece out of my bag and got it running, then looked up at the camera and waved to see if I'd get a response. No one responded. I hadn't really expected it. I just hoped I had audio. At the very least, I'd know when Ahmad entered the building, even if they couldn't track his movements once he went into the basement. And I'd know that Harrison and his team had deployed.

I pulled the guns from my backpack and checked them all once again, then I placed them in different areas around the room, hidden from view. I would have multiple weapons on my body, of course, but if hand-to-hand combat ensued, you never knew where an extra weapon might come in handy. Once the weapons were in place, I paced the room a couple of times before finally settling down on a chair in the far corner. I had instructed Mannie to erect a makeshift barrier in the back of the room, made from concrete blocks that had been stored in the tunnel room.

The blocks were stacked to form a three-foot-high wall. It gave me the perfect cover to have Ahmad in my sights when he walked through the door but not be readily visible to him. Unlike the movies, I didn't plan on some dramatic exchange with him before I fired. I planned on pulling the trigger and getting on with my life.

I heard the telltale click of the earpiece and froze.

"Fortune, this is comm. I don't have visual in your room, but I wanted to let you know that Ida Belle and Gertie are here with me. Gertie says to tell you she has her rabbit's foot and Bible and is wearing her, uh, lucky underwear. Ida Belle says don't hesitate. Harrison and his team are in place and ready to go. I'll signal when Ahmad breaches. I hope you're hearing this."

I smiled. Comm had never seen the likes of Ida Belle and Gertie. I could just imagine what he was thinking when he relayed a message about lucky underwear. I opened a bottle of water and took a sip. This was the part of every mission that was the worst. That point where every second seemed to last an hour. And this time was the worst of all.

I ran through the plan again in my mind, then got off the chair and squatted behind the wall, practicing my aim at the door. Then I got back in the chair and practiced a dive behind the wall and the subsequent positioning for fire. I paced the room a couple of times, checking the hidden weapons and repositioning a couple of them slightly for better access, then flopped down in the chair again.

I looked at my watch. That had taken all of eight minutes and felt as though I'd expended at least thirty. I was just about to pace the room again when comm broke in.

"Ahmad has entered the property through the hedges on the west property line. Deploy aqua team now. Ground force, remain in position until his men appear, then proceed with orders."

I knew the orders were to shoot on sight, but you never said that out loud over the comm.

"Deploying now," Harrison said.

I rose from the chair and walked behind the block wall. If Ahmad was moving at a normal pace, Harrison's team should exit the tunnel about the time he entered the basement. Ahmad would come for me, Harrison's team would move in behind, and in a couple hours, I'd be having a drink with my friends to celebrate. That's exactly how I chose to envision it.

Clenching my pistol, I looked up at the ceiling, silently praying.

If you're listening, I'd appreciate any help you can throw my way. There're a lot of people counting on me to walk out of here, and well, I'm sorta counting on it myself. Thanks in advance.

I drew in a big breath and slowly blew it out, then sank down, one knee up, one down. I inched into the perfect firing position and placed my hands on the blocks, steadying my aim at the door. A head shot was risky in the dim light, even for someone with my ability, but I had no way of knowing if he was strapped with a bomb and couldn't risk a center mass shot. The pistol was CIA issue and had been modified for rapid fire, so I'd have time to get off more than one round. If he attempted to retreat, I would put them in his back if I had to in order to keep him from getting away. I'd just have to risk any explosives at that point.

The seconds ticked away, and I felt the sweat collecting on my brow. I brushed it away with my forearm and focused on the door. On my breathing.

And I slipped back into the world I'd left behind.

All of my senses were heightened as if they'd been amplified by magic, but I knew it was a combination of natural ability and lots of experience. Every sound was as if through stereo. Every glance revealed each minor detail of the surface it covered. My skin tingled with anticipation even as my breathing and heart rate slowed to prepare for the shot.

I was in the zone, and it felt so comfortable. As if I'd come home again.

My overly sensitive hearing picked up the squeak of hinges.

"Ahmad has entered the warehouse," comm said. "He's alone and headed for the basement stairs. Harrison should breach..."

The transmission cut out, but I figured the team must be

close. The timing was perfect. By the time Ahmad got to my room, Harrison and his team should be out of the tunnel and ready to move in behind him. If for any reason I missed my opportunity, or was never presented one, they would be there to ensure success. This was it. My last few seconds of being held prisoner in a fake identity. The last time I'd have to claim a silly name and a past as a beauty queen.

Ahmad was trying to remain quiet and he was good at it, but my hearing was better. The faint shuffle of his feet on the concrete was all I needed to know he was almost there. Any second now, that door would open, and I'd get the chance I'd been praying for. I had a twinge of concern that I hadn't heard Harrison check in, but it was possible his comm system had been damaged during the swim. He said he would be there, and they'd had time to breach. I could only hope they were getting in position to head Ahmad off.

I heard the faint scratch of tools being placed inside the lock, then the *click* when it released. The door moved a tiny bit and my finger tightened on the trigger. I was laser focused as I watched the door. Not blinking. Not breathing. I waited for the moment to strike. I knew he was standing there, listening, but I gave him nothing to hear. A couple seconds later, the door started to open, and I saw a shadow appear on the wall behind the cracked door. He couldn't see me behind my wall. Not yet. I stayed crouched low. I needed him to move farther inside.

Comm started issuing orders, but I only heard pieces. "Ahmad's men in vehicles...inside building...ground troops..."

Then rapid fire broke out inside the warehouse.

Shit!

Ahmad's men must have entered the warehouse after him and had drawn Harrison's unit out from the basement, forcing them to engage. Which sent the team upstairs into the lobby instead of down the hallway to me. Comm was sending ground in to help with the battle inside the warehouse, but that help was some distance away and likely, Ahmad had more men on the outside for ground to deal with.

My pulse ticked up a bit, and I concentrated on my breathing, forcing myself to remain in the zone. I watched as the shadow froze and I shifted a bit, trying to find a way to get off a kill shot. But before I could sight in, he slipped from the doorway and was gone. I jumped up and hurried after him, determined to end this now. I paused next to the door to listen but couldn't make out anything but the exchange of fire coming from above. I peered around into the dim hallway and saw Ahmad slip around the corner.

The only two ways out of the basement were through the gunfire in the entry and the tunnel. Ahmad wouldn't walk into the middle of gunfire, but he'd risk the tunnel, even without gear or knowing how long it was. He was just that side of crazy.

I ran down the hallway, not bothering to mask my footsteps. I had to get to him before he got in that tunnel. When I got to the room, I shoved the door, but it held fast. I knew there wasn't a lock, so I assumed he'd pushed something in front of it. I took a couple steps back and launched at the door, using my shoulder as a battering ram. The door gave and I stumbled into the room just as Ahmad dropped into the tunnel.

Damn!

I ran to the edge of the opening and looked down but I couldn't make out anything in the murky water. I'd left my radio back in the room and had no way of communicating with the team to intercept Ahmad when he exited the tunnel. And the odds of my making it through the gunfire in the entry and across the lawn, which probably contained more of Ahmad's men, were slim to none. At least, not in the time it would take him to get through the tunnel and be gone. I hesitated for a split second, then shoved my pistol in my waistband, took a deep breath, and flipped over the side, headfirst into the tunnel.

CHAPTER NINETEEN

I OPENED my eyes as soon as I entered the water, but it was too dark to see anything. When my hands touched the bottom, I twisted around to change direction and set off down the tunnel. I knew I had the lung capacity to make the swim, but it was pushing it, and I had to remain steady and control my excitement in order to conserve my air. Too much energy spent too soon and I wouldn't have enough air to make it to the surface.

Ahmad had taken a big risk going out this route. He had an indoor pool in his home, and I knew swimming was part of his regular routine, but I didn't know if he'd trained for long-distance underwater swimming. What I did know was that he was the slickest, luckiest target I'd ever pursued. He had more lives than a cat, and if anyone could slip away from this unscathed, it was Ahmad.

Unless I was there to stop him.

I had been counting the seconds since I'd dropped into the water and knew I was over halfway through the tunnel. My lungs were starting to ache, and I knew the excitement of the situation was working against me. I concentrated on the rhythm of my hands and feet, forcing myself not to think about the increasing pain in my chest.

When I was seconds from the end of the tunnel, my lungs started to burn and I let out some air, careful not to release it all at once. As soon as my lungs were empty, my body would start heaving, trying to force me to take in more air. My hands felt what was left of the grate at the end of the tunnel, and I prayed Ahmad had run out of air before surfacing. But I wasn't counting on it.

I swam out of the tunnel and into the canal, letting out more air as I went, and pulled my pistol from my waist. I had to be ready to fire as soon as I surfaced. I could see a glimmer of light above me and I swam for it, my lungs starting to heave. With one final kick, I broke the surface, gasping for air. But as I drew in a breath, I scanned the water and bank, looking for Ahmad.

And then he grabbed me from behind.

His arm snaked around my neck, choking me as I lifted my arm to fire, but he knocked the pistol from my hand. A wave of dizziness passed over me, and I knew that if I didn't get his arm off soon, I'd pass out. With every ounce of strength I could muster, I swung back with my left elbow and struck him in the jaw. His hold loosened on me just enough for me to get my teeth on his arm and bite down with all my might.

I must have channeled Godzilla because he screamed and let go of me. I whirled around as he started to swim away and grabbed his hair, yanking his head back with my left hand. With my right, I pulled a knife from my belt and before he could make a move, I drew it across his throat.

The entire thing seemed to happen in slow motion. I felt the knife slice into his skin and twisted him sideways. I needed to see him die. Blood seeped out of the thin line, making it appear as if it were growing wider and wider. His hands flew up to his neck and his eyes grew large. He stared directly at me—his hate was so clear, so vivid. He gurgled as his lips moved. Still trying to curse me, even as he drew his last breath.

A million thoughts raced through my mind. Things I should say. Things he deserved to take to the grave with him. But ultimately, I said nothing. He didn't deserve anything else from me. I'd already delivered the worst thing possible. Ahmad had died at the hands of a woman. And women weren't supposed to matter at all, much less get the better of a man.

His head bobbled from side to side and as the final breath of air left his body, it dropped forward into the water. His body went limp and started to sink. I grabbed his shirt and began to swim for the bank, dragging him along with me. No way was I letting him float away into oblivion. Thanks to Gertie, I'd seen too many movies that ended that way only for the bad guy to pop up alive and well in a sequel. I wanted Ahmad on an autopsy table, organs removed.

I heard the footsteps when I reached for the canal wall. I looked up to see the end of an AK-47 in my face and one of Ahmad's men staring at me in disbelief. I had another weapon on me, but there was no way I could get it from my ankle strap and fire before he did. Even if I'd been holding it, I couldn't have gotten off a shot.

"I can't believe it," he said. "You. It's not possible."

"Oh, it's possible all right," I said, trying to distract him as I reached for the pistol on my ankle. I probably couldn't get off a shot, but I wasn't about to go out easy.

When the shot sounded, I flinched, waiting for the pain to hit the instant before the lights went out. Instead, I saw an exit hole appear in the man's forehead. His eyes widened and he fell forward into the canal. A couple seconds later, Carter rushed up to the edge of the bank wall and looked down at me.

"Are you all right?" he said. "Is that Ahmad?"

"Yes and yes," I said as I reached out for the iron rungs cemented into the canal wall.

"Is he dead?"

"Hell yes!" I lifted Ahmad's shirt and hung it on a broken rung, letting him dangle for a moment while I rested my arms.

"What are you doing with him?"

"I was thinking about stuffing him and putting him over the sofa. What do you think I'm doing? I want proof on a cold table in a morgue. Can you give me a hand? He's getting heavy and I'm a little tired."

Before he could kneel down, a shot fired and I saw him flinch as it hit his arm. He dropped to the ground as a second shot rang out. From my position in the water, I couldn't see the shooter. but I knew the shot had come from somewhere behind him. What I didn't know was if the second shot had hit him or how badly he was hurt.

I scrambled up the ladder and peered over the edge. Carter was reaching for his rifle, which he must have dropped when he fell. I saw movement in the shrubs behind him and grabbed the weapon in my ankle strap. At the same time, the man in the shrubs leveled his gun at Carter. The shot rang out and I screamed, then the man in the shrubs fell to the ground and I realized the shot had come from behind me.

I whipped around and saw Mannie in the water on the other side of the canal, a rifle in his hand. He winked and slipped below the surface, disappearing completely. I hefted myself over the side of the wall as Carter grabbed his rifle and scanned the bushes.

"Did you shoot him?" he asked.

I shook my head. "I don't know where the shot came from. Must have been one of the team."

I heard running and whipped the pistol from my ankle, but

when I looked toward the sound, I saw Harrison crossing the lawn. I slumped in relief and checked Carter up and down.

"Were you hit anywhere but the arm?" I asked.

"No. I was lucky. That second shot hit the ground not an inch from my head."

Harrison slid to a stop in the dirt as Carter rose, then leaned over to give me a hand up. He did a double take when he peered into the canal and saw Ahmad hanging on the broken rung.

"You did it," he said. "You crazy, insane woman. You followed him through that tunnel and killed him." He grabbed me in a hug and lifted me off the ground, twirling me around. The agents who'd come up behind him started laughing and cheering and everyone shared high fives.

When he finally set me down, his grin was so big it was probably hurting his face. "I can't believe it. They're going to be talking about this one at the agency for the next fifty years."

He looked at Carter and clasped his good shoulder. "Thank you for being part of the team."

"Were there any casualties?" I asked.

"Only the bad guys," Harrison said. "Two of Ahmad's men were already going down the hallway when we exited the tunnel. They engaged, and we retreated to the lobby where two more were waiting. I lost comm in the water and didn't know where Ahmad was. A couple of my men took a round, but nothing life-threatening. Paramedics are on the way. Let's get your man some medical attention. I'll get that body up. I've never been this happy to carry a corpse."

Harrison headed down the canal wall, and Carter and I stood staring at each other for a couple seconds. I think we were both in shock, or at least a form of mild disbelief. It was over. My long nightmare had come to a bloody but successful end. He took one step toward me and I ran into his arms, tears already flowing.

"Let's go home," he said.

Home.

That word meant something completely different now than it had before.

It meant everything.

As a paramedic attended to Carter's arm, a car pulled up and Ida Belle and Gertie jumped out. They ran over, both tackling me in a hug, while laughing and crying at the same time. When we finally broke lose, they made a fuss over Carter, who, despite being shot, was in as good a mood as they were.

"It's only a scratch," he said. "Doesn't even need stitches."

"It was so scary," Gertie said. "Hearing part of what was going on, but having to guess at the rest."

Ida Belle nodded. "And then when the shooting broke out...well, it was rough."

"Ida Belle grabbed my rabbit's foot and started praying."

"I wanted to double down on it," Ida Belle said.

"And then when Harrison came on and said everyone was alive, we started cheering," Gertie said.

"And when he said Ahmad was dead, we cheered ourselves hoarse," Ida Belle said. "The comm guy was jumping up and down, whooping like a crazy person. I don't think I've ever cried tears of joy, but I did today, and I'm thrilled to say that."

"The Ahmad end of things was a surprise for the rest of the team," I said. "But ultimately, a great one given the way things turned out."

"Are they mad at Harrison?" Gertie asked.

"No. They're professionals. Harrison did what was necessary for a successful mission, and this one was huge. They're all happy they played a role in it. It's a big feather in their caps at the agency. Ahmad is a huge score."

"Harrison said you did the honors," Ida Belle said. "That you jumped in the tunnel after him and fought him in the canal."

I nodded.

"It sounds insane," Gertie said, "but we get why you did it. And since it all turned out all right, we're really happy you did." Gertie teared up again. "Oh Fortune, this is it. The first moments of the rest of your new life."

She flung her arms around me and I hugged her tightly, smiling at Ida Belle and Carter over her shoulder. I thought that I'd be nervous about moving forward. About having a life without the CIA directing my every move. But now that it stretched in front of me, all I saw was a big, open canvas, with my new family standing right in the middle.

CHAPTER TWENTY

It took several hours to wrap things up with the New Orleans police, who'd received a ton of calls about gunfire and shown up to the culmination of a massacre. Harrison shuffled Carter, Ida Belle, Gertie, and me out of the way and took point, claiming we were locals accidentally caught in the fray. The police chief talked to Director Morrow and eventually, everything calmed down and the questioning stopped. The paramedics hauled the bodies off with instructions that they were all to be flown to DC for processing.

Once we were hustled off scene, we went back to the hotel. Carter and I had a hot shower—separately—and a change of clothes, then we all headed out for a much-needed meal. No one had eaten much that day, and now we were all starving. The dinner was full of excited talk as I recounted exactly what had happened, leaving out the part about Mannie delivering the final shot. It was better that everyone assumed it came from one of Harrison's team, although I knew the forensic team back in DC would run ballistics and figure out that couldn't be the case. It didn't matter, though. They had no idea where to start looking for the other shooter, and I wasn't about to help. My guess was they'd give it a cursory questioning, type up a report, and shelve it under "sometimes cool things happen."

After dinner, Gertie and Ida Belle took off for Sinful in Ida Belle's SUV, and Carter and I followed in his truck. During the meal, no one had mentioned the future, and it had been the elephant in the room. All the "what now" questions I'd expected were strangely absent as the three who wanted answers the most seemed to dance around the subject.

At first, I didn't understand, but the longer I thought about it, I started to. I'd talked to some extent about what I would do when this was over, but now that it actually was, I think everyone was afraid I'd change my mind. That I'd slip back into my old life and disappear from theirs as quickly as I'd appeared.

And then there was the timing of it all. There was certainly no shortage of things to process that had happened that day. For all of us. And now that everyone knew the details of what I'd done during the takedown, all the gaps had been filled. But it was a lot for them to process and it would take time. I wasn't done processing it and I'd lived it, so my friends' spending time in silent contemplation wasn't odd.

But I knew the thing keeping them from asking the most was fear.

I owed them answers, and I saw no reason to leave them hanging. I hadn't broached the subject over dinner because I felt we all needed to talk about what had happened and get that all out of our systems. And I didn't feel a public place was a good location for such an emotional and private discussion. Nor did I wish to have the discussion with them as a group. But now, in the quiet of the truck cab, alone with Carter, that single unasked question seemed to be taking up every available inch of space.

"I'm not going back to the CIA," I said quietly.

His relief was visible. "You're sure."

I nodded. "I'm not going to lie. When I was preparing for Ahmad to enter the room—when I got into the zone—it felt good. Familiar and right."

"I can see that. I felt the same way this afternoon working with Harrison's team."

"But it's not what I want for myself. Not anymore."

"Can I ask why? I mean, I'm thrilled you're not going back, but I just wondered..."

I knew he was thinking about his own exit from the military and his time in Special Forces. He'd taken a lot of time afterward to figure out what he wanted out of life and knew better than most people exactly the kind of thoughts that I had been dealing with. He also knew that a lot of people made a rash decision about quitting and ended up going back.

"I found something I like better. Something that I believe is sustainable, and that life isn't." I blew out a breath, Ida Belle's recent words to me echoing in my head.

Be true to yourself.

"The truth is I didn't have much of the life like you did before your time in the service," I said. "Once my mom died, everything was different and none of it something I'd want to revisit as an adult. I adapted because I didn't have a choice, and I moved forward with my career because I'd been raised not to consider anything else. Don't get me wrong—I don't regret my career. Not at all. It was what I needed to do then, and I excelled at it. I needed that as well."

"And now?"

"Now I know I can have the life I had before my mom passed. One with friends and hobbies and not having to shoot someone every week."

He smiled. "You sure about that shooting part?"

"Warning shots and shoes don't count. And yeah, I know my time in Sinful hasn't been exactly normal by average US standards, but it seemed fairly normal by Sinful standards."

"If you're besties with Ida Belle and Gertie, maybe."

I shrugged. "There are way worse things. To be honest, coming to Sinful and meeting them is the best thing that ever happened to me. They've helped me in ways you'll never know and that I could never explain."

He nodded. "I can see that. I had a couple people who did the same for me...Walter being one of them. So you're resigning your position at the CIA, and then what?"

He tried to sound nonchalant, but I could hear the strain in his voice. My heart clenched a little even as I felt a sense of relief. Despite everything—even the strain our relationship had been under lately—he still wanted me to stay. He might not feel that way tomorrow or the next day or the next time we butted heads, and it was sure to happen. But today, right now, the thought of my leaving had him in knots. I could see it in every flex of his jaw. In the way he clutched the steering wheel. In the way he sat so rigid in his seat.

"I'm going to stay in Sinful," I said.

He looked over at me, his expression one of both excitement and partial disbelief. "You are? You're sure?"

"It's one of the only things I am sure about. I don't know where I'll live, or what I'll do for a job, or if I will have any friends besides Ida Belle and Gertie once everyone learns the truth. But I'm going to take the risk and see."

"You know you can stay with me," Carter said.

"I appreciate the offer, but neither one of us is ready for that, and the truth is we don't know that we ever will be. No use putting a strain on things when we're already working around a lot of stuff to begin with. Besides, Ida Belle and Gertie have both offered me a place as long as I need. Having a roof over my head isn't a big concern of mine. Not at the moment. I'll figure something out."

I already had some ideas on that one, but I didn't want to say anything unless it was viable.

"I guess working in a library is out," Carter said.

"Since I can count on one hand the number of times I've been in one, I'm going to go out on a limb and say yes. But I'm not worried about the job thing, either. I have money saved—life insurance from my parents, and their estate—so I'm good for a while. And it's not like I have big expenses. I used to spend the bulk of my money on ammo and range fees. And rent. DC isn't cheap."

He reached over and took my hand in his. "I know we've had a rough time of things lately, and we never cleared the air, even though we said we would. But I want you to know that I always wanted you to stay, and have been afraid from the beginning that you wouldn't. Ever since you told me about the takedown, I've been worried that it was over. I want a chance with you, Fortune. Even if we ultimately can't make it work, I think it's worth trying to."

"I do too, but it's not going to be easy. You can't have the simple, easy life you were looking for—not if you're going to be with me. I could tell you I'd try to tone things down, but I'd be lying. I am who I am, and I've accepted that. Now it's on you."

He nodded. "I'm working on it. But there still has to be some sort of compromise. Some form of truce on certain things."

"I'm working on *that*. And I'm not going to lie to you. It's not easy for me. I'm not only used to being responsible only for myself, I prefer it. Taking other people into consideration has never come naturally for me. So all this is new territory. I'm going to make mistakes. And I'm going to have some lines in the sand that your average person probably wouldn't have. I can't promise you how far those lines will move, if they move at all."

He squeezed my hand. "Tell you what, let's just deal with it one day at a time."

I looked over at him and smiled. "Perfect."

THE FOUR OF us gathered at my house for a while, and I knew no one wanted to return home alone. Being in the same room was a comfort, even when no one was talking. We rambled on about everything and nothing until Harrison showed up for a debriefing. The three excused themselves, but I could tell they still didn't want to leave. But this was business, and it was confidential business.

My last business with the CIA.

Harrison was as exuberant as the rest of us and I couldn't blame him. He'd already confided in me that he was leaving the agency once Ahmad was out of play, so this was the start of the next stage of his life as well.

"Morrow is beside himself," Harrison said as he sat at the kitchen table.

I put two beers on the table and sat across from him. "I can imagine. So many good things in one day. Ahmad is gone. Morrow doesn't have to worry about hiding me anymore. Lots of things for him to be excited about."

"He's not as thrilled about both of us leaving the agency."

"You told him you were resigning?"

"Yeah. I didn't see any reason to wait." He looked me directly in the eyes, his expression serious. "I'm thrilled that I ran the mission today. As far as I'm concerned, it's the most important job I've ever been on, and there is no place else I would have preferred to be."

"But?"

"But I want it to be my last." He took a drink of beer and nodded. "The last time people who love me have to wonder if I'm coming home and have no idea when they'll find out."

"I get that, and you earned it. I will never be able to repay you for what you did for me. I couldn't have done this without you."

Harrison lifted his beer and I clinked mine to his. "We made a great team," he said. "And beyond my personal reasons for wanting to leave, I wouldn't have wanted to do the job without you. It would have never felt right."

I nodded. We had both worked with other agents and teams, but from the moment Harrison and I had been partnered, we'd known our pairing was something special.

"Morrow knew it was coming," I said. "At least from me, and honestly, I doubt he was surprised to hear it from you."

"Probably not. But I'm sure he thinks I'll change my mind."

"Will you?"

"Not a chance in hell. You?"

"Same chance here. I don't know for sure what I want for my future, but I know what I don't want. If that makes sense."

"Perfectly. I've got some soul-searching to do as well. Fortunately, I have a ton of vacation and sick time and plenty of money saved. I plan on taking some time off to figure it all out."

I grinned. "You just want to hang out with Cassidy all day."

"I would love to, but as she has her own career, that's not possible. However, I predict I'll see her ten times as much as I used to. And that makes me a happy man."

"I'm really glad for you, Harrison. You deserve everything

good. You've been an awesome partner and an even better friend."

He grinned. "You're one of a kind, Fortune Redding. And you're going to go down in CIA history."

"Maybe." At one time I would have cared. I would have been glowing over the boost to my reputation that taking down Ahmad would bring. I would have reveled in the fact that I'd taken out one of the agency's most wanted in hand-to-hand combat, something even my revered father had never done.

But now...now it was simply part of my past.

Harrison spent a couple hours documenting my version of what happened during the takedown, and we had a long Skype session with Director Morrow. By that time, we were both ready to call it a night. I'd told the story so many times now that I could probably do it in my sleep. But everything about the mission had to be recorded, even though I figured some of the "facts" would be slightly different before they went into the file at headquarters.

After Harrison left, I considered hopping into bed. It was late, and it had been an incredibly exhausting day. And God knows my sleep hadn't been all that grand for a long time. But I was too restless to settle. I knew if I got in bed, I'd lie staring at the ceiling until I couldn't stand it anymore. So I did what I'd been wanting to do all evening.

I headed out to see Big and Little.

I sent them a text asking to meet. It was late, but I figured they were anxious to hear the details and were probably waiting up to see if I had a chance to call. The response was immediate.

Looking forward to it. See you soon.

Their Hummer was parked in front of the warehouse. I

headed for the front door and Mannie opened it, grinning at me.

"Big and Little were very excited to get your text," he said. "They've been talking about the coup all night. You were something else. I mean, I'd heard through channels, of course, but hearing about it and seeing what you accomplished are two entirely different things. Following Ahmad into that tunnel was a move most people wouldn't have even tried, much less come out of successfully."

"How do you know what I did?"

"I saw both of you break the surface, but I was too far up the canal to help. By the time I got there, you'd already taken care of business."

I nodded. "I want to thank you for shooting that guy. You saved Carter."

He shrugged. "One of the team might have taken him out before he got off another round, but I figured why take that chance when I had the shot."

"And at the moment, another team member shooting that man is exactly what they assume happened. I'm not telling them any different."

"I appreciate it."

"It's the least I can do." I tilted my head to one side and studied him for a moment. "You weren't wearing a mask or a regulator."

"No."

"And I saw no snorkel or bubbles despite the fact that I had plenty of the canal in my line of sight. You simply disappeared. Tell me the truth. You're Aquaman, right?"

He grinned. "Let's just say swimming might have been a big part of my previous profession."

I smiled. I knew it. "SEAL. I can totally see that. And your secret's safe with me."

"I know. Now, let's get you upstairs before the Heberts burst from anticipation."

We headed to the office where a very excited Big and Little greeted me as soon as I walked in. I took a seat, and Little opened a bottle of champagne and poured us all a glass. I sipped the champagne and told my story one more time. The last time, because no one else could ever know the details.

When I was finished, they looked at each other, then back at me.

"You are one of a kind," Big said.

"Some would say that's a good thing," I said.

Little nodded. "It most certainly is for the bad guys."

"I want you to know that your identity is still a secret. I refused to give that information to the CIA, or anyone else for that matter, and I won't. The only people who know the building was yours are Ida Belle and Gertie, and you can trust them."

"If you trust them, then we do as well," Big said. "As to the other, we knew you were a woman of your word. We were never worried."

"I wanted to tell you again how much I appreciate everything you've done for me. Without your help, this couldn't have happened and I'd still be in limbo. You stuck your neck out for me, more than once, and I'm not going to forget it. I owe you and Mannie big-time. Whenever you need to cash that marker in, you let me know."

"No questions asked?" Big asked.

"I'm a woman, and CIA. What do you think?"

They both laughed.

"I also want to apologize for the damage to the building. I am happy to pay for the repairs, if you'd just get some estimates and let me know the cost."

Big waved a hand in dismissal. "You did us a favor."

"I don't understand."

"We've been wanting to unload that warehouse for years, but with that meatpacking plant upwind, no one would bite. Since you conducted a small war on the property, I've heard through my sources that the plant is moving forward with a plan to consolidate operations at their remote location. They should be cleared out in a couple of months. I expect the property value to soar, and Little and I will make out extremely well."

"Then I guess this has worked out for everyone," I said.

"Fabulously so," Big said. "So what's up next for the now-infamous CIA agent Fortune Redding? Another impossible mission in a foreign locale?"

I shook my head. "Not anymore. I resigned."

Big's eyes widened and he glanced over at Little, who'd leaned forward in his chair.

"And may I ask your plans?" Big asked.

"I think I might stick around a while. See how I fare here as the real me."

Big laughed. "I think the better question is how Sinful is going to fare." He rose from his desk and extended his hand. "Let me be the first to officially welcome you to southern Louisiana."

CHAPTER TWENTY-ONE

I WAS up early the next morning, but not as early as Gertie. It was only 6:00 a.m. but Gertie had sent a text at five thirty asking me to let her know when I was awake. I figured she and Ida Belle were probably as antsy as I was, so I texted back for them to come over for coffee.

In theory, one would think we'd all be sleeping late, relaxing in the glory of all that was now behind us. But the reality was, there was so much in front of me that I couldn't stay asleep a minute longer, despite the fact that I'd only put in a couple hours. It had taken forever for my mind to settle enough for me to sleep and even then, it hadn't been restful. I'd tossed and turned and dreamed until I'd finally given up and decided I had the rest of my life to snooze. Sooner or later, I'd feel like it.

They arrived fully dressed and completely alert, proving my theory that all of us had been up at the crack of dawn. Gertie had a blackberry cobbler with her that had just come out of the oven, so we headed back to the kitchen for coffee and an unorthodox breakfast. I figured it had fruit, so that was at least one food group.

Ida Belle and Gertie were silent when they sat, but I could tell they were both bursting to ask me about what had happened with Carter and Harrison. I didn't make them wait.

"I gave my official notice to Morrow while Harrison was here," I said. "He accepted and allowed my time served here in Sinful to count as the month I gave him. I did a debriefing with Harrison last night, but there will be some follow-up, I'm sure. I have some paperwork to attend to in DC, so I'll be headed back there in a couple weeks probably. But it's official. I'm regular people."

Gertie jumped up from her chair, whooping and hopping. Ida Belle grinned so hard I was afraid she'd strained something. When Gertie finally ran out of breath—about five seconds into the whooping and hopping—she flopped back into the chair and drew in a big breath.

"We were afraid you'd change your mind," she said.

I nodded. "So was Carter. I won't lie, there was a moment, when I was waiting for Ahmad to enter the room, that I thought 'this is where I belong.' But it didn't last. And it wasn't real. It was just my body and mind returning to the one thing I know more than anything else. One day, that won't be the case. I'm looking forward to that."

Ida Belle nodded. "Sometimes I dream about Vietnam. They're so vivid that I wake up confused that I'm not on a cot. And I feel this ache...not because I want to be there again, but because it was the place where my emotions ran so high. Where every little thing I did and said could be life or death. I think sometimes I miss the intensity—the way a junkie does a fix—but not enough to want to relive it."

"Well, I've found there's no shortage of life-or-death decisions right here in Sinful," I said, "so although it won't be at all like what I'm used to, I think I'll manage not to be bored. At least most of the time."

"You're staying!" Gertie jumped up from her chair again and grabbed me around my shoulder, doing round two of the hopping thing. Ida Belle and I couldn't help laughing.

"You know you're welcome at my place," Ida Belle said. "As long as you want. Hell, you can make it permanent."

"Mine too," Gertie said.

"I appreciate it," I said, "and I might have to take you up on the offer, but I'm working on something that looks promising."

Gertie sucked in a breath. "You're going to buy Carl's house and live next to Celia!"

"Good Lord no!" I said. "Living next to Ronald is enough of a trial. I asked Morrow to talk to Sandy-Sue about selling me this house."

"You want to buy Marge's house?" Gertie asked.

"Why not?" I said. "It's a great place and I'm comfortable here. Merlin likes it and it comes with a stash of weapons better than what I have back at my condo in DC. I don't figure Sandy-Sue ever plans on living here, which means she'd be selling anyway. Might as well save the Realtor commission and the hassle and sell to me."

"And does Morrow think she'll go for it?" Ida Belle asked.

"He's pretty sure she will and if she isn't sure, he says he can convince her. Especially as it will be a cash offer, at market, for everything. So no boxes for her to pack, no attics for her to clear. She was never close to Marge anyway, so it's not like anything here has sentimental value. It's not a sure thing, but I think it looks good. And if it doesn't work out, then I'll figure out something else."

Gertie sniffed. "I think you living in Marge's house would be perfect. I think it's exactly what Marge would want. I wish she'd been able to meet you. And you her."

Ida Belle nodded. "Kindred spirits. Maybe that's why you

feel comfortable here. Marge wasn't your typical woman and neither are you. You have a lot in common. Far more than the one related to her."

"Well, it's in the works, so all we can do now is wait and hope," I said. "But don't say anything until I know. Not even to Carter. I haven't had a chance to tell him yet."

Gertie looked over at Ida Belle and then back at me. "And what about Carter? Did you finally have the talk?"

"We had part of the talk, but I'm guessing that given the nature of our relationship and both our personalities, that talk will be ongoing."

Ida Belle nodded. "I think it's smart that you realize that. You and Carter are two intelligent, strong-willed, independent people. I don't think it will be easy, and there will probably be times you'd rather throw your hands in the air than deal with it, but I think you two are really good together. In fact, I don't know that there's a better fit for either of you."

"So make it work or we both die alone and lonely?" I asked.

"Not necessarily lonely," Ida Belle said, "but maybe alone. It's not so bad, mind you."

"So what are we going to do today?" Gertie asked. "If Fortune's going to live here, we have shopping to do. I mean, you can't continue to wear the same couple outfits everywhere. And surely you want your own linens...something your style. Even if you don't get the house, those things can be taken anywhere."

Ida Belle gave her a pained look and I could tell she was as enthusiastic about a day of shopping as I was.

"Actually," I said, "I'd like to address that missing food case again."

"Really?" Ida Belle said. "Did you think of something new?"

I nodded. "I think I know who did it and I'd like to

confront them before Francine puts those cameras up and is forced to do something about what she finds."

"I thought we'd settled on Cora being the one," Gertie said.

"And she might be," I said. "But I'd like to try something."

Ida Belle nodded. "Great. Let's go."

"This early?" Gertie asked.

"Oh yeah," Ida Belle said. "I forgot."

"Now is fine," I said. "We're going to the café."

I parked my Jeep on Main Street and we headed for the café. Gertie was practically jumping out of her shoes because I wouldn't tell her my suspicions on the way over. But I wanted to see if I was right first, and I wanted to test my theory without getting input. I thought the pieces fit together. I wanted to make sure.

"Around back," I said. "I don't want to do this in the dining area."

We headed to the back door and stepped inside, walking past the office and the cooler and into the kitchen. I scanned the room, hoping the person I wanted to speak to was on shift this morning. Then I spotted Jordan rinsing dishes in a huge sink and waved him over when he looked our way. He frowned, but put the dishes down and dried his hands before heading toward us. I motioned for Ida Belle and Gertie to retreat and we all walked out the back door.

"Is something wrong?" Jordan asked as he stepped outside. "Is it my uncle?"

"No," I said, reassuring him. "Your uncle is fine. But he might not be if he finds out what you've been doing."

"What are you talking about?"

"Francine has noticed food missing from the café. Food that wasn't sold to diners."

"I don't know anything about that," he said, but I could tell by the way he avoided my gaze that he was lying.

"I think you do, and I think I know why. You've been using the food for bait, trying to draw Godzilla into town."

Gertie's eyes widened. "Why would you do that?"

"Because of Celia," I said. "You said he's having trouble selling his house because Celia lives next door. And until he sells the house, you're stuck here in Sinful, putting school on hold and shuffling dishes at the café. You overheard Celia's complaints about the alligator and thought if he harassed her, she might move."

"So I took some food," he said. "I was gonna pay Francine back as soon as the house sold, but if I took from my savings now, I wouldn't be able to afford the next semester, and it's about to start." His shoulders slumped. "I got desperate. I know it was stupid."

"And dangerous," I said. "What if Godzilla had injured someone? Not to mention someone could have shot him. I don't think that's what you want."

He stared down at the ground, clearly miserable. "No. I guess I didn't think that far."

"This doesn't have to go any further than right here," I said. "Put the money for the food and an apology in an envelope on Francine's desk, and don't ever do it again." I reached up to squeeze his shoulder. "I'm sorry about school, but you just have to be patient. Someone will come along who wants to buy your uncle's house. And school will still be there waiting for you when it does."

He looked up at me and nodded. "Thanks for not telling. It would have killed Uncle Carl, and he's been so good to me. I didn't mean to make trouble. Well, at least, not the way I did." He looked at Gertie. "And I'm sorry I put Godzilla in danger. That wasn't my intention."

"That's okay," Gertie said. "Nobody got hurt."

"Maybe Carter," Jordan said. "Celia probably broke a rib when she fell on him. And he did get those panties in his face."

"True," I agreed. "Maybe next time Carter comes in, he gets the biggest piece of pie available? On you?"

"I can do that," Jordan said. "Thanks again. I better get back to work before the dishes start piling up."

He headed inside and Ida Belle and Gertie stared at me.

"Spill," Gertie said. "How did you know it was him? I was certain it was going to be Cora. All that Goody Two-shoeing around. It's got to be a cover for something."

"Last night after I talked to Harrison, I went to see Big and Little and clear things with them," I said. "It was something Big said that started me thinking, and then everything started to fall into place."

"What did he say?" Ida Belle asked.

"When I offered to pay for the damage to the warehouse, he said he was happy because the shoot-out had prompted the meatpacking plant to relocate and now he'd be able to sell the property for a big profit."

"And Carl is having trouble selling his house," Ida Belle said. "That part I get, but you said everything. What else was there?"

"It's mostly circumstantial," I said, "but it all made sense. There was the house sale, then the bacon box in Jordan's neighborhood, and the complaint about something smelling under Celia's house. Then there was your comment about how the Lowery brothers might have used the bacon for bait."

"You think Jordan put the stolen meat under Celia's house to draw Godzilla there?" Gertie asked.

"It's not completely absurd," I said. "The bayou isn't that far away and Godzilla has been spotted roaming the neighborhood more than once."

"Because that's where casseroles come from," Ida Belle said drily.

I nodded. "And remember what Ally said about Celia smelling? I don't think it was Celia that smelled. It was her purse. I think Jordan dropped food in it when she ate at the café that morning, knowing that he'd already lined the bank behind the shops with bait before coming to work. Remember, he was the one holding the purse after Godzilla chased Celia up the lamppost."

"He wasn't retrieving it for Celia," Gertie said. "He was removing the evidence before Celia found it."

I nodded. "Celia buying those deer steaks was just a lucky break. Godzilla would have been automatically attracted to the butcher and then she waltzed out the door, smelling of steak and probably bacon. I'm not saying it was all the greatest plan on Jordan's part, but he's young and was desperate. So I made a leap and figured I'd just come right out and ask him."

Ida Belle smiled. "Pretty smart. I'd bet you got it all exactly right."

"Including your solution," Gertie said. "He won't do it again, and Carl is better off never knowing."

"So if Jordan was the one stealing the food," Ida Belle said, "I wonder why Cora looked so guilty when we asked her about those bacon-wrapped shrimp."

"I don't know," I said. "Maybe we need to figure that out."

Gertie grinned. "You're going to fit in just fine here, Fortune. Wait and see."

I took in a breath and blew it out. So much stretched before me—permanent housing, employment, so many honest conversations with so many people, and hopefully plenty of challenges. Finding a casserole-eating alligator topped the list at the moment, but otherwise, I had no idea what the future held. But I was sure of one thing.

There would be a lot of laughs along the way.
And it would never be boring.

What's in store for Fortune now that she's a free agent? Look for the next Miss Fortune book, coming later this year.

Get release notice for the next Miss Fortune adventure by signing up for Jana's newsletter.

If you're on Facebook, join Jana's reader group, the Insta-Gators, for updated release information, sneak previews and more.

Made in the USA
Coppell, TX
31 August 2020

35977930R00154